DAMAGED SOULS

EVERNIGHT PUBLISHING ®

www.evernightpublishing.com

DAMAGED SOULS

DAMAGED SOULS

Chaos and Carnage MC, 2

Sam Crescent

Copyright © 2023

❖ ◆ ❖

Chapter One

Aria Taylor stared down at the wedding photos and she wasn't even surprised. If she looked closely enough in the corner, she saw part of her body and her *chunky* arm. No matter what she did, her mother would criticize her. She had attempted to diet for that day. The weight she had lost was never enough.

Staring at the pictures, she felt the tears well, which she hated. Two attacks in the past twenty-four hours was just too much.

Last night had been Halloween, and she had dressed up as a sexy witch, per her best friend's suggestion. Lidia was constantly telling her how beautiful she was, and that she needed to ignore what people said.

She'd been trying to get into the party, but Lidia's current boyfriend Sean had told her to leave.

"Yeah, that is not coming to my party. Take your

ugly ass away. Lidia is too fucking nice to tell you this, but your fat fucking face is no longer welcome here. She can do so much better than you. Leave."

It was no shock that her and Sean didn't get along, but this was the first time he'd verbally attacked her. His friends had been around, and they'd laughed at her.

Humiliated, she had forced a smile and then left.

Now, she opened up the photos her mother had sent her and had to wonder if this had been done on purpose. It was no secret in their family that her sister Isabella was the star. Thin, beautiful, perfect in every single way, and had even scored herself a lawyer. A wealthy man that didn't seem to mind coming to live in the town of Carnage.

Tears filled her eyes, and she quickly placed the pictures back into the envelope and rushed toward her bedroom.

This was not a hard thing for her.

Her mother was constantly telling her she wasn't good enough. She opened her closet, gripped the edge of her clothes, and shoved them all to one side, finding what she was looking for, and feeling a little crazy as she grabbed it off the shelf.

The box had once started as a shoebox, but as the years moved on, it had developed into a proper box. Lifting off the lid, Aria didn't dare look inside. She added the envelope, hoping it would take the memories of the previous night with it as well. She placed the lid back on, lifted it up, and slid it into place on the shelf. Stepping back, she didn't feel any better. Like so many gifts and horrible reminders before, it made her feel sick to her stomach.

Aria arranged her clothes, running her hands down them and trying to remain calm as she did so.

Nibbling her lip, she tried to ignore the sick feeling that swirled in her gut. She closed her closet door, and instead of going to the kitchen, she went straight toward her en suite bathroom. She stopped once she stood directly in front of the mirror, lifted her gaze, and then looked at herself.

Like her sister, she possessed long, blonde hair and blue eyes, but that was where the resemblance ended. She had started to gain weight as a youngster, much to their mother's misery. Where Isabella was slender, with curves in all the right places, Aria was bigger. Much bigger. Her tits were larger, as were her thighs, hips, ass, arms, just about every single part of her.

"Ugh, why can't you be more like your sister?"

"I swear, Aria, if they don't fit, you're going on a diet."

"Do you need more fat and sugar? You have enough."

"No one is going to want to marry the fat girl."

"Seriously, Aria, enough. You're fat enough."

She closed her eyes as the years upon years of insults added up. At twenty-five years old, she had come to dread going to her family's house. Her dad wasn't too bad, but then, he always sided with his wife, as she knew best.

He'd always wanted sons, as he felt there was no way he could handle girls. So, he often left them alone to go and have a round of golf, or go to the bar, or anything that stopped him from interfering with his wife's way of raising two girls.

Aria had lost count of the number of diets she'd been on. How she'd be banned from having cake, pastas, bread. There was even a Christmas her mother would only allow her to eat vegetables. Just the memories of those times had her eyes welling up in tears.

So, staring at her reflection, she grabbed her shirt and lifted it up over her head, before throwing it to the floor.

She opened the button of her jeans and wriggled them off her hips, and after that was done, she simply stared at herself and then thought of all the insults she had been given. Even the one from last night. Each one chipping away at her.

"You're a fat, ugly person, Aria Taylor, and it's time for you to change." She pushed a finger into her rounded stomach, slapped her thick, cellulite thighs, and then the tears truly started to fall.

No one loved her.

No one liked her.

She was too fat.

Too ugly.

And she was never going to be good enough.

It was time for her to change.

Pressing her hands on the bathroom counter, she glared at her reflection. "You are useless and you're not good enough. You are going to change this, for good."

She nodded at her reflection, changed back into her clothes, and then headed toward the kitchen. She refused to listen to that part of her brain that seemed to be asking her why, that there was nothing wrong with the way she ate or the way she looked.

Those pictures were the last straw. There was no way she could endure another Christmas of being berated for just existing on more than a celery stick. It was time to change.

Those diets her mother had put her on filled her with misery, but she had a way of doing it herself. She'd find something and some way to make this all work.

Once in her kitchen, she found a large box and then opened each cupboard, taking out the cans of food that were not healthy—even soup that registered too many calories or fat.

Filling the box, she found another and did the same. Once she was finished, she had three boxes of food. She lifted one in her arms and made her way out to her car. One by one, the three boxes were loaded into her car. There was no way she was throwing the food out. She needed to get to work, and on the way was a food bank.

Checking the time, she saw it was a little after seven, so she would simply leave the food boxes outside the door. Aria looked over the boxes to make sure there was no indication they had come from her. She went back into her home, grabbed a couple of apples for lunch, her bag, and went back outside.

On a Saturday, it was always a slow day but a casual one at the veterinary practice where she worked. It was a new one that had been set up on the outskirts of town, and when she had seen they were looking for reception staff, she had jumped at the chance and gotten the job.

She made the journey into town, leaving the boxes of food outside the food bank. It was early enough so no one would see her.

Aria drove toward the outskirts of town where the veterinary practice was and parked in one of the few available parking spaces. The building was quite small, and she had heard that some of the vets were hoping to expand.

She didn't know much about veterinary medicine, but answering phones, booking appointments and stuff like that, she could do. She'd been working for the practice for six months, and it had been an emotional six months. Aria hadn't realized how many animal lovers there were in Carnage.

She didn't know where they went before Animal Lovers opened, but now they brought their pets to them, and she was thankful for it. They also didn't mind paying, which was a bonus. The more people that came, the longer the practice would remain open, and she'd have a job. Yay.

The practice was closed as she arrived, but that was fine. She had been given a key by Phil, the man who had set the practice up with his wife, Andy. Both were vets, and both were amazing people.

They helped to put not only the owners at ease, but also the pets as well. They saw a great deal as well—dogs, cats, rabbits, guinea pigs, there had even been a snake—and a few other things Aria had struggled to deal with.

The tarantula had terrified her. She had wanted to put tape or some other adhesive all over the box to keep that furry thing contained. Instead, she just avoided looking at it. Gross.

She opened the doors, switched on the light, and listened to the few animals that had to stay overnight. Two dogs and three cats.

Locking the door behind her, she walked toward the back and stepped into the small kennels. The heat had been put on low. Whenever they had patients, Phil and Andy insisted on there being heating, as well as cameras. She was aware of someone watching the pets at all times.

They had asked her whenever she came in to open, if she would just check on them first before opening any other part of the shop. So, that is what she did. She never wanted to startle the pets. They were wonderful.

"Good morning," she said softly. "I hope you guys remember me. I'm Aria Taylor, from the front desk, and I cannot believe I'm even talking to you like this." She rolled her eyes, but this is what she did. She always talked to the pets as if they were people who understood what she said.

She had always wanted a dog, a cat, or both. The first kennel had a cocker spaniel doggy, Billie. She smiled in at him, and his tail flicked from side to side. "I hope you're feeling better." His tail wagged.

She moved down to the Jack Russell, Martha, and did the same, before heading to the three cats, Trixie, Ainsley, and Betty. After her visit with them, she made her way through the practice and began to open and check the rooms.

The main heating wasn't on, so she made her way toward the back, where Phil and Andy had given her the tour. After flicking on the heat, her next place was the staff room. She set up the coffeepot, flicked it on, and waited for a cup.

She opened the fridge, only to pause as she thought about it. There was no cream or milk. She closed the fridge, grabbed a mug, and waited for the coffee. Pouring herself a generous cup, she walked out toward her desk. She was the only receptionist they had on staff, and she didn't mind working the six days a week they were open.

Phil and Andy did also work on Sundays but that was for emergency calls. They didn't ask her to work, but she was more than happy to.

Making excuses for not attending Sunday lunch with her family was imperative. She had yet to find something reasonable. Working sounded a lot better than listening to her parents moan about what she had or hadn't done.

Shaking her head, she took a deep breath and then sat down in her chair. It was no good thinking about her parents. That was not the best way to start her morning. Blowing across the rim of her cup, she took a sip and wrinkled her nose.

This was a new leaf of her life. There was no time for moaning or hating black coffee. She would learn to like it. Taking another sip, she attempted not to shudder. By the sixth sip, she was more than used to it.

Smiling to herself, she flicked open the appointment book and saw they were already fully booked. With the appointments open, she got to her feet and made her way toward the filing cabinet. Phil and Andy insisted on keeping a record of their patients. She flicked the lock from the set of keys she was given and found the appointments for that day, lining them up in the tray. As she finished, Andy arrived, shaking as she did so.

"I swear it's going to snow soon."

Andy was a lovely woman, who also happened to feel the cold, even in August in the height of summer.

"You've been saying that since June."

"Trust me, one of these days I'm going to be right."

Aria couldn't help but laugh.

"Please tell me we have a busy day?" Andy asked, removing her hat, gloves, scarf, and coming toward the desk.

"We certainly do."

"Good news. Very good news."

"Where's Phil?" Aria asked, getting to her feet.

"He had to take a call during the night. One of the ranchers wanted his cow to be attended to. I would have gone with him, but Phil insisted I stay home so I could make it here."

"Is the cow okay?"

"I'm not sure. He'll give us an update when he

arrives."

"Would you like a cup of coffee?" Aria asked.

"You're a precious woman, Aria. Absolutely. I feel I need it."

Aria smiled and made her way back into the staff room while Andy walked to the back office.

Without Phil in the office, it would get hectic quickly. They were both amazing vets, but where Phil was able to calm people's fears and stop panicked conversation, Andy was not the same. She would chat for hours, and of course she was an animal lover, so it meant they were going to be here for a long time, until Phil arrived. Aria didn't mind. The idea of going back to her home, the one once owned by her grandparents, didn't appeal.

Her grandparents on her father's side had left her the house in their will, much to her parents' dismay. They had hoped to either use the property as a rental, bringing in money, or to sell it. They had tried to contest the will, but her grandparents' lawyers had warned in that event, all other property granted to her parents and Isabella would revert to Aria. That had been an awkward meeting.

Anyway, she moved out of her small apartment the next day and hadn't looked back since.

****

Grant stared around at the kennels. Once again, he'd been given kennel duty, not for the first time either.

He was starting to recognize these dogs, including their names and their reasons for being at the kennel, and why they had to find this location. Running a hand down his face, he tried to convince himself that he didn't care. Dogfighting happened.

Nope, he couldn't do it. Dogfighting was a fucking weak man's sport. Allowing dogs to kill each other for sport was not a fucking sport in his book. Evil bastards. Not that he'd ever admit it to anyone. If men wanted to bet over fighting, then do it man to man.

Grant refused to think about what had happened in Carnage less than a year ago. How he'd ended up pretending to have been removed from the club in order to go and protect his brother's woman. Bull, his brother, as well as his prez from the Chaos and Carnage MC, had then forgiven him for all the shit he'd put him through over the years, including but not limited to the potential overthrowing of power.

Not that Grant even wanted to be leader of the fucking club. Far from it. He was just pissed at Bull. Only a guy who had a brother would understand. Older brothers had that chip on their shoulders, that feeling that they knew best, and when it came to Bull, Grant sometimes found it hard to differentiate between brother and prez. He was working on it.

Since then, Bull had given him shitty assignments, most of them about the dogs. Going to the kennels, keeping an eye on the workings for any sign of the Vito Crew or the Cartel. So far, nothing.

He did know, although he'd not been invited along for the meetings, that his brother was talking to William Ranford, who was the crime boss whose brother got killed after getting involved with the dog fighting ring. Again, he was out of the loop, other than what they discussed at church, but on their personal front, nothing was going on, and Bull wasn't talking.

Grant was the first person at their kennels, and the first thing he did every single morning was go and check the security. The dogs had their own kennels in one of the buildings out back, and they always made sure the heat was on low. In the past few days, it had gotten cold and Maddie had been riding his ass to keep the dogs safe. Like he wouldn't.

She should be focusing on her baby, not on him. It wouldn't be long before his niece was too big and running around. She should enjoy this baby stage and all that entailed. She had to stop worrying about him doing a good job. He was more than competent at what he did and didn't need to have the woman babysitting.

Grant couldn't believe that in the past two years, he and Maddie had become friends. Maddie was a sweet woman, beautiful as well. He had a nasty history with her, and he didn't even want to think about it seeing as everything he'd said to her was bullshit. Not that he'd ever admit that to anyone.

There was no way he'd admit to being a fucking pussy and falling in with a crowd. He was a grown-ass man, not a coward. Not that he'd been a coward as a kid, but it had gotten some cheap laughs.

Grant checked the security gates, quickly looked around the perimeter, checked the security logs, and when he was happy, he stepped into the kennels and looked in at the dogs. The moment he opened the door, like so many times before, the dogs moved to the front of their kennels. He had attempted to take them all for a walk at the same time, but that hadn't worked. So, he managed about three big dogs at a time, or four small ones.

Walking down the main aisle, he talked to each of the dogs, wishing them a good morning. When he came to the last kennel, he paused. Wanda, the big German shepherd with a heart of gold, was curled up at the back of her kennel. Not even on the bed he'd gotten for her.

"Wanda, girl, what's the matter?" He didn't like this.

When he was first assigned to dog duty, he didn't have a clue what he was doing. He ended up going to

Maddie for advice, and she said to constantly pay attention to the dogs. He would eventually learn their habits—what they liked, how they reacted—and he'd know when something was wrong. Something was definitely wrong right now, and he wasn't happy.

Pulling out his keys, he found Wanda's key and flicked the lock of the cage. There was no wagging tail. No sign of her even knowing who he was.

His heart raced. This was bullshit.

As per Maddie's instructions, even though he and Wanda had been getting to know each other over the months, he took his time approaching. The dogs had come from illegal dogfights and he was aware Bull had stuck his neck out to stop them from being euthanized. They had even gotten a dog trainer and were doing what they could to help the dogs.

Grant couldn't do it. He couldn't end a dog's life. It wasn't their fucking fault. Now, the men who were responsible, most of them, if not all, were fucking dead. Six feet under. And he was fucking glad of it.

Only, on moments like this when one of the dogs was not acting their usual way, he wanted to raise them back up from the dead and kill them all over again. Now that would be fun. A lot of fucking fun. He could totally handle that kind of death and torture.

Wanda didn't sniff his hand, didn't come to him. He had no choice but to shuffle forward on his knees and as he did so, he started to feel fucking old. The cold floor on his knees was not a fun experience, not by a long shot.

"Hey, girl, come on, are you going to give me a smile?" he said.

Nothing. Wanda kept her head on her paws and didn't move.

Gritting his teeth, he cut the crap and went to her. He ran his hand down her back and she did nothing. That was it. He was taking her to the vet. He had no choice.

He pulled up Bull's number on his cell phone but then hesitated. Bull was an irritating bastard and would tell him he was worrying for no good reason.

"Fucker," Grant said.

There was one person who would understand his issues, and as soon as he dialed Maddie's number, he felt a million times better. He did so with a smile.

"Grant, what's up?" she asked, her voice low.

There was so much he could say to wind her up but Wanda was the priority right now.

"Wanda's acting strange. I don't like it. I need to take her to the vet. Can you phone Bull, get him to send a couple of the guys over while I deal with her?"

"Wanda, is she okay? She has struggled over the past few months," Maddie said.

"I know, and I'm not liking this behavior. She's never been like this."

"Understood. Take Wanda to the vet. I'll deal with Bull."

"He's … er, going to be pissed."

"I don't care. You're doing what I've asked."

He smiled. "Love you, Maddie," he said.

"Shut up, Grant. You know Bull will be pissed with you for calling me. I'm not an idiot. Go and take care of her."

He said his goodbyes, hung up his cell phone, pocketed it, and then looked at the task ahead of him. Wanda wasn't going to be helpful. He had no choice but to try and get the dog up into his arms and then out toward his truck. Now he was glad he arrived in his truck rather than his bike.

With Wanda in his arms, and she was fucking heavy, Grant managed to get her out to his truck. He hated the idea of leaving the other dogs, but didn't have a choice. He locked the doors and pocketed his keys. The brothers all had keys of their own.

There was a new veterinary practice on the outskirts of town, and he had started to use that one rather than calling one of the city vets. The last practice had been shut down years ago.

With Wanda in the back seat of his truck, he climbed behind the wheel and took off, heading toward the outskirts of town where Animal Lovers was. Fucking lame name, but so far he didn't see a problem with Andy and Phil.

The club was going to look into them. At least, he had asked Bull to check them out, and so far, nothing. He and Bull always had that kind of relationship, and at moments like this it pissed him off. They rarely saw eye to eye, most of the time because Grant believed Bull had a stick up his ass, and Bull thought he was irresponsible. None of that was a lie.

Grant had a history of partying, being the wild animal and all that, but he was changing. He'd proven time and time again that he was good for the club. Okay, so there were a few times he was an asshole. Not his fault. He couldn't help it. Bull pissed him off and he just reacted. But, he was more than willing to give his life for the club and for his brother. That wasn't going to change.

Arriving at the practice, he saw there were only two other cars parked in the lot. Hopefully, they were Maddie's and Andy's cars.

He parked his truck, then went to the back and had to pull Wanda into his arms and carry her across the cold parking lot. The front door wasn't open.

"Fuck!" he growled in annoyance, and kicked at the base of the door. He did so repeatedly until he saw Aria. She frowned at him and then saw the fur baby in his arms, and she immediately opened the doors.

"Mr. Reynolds," she said. "Is this Wanda?"

"Yes, and how many times do I have to tell you to call me fucking Grant."

"Well, fucking Grant, it is rude of me to call you that."

He would have laughed any other time. Aria never swore, at least he hadn't heard her do so before. She certainly wouldn't say anything in front of customers and had even on occasion asked him to be more polite. He found it so cute when she asked him politely to be that way. So fucking adorable.

Aria Taylor was a beautiful woman. It was the blonde hair. No, it wasn't the blonde hair. It was the … curves.

His teeny, tiny little secret, one he would never tell Bull or anyone else about. Grant gritted his teeth and stopped those memories from building. The past was firmly in the fucking past, and he wasn't going to allow them to resurface. He hadn't thought about his pop in years.

"What's wrong with Wanda?" Aria asked, stepping out of the way so he could pass.

"I have no fucking clue. Trust me, I wouldn't have come here if I knew what was wrong with her. I went to the kennels like I do all the time, and she was just … like this. So resigned and reserved. Her tail won't wag. I need to see the vet."

"Andy's here. Let me go and get her."

Grant wasn't taking no for an answer, so as Aria made her way toward the vet, he went straight into one of the exam rooms and laid Wanda on the table.

"I've got you, girl. You don't worry about a thing. I've got you."

He wouldn't let her go.

Seconds later Andy was in the room. Like so many other times, she looked disapproving, but he didn't give a fuck what was going through the vet's mind. The dog was what mattered.

She asked all the usual questions and then took her time taking Wanda's temperature and checking her over. By the end of it, Andy shook her head.

"What the fuck is that? There's nothing wrong with Wanda. She was a perfectly healthy dog. Don't just shake your head like you don't have a fucking clue. Do something." He did not like this pain that filled his chest or his gut. He didn't give a fuck about the dog. They meant nothing to him, and hell no, he wasn't going to cry. Crying was for fucking pussies.

"No son of mine will ever shed fucking tears."

Grant stared at Andy and sighed.

"She is sad," Andy said. "Physically, she's more than fine, but it happens to some dogs at shelters for a long period of time—even though I know your kennels are not a shelter and you take care of them. Wanda is clearly miserable. She wants company, a best friend."

"So ... there's nothing I can do?"

"Can you adopt her?" Andy asked.

Grant opened his mouth and closed it. There was no reason he couldn't adopt her. Maddie and the guys were always checking out applicants, but the dogs at the shelter had been impossible to rehome, so they were waiting for their forever homes.

"Er, you mean like take her home with me?"

"Yes. If Wanda improves, then it's down to the shelter, and she's needing a little extra care. Maybe a foster family or something. If she doesn't improve, then please bring her back in and I'll conduct more tests and see if I can find something."

"Can't you do those tests now?"

"I try not to put the dogs through unnecessary testing when I don't believe they will help. I don't think they will help in Wanda's case."

He didn't like this.

"I know you don't like that, Mr. Reynolds, but it's the best I can do for now."

Stroking Wanda's head, he crouched down and looked into the dog's eyes. "What am I going to do with you, huh?"

He was going to fucking adopt her for some time.

"How about you stay with me?" he asked.

He was currently living in Maddie's old apartment, and seeing as he didn't need to leave, it would be a nice place for Wanda.

"I truly think it would help."

Chapter Two

Aria sipped at her coffee, which had cooled down a lot. She had just finished a phone call, helped a troubled cat owner, and had her booked for that evening. There were a few minor ailments Aria had been trained to help with. There was also a list of possible remedies that Phil and Andy have given her to use.

With the appointments booked for the day, she got out of her seat and walked around the desk, checking out the waiting room to make sure it was clean. There was no cat or dog hair, but each night she made sure to run the vacuum around the building. She liked to keep it clean and welcoming. She was opening the curtains when Grant and Wanda appeared. He was no longer carrying the large dog, but Wanda was by his side.

"Is everything okay?" Aria asked.

"Yeah, according to the fucking fake doc," Grant said.

The doors had already closed, but Aria winced. Andy would have heard that insult. It wasn't the first time the vets had been called fake doctors. Not good enough to take care of humans, so they became vets. It was an insult, and she knew it upset Andy. The woman worked hard at being a vet. Andy had once told her that she became a vet because she couldn't stand people. Humans were cruel, and there were plenty of other people to take care of them. She was only interested in animals, as they loved with all their being, and were not manipulative or cruel.

Aria had to wonder if it was time she got a dog. She had always wanted a dog, but her sister hated them because they crapped, so they never got one. No matter how many times Aria asked for one growing up, the answer was always *no*.

Then she moved into an apartment, where no pets were allowed. But now, she had her own place. Her own home. Without her parents. She could have a dog if she wanted.

"Shit, fuck, I shouldn't have said that crap. Andy's great. I'm sorry."

"Is Wanda okay?" she asked.

"I hope the doc is right." He ran a hand down his face. "I'm going to take her home with me."

Aria had no idea what the diagnosis was, and so she smiled.

"I … er … your hair is pretty."

She frowned and ran her hand through her hair. "Thank you." This was new. She forced a smile to her lips. "Well, you know the drill."

"You want me for my fucking money again."

Aria laughed. "You can always send the bill to your brother."

Grant wrinkled his nose. "Fuck that. He's already going to be pissed at me for the shit I pulled this morning."

Aria didn't have a clue how the Chaos and Carnage MC worked. She was aware Grant was a member. Her parents didn't like the club. Her mother called them a bunch of thieving thugs. Aria didn't mind Grant or the other MC members she had seen, which in the past few months had been a lot of them, seeing as they all helped out at the shelter. Grant was the main person she saw, but Bull was terrifying, especially as she had to take payment from him.

Walking around the counter, she sat and typed into the computer. She saw the note from Andy for payment. There was no medication. Just a bill for the time.

She set up the payment and handed the device to

Grant for him to swipe his card and type in the number. Once that was done and payment had been processed, she got him the receipts he'd need and smiled.

"It was a pleasure seeing you again this morning, Aria," he said. He rested his elbow on the counter. "Did you have a good Halloween?"

The memory of Sean struck her.

"Nah, not really. I was supposed to go to a party but that didn't pan out."

"How come?"

"I … it doesn't matter." There was no way she would admit to Grant that her best friend's boyfriend had told her she was too fat and lazy. "How was your … er … Halloween?"

"Partied at the clubhouse. You should have come, by the way, it would have been a hoot."

Aria chuckled. She wouldn't have dreamed of going to his clubhouse. Her parents had often told her to stay well clear of the place. Some of the girls she had gone to high school with had partied there, and some of them had looked a little rough afterward. None of them had complained, though. All the women had said the same thing—that Chaos and Carnage know how to party.

"Oh, well, maybe next year."

"Or at Thanksgiving."

"Thanksgiving?"

"Yeah, we have a party then as well. Actually, that might be different this year. Bull is with Maddie and all that. Anyway, if you're not doing anything, we should call it a date."

Aria forced a smile to her lips, not taking him seriously. Grant had a way of rambling at his visits to the vets. His cell phone went off, and she kept the smile on her face.

"Fuck me," he said, shaking his head. "See you

around, Aria."

She held her hand up and waved. "Bye, Grant."

He left with Wanda beside him.

Andy came out of the room and chuckled. "That man has the hots for you," Andy said.

Aria shook her head. "No, he doesn't. He's just being polite."

"You do know that I can hear everything that's going on in that room, right? I hear when he asks you on dates, and what you're doing. He makes small talk with you all the time. Also, I've noticed he arrives whenever we're not busy. Have you noticed that?"

"He helps out at the shelter that the club has set up." Aria shrugged. "It's nothing."

Andy sighed. "He did invite you over for Halloween, you do know that."

"No, it was a passing comment. It wasn't an invite." Aria didn't want to talk about Grant Reynolds.

He was an interesting man. Older than her by six years, but she had recognized him around town. He was a player. Most of the women had taken him out for a test drive.

"Grant likes to sleep around. He's just being nice. He's a flirt."

Andy snorted. "That man is not flirting with you in the way you think."

"Can we drop it?" Aria asked.

"Fine. Fine. Phil called. He's on his way. The cow thing was a birthing that was a bit difficult, but cow and calf are now fine."

"That's good news," Aria said.

They both looked toward the parking lot as the sound of a car arrived.

"Is that Phil?" Aria asked.

"Nope, that's Mr. Peters, come to collect Billie."

Andy smiled. "We'll take a rain check on this. We'll talk more."

"It's nothing."

"Come on, are you telling me you're not attracted to Grant?"

"No, I'm not. I don't know anything about him." She didn't want to get into Grant's reputation. Instead, she kept a smile on her lips and tried to ignore the hunger that had started to build.

Mr. Peters arrived, and Andy took him through to the consultant room.

Aria made a quick dash to the staff room. The fridge looked appealing, but she wasn't going to just eat anything. She hadn't taken time for breakfast. How was she going to lose weight when she constantly thought about food? There was no way for her to survive without food.

She grabbed her cell phone from her back pocket, did a quick search, and poured herself another black coffee. There was not much time for her to read, as the phone began to ring and customers arrived for their appointments. Phil made it in an hour later. He didn't look like he'd been awake all night, but the moment he entered, he greeted her and got stuck in. There was no lull until lunchtime.

Phil and Andy always insisted she take an hour for lunch, so she headed into town toward the diner. Carl and Beatrice were a lovely pair who ran the diner. The food was always to die for. Stepping inside, the guilt ate at her. She would have loved a cheeseburger with fries, but the calories were already adding up.

She stepped up to the counter, ordered a plain salad, no dressing, and a black coffee again, then quickly changed it to water. She took a seat at the back of the diner. It was already busy, so finding a small table was a miracle.

Pulling out her cell phone again, she began to read through the websites on losing weight. Cutting out all fats and carbs was the answer. Drinking more water. Eating fiber and grains. More exercise. The list went on and on. She knew there was a gym in town. Her mother had purchased a year's subscription for her, which she could use at any time. It was at the back of her purse. All she had to do to activate it was to go in and use it.

Beatrice brought over her salad. "Hey, sweetie," she said.

"Hi, Beatrice."

"Are you okay?" the other woman asked.

Aria smiled. "Yes, thank you. Did you have a good Halloween?"

"Business was booming. I don't mean to pry but it's not like you to order a salad."

Glancing down at her plate, she avoided wrinkling her nose. "I'm not very hungry today." The lie fell easily from her lips. She was starving.

"Ah, okay. Well, I'll let you enjoy it."

Aria nodded and watched Beatrice go.

She hated salad. Another meal she was going to have to love. Leafy vegetables, salads, they were everything she needed to eat.

All the diets she'd been on before were because of her mother. Aria didn't have a goal weight. She didn't have any goals when it came to fitness. The truth was, all she wanted was for her mother and everyone to leave her alone. All her life, people had judged her because of her weight.

"You'd be so beautiful if you just lost some weight."

"It's a shame you're so … big."

Picking up her fork, she stabbed it through the

leaves and then shoved it into her mouth. Was it so wrong for her to be happy being herself? Yes, she knew she was big, but she was happy.

No! She yelled at herself inside her head. This was the problem. This was why her mother was the way she was, why people like Sean did what they did.

There was no excuse.

She couldn't be happy with herself. That was the problem. Her body was the issue.

Her body was disgusting. She had to stop thinking how happy she was with herself. Something had to change.

Aria looked down at her plate, and when she couldn't eat another piece of leafy lettuce, she got up and carried her used plates to the counter. She thanked Beatrice, as she had already paid her bill. She left the diner and stepped out into the cold.

The gym wasn't too far from the diner. She had to wonder if there was a reason they had placed the gym there. Enjoy Carl's amazing food, step out, and see the guilt sign that if you don't do something, you'll be gaining pounds.

Aria walked down the street, and she had already seen the sign.

She opened her bag, pulled out her purse, and found the gift card for the gym. One year of membership already paid for. This was the gift her mother had been excited about. The moment she stepped through those doors, she'd be making her mother happy.

She thought about those wedding photos, as well as Sean's cruel comments. The only way for this to work was if she took that giant step. Going to work out. Exercise.

Nibbling her lip, she looked at the gym, and then stepped inside the building. She expected to step inside the doors and have people point at her and laugh. Instead, there was no one around.

There was a main reception desk with a man at the front. He was on the phone. He looked up as she entered and any chance of escaping disappeared. She made her way toward the main desk and waited. He held up a hand. She saw his badge read "Jase," and she waited.

Licking her dry lips, she glanced around the reception. No one was present. There was soft music playing in the background. Was there a way for her to politely leave without looking bad? Just when she was about to leave, Jase put down the phone. Of course he did.

"I'm so sorry about that. How can I help you?" he asked.

"Er … my … erm, my mom got me this, and I haven't had time to use it. I don't know if it's still valid."

Jase took the gift certificate from her, turned it over, and typed in the card. "Yes, absolutely. Are you applying for your year's membership?" he asked. "Also, I don't know if you're aware but this also includes a personal trainer."

"A personal trainer?" Why was she even surprised? Her mother would always go that extra mile to make sure her daughter did the right thing. "I had no idea."

"I don't have any trainers available at the moment. However, I can take you as a client."

"Er, are you sure?" she asked.

"Yes, I own this gym. I can show you all my relevant qualifications. We can set this up, if this is what you want," he said.

Aria nibbled her lip. Looking up, she realized there was a mirror behind him, and she caught sight of her reflection.

"You're not good enough."
"You're fat."
"You're ugly."
"No one will ever want you."

The same words kept ringing in her head, in her mother's voice. The constant, annoying sound.

Forcing a smile to her lips, she nodded. "Yes, I would like that. I'd like to set this up, and then we can do whatever comes next. If you don't mind."

"No problem! Give me a moment. I'll have someone come and deal with the desk, and then we'll go and get you set up."

This was it. This was really happening.

"Will the … er, the person who gave me this certificate, will they know?"

Jase shook his head. "No, they won't be notified that it's being used."

"That's good."

She didn't want her mother to know. If she did, it would just make this worse.

****

Grant rubbed at Wanda's head. She had managed the steps leading up to the apartment with no problem. She also had no issues with taking her seat in the corner of the sofa.

"You're not a bad dog at all. You're just a giant pain in my ass because I fucking care." He shook his head. The last thing he wanted was for anything to happen to Wanda.

So far, Andy's assessment hadn't been quite so accurate. Wanda had joined him back at the kennel. She'd stayed in the large bed he'd purchased in the main reception room, and she hadn't moved even as he took the other dogs for a walk.

Bull had left a nice, threatening voicemail on his cell phone, and he knew he would get an earful when they met.

After spending all day at the shelter, he'd put Wanda into the back of his truck and drove back to his apartment. He couldn't stand the idea of noodles from a packet again for dinner, so he'd ordered takeout from the diner. He was starving.

Wanda hadn't eaten the food he'd gotten for her either. He didn't know the last time Wanda ate. He was tempted to phone the vet. Glancing at the time, it was a little after 7:00. They were open until 8:00, but they would also answer emergency phone calls.

There was a break in his worrying as someone banged on his front door. He hoped it was food. Wanda lifted her head but didn't make a move.

"I can see that I'm going to be your guard dog." He shook his head and made his way to the front door, expecting to be greeted by the delightful smell of food, only to see the ugly-ass face of his brother.

"Bull," he said.

"What game are you playing?" Bull asked.

"Game?"

"Calling Maddie to get her to do your dirty work."

"Oh, that."

"Oh, yes, fucking that, Grant."

"I wasn't … come on, I needed to get Wanda to the vet's and I know you'd have told me to wait."

Bull looked toward the sofa and shook his head. "And what is wrong with fucking Wanda?"

"The vet thinks it could be the shelter. That she's sad."

"Seriously, you disturbed Maddie because of this."

Grant wanted to argue with his brother but he also knew that Bull was in one of those moods. The kind that meant he needed to get something off his chest. So, he stood and waited.

"Do you have any idea how tired Maddie is? The baby is not fucking sleeping through the night. Maddie is always there. She's not getting much sleep, and I took Lindsey with me today to give her a chance to rest, and then you call her up!"

He hadn't realized that Maddie was still having issues sleeping. Whenever they talked, which wasn't often since the baby had arrived, she hadn't said anything. If he'd known, he wouldn't have gotten her involved. He held his hands up in surrender.

"I'm sorry."

"You're always so fucking sorry, but I'm getting tired of this shit, Grant. When are you going to grow up?"

This was normal. Bull often asked him this question, and the truth was, he didn't have a fucking clue.

"You flit through life like nothing matters. You're supposed to be working at my fucking garage. You're one of the best mechanics I've got, and you rarely turn up. The only consistency you have is when it comes to the club, and even then, you try to take my fucking place."

"Look, I told you, I wasn't thinking—"

"You never fucking think!"

He'd expected Bull to be pissed at him, but this was a whole new level of fucked off, and he didn't know what to do, so he just waited, and waited.

Bull paced back and forth, running fingers through his hair, seeming even more pissed off with every second he was there.

"How is Maddie?" Grant asked.

"She's fucking tired."

He deserved that one.

Suddenly, Bull stopped. "You know what, enough. Enough of your shit, Grant. Until you get your act together, you're on dog duty. That's all. I don't want you at the clubhouse. I don't want you fucking near me or the garage, or anything."

Grant stopped. "Fuck, no. You're not kicking me out of the club. I've always been this fucking way, and so what if I don't get to the garage. You've got Pat and the other guys. You don't fucking need me."

Bull stepped up to him and pointed a finger at his head. "That's your problem. You don't fucking think, and maybe, just fucking maybe, if you gave yourself time to think, you'd realize that there are a lot of us waiting for you. I mean it, Grant. Until further notice, you're on suspension."

"Suspension?" Grant shook his head. "This is bullshit."

"It is what it is. I've already spoken to the boys. You're not to come by the club. You want me or one of the brothers, you fucking call me and I'll deal with it, but you need a wake-up call and I hope this is it."

Grant didn't get a chance to stop Bull. He was already out the door.

Suspended. From the club. He'd never heard anything so fucking stupid in his life. After locking the main door, he made his way back to the sitting room.

Wanda waited for him. There was a little whimper and he crouched down and started to stroke her fur. "What the fuck do you think that was about?" he asked.

He was tempted to call Maddie to piss his brother off, but decided against it.

This was classic Bull behavior. It wasn't the first time he'd been pissed and made a judgement call without thinking about it, and he doubted it would be the last. There was no way Bull could suspend him from the club. It just wasn't possible.

Wanda continued to whimper and he sighed.

"Are you needing a walk, girl?" he asked.

Another whimper followed by a head tilt.

"Yeah, let's go for a walk. I don't want to stay locked up in this apartment either." He grabbed her walking lead, attached it to her collar, and left the apartment.

The moment he stepped outside, he gritted his teeth. It was fucking freezing. Glancing down at Wanda, he wondered if she was too cold to go for this walk, or just needed to squat down outside. He saw something precious—her tail wagged—and he was going for a walk. They walked down the long staircase, heading out toward the town. It was dark, as it was quite late.

The diner was still open since it did serve the late-shift workers. Grant was tempted to head in, and then he realized he had ordered a pizza. He was about to head back when Wanda whimpered again, so no hot pizza for him, if they even bothered to leave it outside.

Walking through town, he came to a stop outside the gym. He thought about Maddie and wondered if she was still visiting. Maddie had decided it was time to lose some weight, after Bull created a scene in order to push her away, but whatever the reason, it had sent her to the gym.

He wasn't too fond of the gym member, Jase, not that there was anything wrong with him. From what Maddie had told him, Jase was a good guy.

"You're always so fucking sorry, but I'm getting tired of this shit, Grant. When are you going to grow

up?" He couldn't help but think of Bull's accusation earlier. He *was* fucking grown up. So, he didn't always show up at the garage, but what was the fucking point? His brother had ordered him to go to the mechanics course. Fixing cars wasn't something he wanted to do.

He was good at club work—fighting, working with his hands, doing shit. He was good at all of it, but working at the garage was fucking boring.

"You're always so fucking sorry, but I'm getting tired of this shit, Grant. When are you going to grow up?" Once again, Bull got into his head. He was a fucking grown-up and had been for a long time.

Wanda whimpered again, and he glanced down at her. "Do you think I should go and ask for a job here?" he asked.

Working at the kennels through the day and the gym at night. It sounded doable.

He stepped into the building and as soon as he did, the man on the counter looked at the dog and shook his head.

"We don't allow animals in the building."

"Then why call yourself a fucking gym?" Grant asked. Where he went, Wanda went, and he'd have it out with anyone who tried to force his dog out in the cold. "Where's Jase?"

"I mean it. That dog is not allowed inside. It carries diseases and is just gross." The man named Ben, according to his name tag, swatted his hand as if to ward off whatever Wanda had.

Grant was not in a good mood. He still wore the Chaos and Carnage MC leather cut, but he was possibly the first club member to ever be suspended.

He was pissed off. There was nothing funny about what had just happened. Leaning on the counter of the desk, he curled his finger, as if he was drawing him close.

Ben stepped closer and Grant grabbed the front of his jacket and yanked on it. "Listen to me, fucker, my dog stays, and if you've got an issue with it, I'll beat you black and fucking blue so your eyes swell shut, and then you don't have to see my dog. Now, where is Jase?"

As if his request had conjured him up, Jase stepped out of a side door, with none other than Aria Taylor. Her face was bright red.

"I'll see you the day after tomorrow," Jase said.

Aria nodded.

Grant looked at her. She hadn't seen him. Why was Aria at the gym? What the fuck was happening in town?

"Sir, there's a gentle ... man here to see you."

Grant nearly burst out laughing, and if it wasn't for Aria's disappearing ass, he would have. Right now, he had a whole load of questions.

Jase turned to him and the smile faded a little. It was nice to see he'd made an impression the last time they met.

"Grant," Jase said. His gaze slid down toward Wanda and instead of telling him to get out, he merely crouched down.

He expected Wanda to go and greet Jase but she didn't. Instead, she stayed at his side, and he was so fucking pleased with that. Hah. The dog wanted him.

Jase smiled and stood. "You want to see me?"

"Yes."

"Let me take you to my office."

"The dog, sir," Ben said.

"The dog clearly stays." Jase walked to his office and Grant moved with Wanda at his side.

They stepped inside Jase's office, which wasn't the door he'd come through with Aria.

"What is Aria doing here?" Grant asked, more interested in her reasons for being there.

"I can't discuss clients with you, Grant."

"Client. She's using this place?"

Jase sighed and sat down. "You're already breaking rules with your dog. I won't be discussing people who visit here."

Grant sat down and Wanda sat beside him. They looked at Jase.

"Just so you know, it doesn't say anywhere on the building that dogs aren't allowed."

"Grant, it's a gym. Dogs at gyms could get hurt."

"I came to see you."

"What can I do for you?"

"I want a job."

Jase laughed. And continued to laugh.

He waited.

Eventually, the laughter died down, but Grant wasn't entertained. In fact, he was pissed off. Before his brother's visit, he was handling shit fine, and now he was at the end of his tether.

"You're not joking."

"I'm not joking. You're hiring. I want a job."

"The job description is for a personal trainer, Grant. Not for … I don't even know what you do."

"I can train on the job."

Jase shook his head.

"Come on, what do you need me to do?" Grant asked.

"First of all, you'd need to follow the rules, and to do things properly, not how you think they should be done."

"I can do that."

Jase shook his head.

"I don't see many people applying," Grant said.

"Look, I get it, I'm not the perfect choice, but I am one of the best. I'll work on the job, and how about this? I help you out when you need it."

Jase frowned. "I don't need a member of Chaos and Carnage in my gym. It'll scare my clients away."

"I won't wear the patch while I'm here."

The other man shook his head but Grant saw that he was wearing him down, which was all he needed to do. He tried not to smile.

Jase sighed. "Fine. You can have three weeks and we'll see if it's even worth you applying for a personal training course. I can invest in one if I feel you have what it takes and it can be dealt with through the gym."

Grant smiled. That was all he needed.

Getting to his feet, he held his hand out for Jase to take, and he shook it strongly. He was surprised by the firm grip Jase had, but then again, the guy probably spent every waking moment working out.

He left the gym, taking Wanda with him, and they headed back to his apartment, where there was a pizza waiting on the doorstep. Fucking assholes. Opening the box, he saw nothing had touched it, so he carried it into the house. He pulled off a large slice, dropped the pizza box onto the main table, and then took a bite.

Wanda was sitting next to him, and he felt her eyes on him, looking. "You want a bite?"

There was a small bark, and he held the pizza out to her, and she took it.

He laughed. "Attagirl. Do we think that crazy vet was right? You just need some lovin'." He rubbed at the back of her neck.

Grant knew what that was like, not that he'd say it out loud.

Chapter Three

Ouch!

Ouch!

Really fucking *ouch!*

It was taking every single part of her strength not to whimper at what was happening to her body. Jase had warned her at the beginning she would feel it. He'd only wanted her to do some warm-up exercises. Her body was already in protest. The first day.

But she wouldn't quit.

She refused to quit.

Opening the vet practice, she kept moving as she didn't want her body to stiffen up. After she left the gym last night, it had felt good, like she was on the right path. Jase had told her they would work out a meal plan and sort through a way of making this work. He seemed so confident he could help her, which was a relief. She didn't have a clue what she was doing.

Growing up, her mother simply took all the good things away from her, and she ended up eating cardboard, which sucked.

She'd gone home, enjoyed a salad, gone to bed, and this morning, she had woken up with her body in a full-on aching zone. Now she hurt all over. It didn't matter, though. She could handle a little pain.

With the practice open, she lifted her thighs close to her chest and placed them on the floor. She did this repeatedly until they started to feel good. The chair looked tempting, but she refused to cave so quickly.

"Are you okay?"

She turned to find Andy watching her.

"Yeah, yeah, I'm fine. I went to the gym, and I'm … well, just a little sore."

"I had no idea you frequented the gym."

"I didn't, but I do now."

"Huh, okay."

Aria felt the heat fill her cheeks. Andy was one of the few people who had never judged her on her weight. Staring at her boss, she wondered if this was about to change.

"Well, if that's what you want to do," Andy said, stepping closer and handing her a mug of coffee. "I, for one, couldn't go to the gym."

"Andy, you don't need to go to the gym."

Andy laughed. "Yeah, I may be thin, honey, but trust me, I am unfit. You tell me to climb a hill and I'd be puffing within a few feet." She wrinkled her nose. "Gyms are not for me."

Aria didn't want to talk about her experiences yet, so she smiled.

"Where's Phil?" Aria asked.

"Another late-night call. This time to the dog shelter in town. It was only an hour ago, but he went anyway."

"The one with Grant?"

"Nah, the other one owned by the club." Andy sighed. "Do you know anything about the club?"

"What do you mean?"

Andy and Phil were new to town.

"You know, anything about them? I've seen them riding through town with their leather jackets, and of course coming here with the dogs. What do you know about them?"

Aria frowned. "There's nothing to know, or at least I don't think there is. They've been here my whole life."

She wasn't going to tell this woman that her parents hated them, and wanted them ridden out of town. She never had an issue with any members of the club.

Everyone she had met seemed nice to her, or at least reasonable. A little rough around the edges, but then, wasn't everyone? Grant was nice too.

"Any news from our little dog lover?" Andy asked.

"Grant? No, unless you got a call about Wanda?"

"No, silly. Him asking you out on a date."

She rolled her eyes. "That is not going to happen."

"I heard him and I saw him. That man wants you."

No man ever wants her.

"Hopefully, there's nothing wrong with the dogs," Aria said, trying to change the subject.

"Yeah, they're not the ones that were involved with the dogfighting, were they?"

Aria looked toward Andy. This was the first time she had seemed curious about the dogfighting.

"I don't know the complete story but the rumor around town was that they stopped the dogfighting and helped with the overrun shelter." To Aria, it had always sounded like the club were good guys.

"Huh."

"What?" Aria asked.

"Nothing. Just learning more about the town and seeing as they're turning into regular clients, I want to know more about them. I want to make sure the dogs are in good hands."

"I don't think you'll have an issue with that. They're good people." Aria wasn't sure if she was the right person to judge the club.

Phil chose that moment to come into the veterinary practice. He was humming as he walked up to Andy, wrapped his arm around her waist, and kissed her on the cheek.

"Good morning, my love. Morning, Aria."

"Morning."

"You had a good morning?" Andy asked.

"Yes."

"What was the verdict?"

Aria stood up and hesitated as the pain rushed down her thighs, but she was more than fine. She loved the pain. The burn. Yay for weight loss.

The humiliation was over, seeing as Jase had weighed and measured every single part of her last night. He didn't tell her the number on the tape and she hadn't asked. What she had done, though, was go and buy some scales and read her starting weight.

"There is no verdict. The dogs are all in good health. Some are happier than others, but from what I can see, they run a tight ship." Phil took his wife's coffee and had a giant sip. "Love, you always do this too sweet."

"I'll go and make you some coffee."

"Aria was telling me that they were not the cause of the dogfighting ring."

"I can see that. They care too much. People who use the dogs in such a callous way don't care how they're doing."

Andy nodded. Phil smiled.

Aria made her way into the staff room and made him a cup of coffee, minus the additional sugar his wife enjoyed. The sound of the bell alerted her to a customer.

"Don't worry about it, Andy has taken care of Miss Philips and her cat," Phil said as he stepped into the staff room.

"Ah, that's good." She had already arranged the filing for the customers that Phil and Andy preferred. She didn't know if this was how all veterinary practices were handled, but it was their way.

"Don't mind my wife prying. She wants us to

stay here, and she likes to know as much as she can about a place."

"You've moved around a lot?" she asked.

"Yes. We both love animals. The dogfighting ring has her unnerved. It destroys a part of us, you know, when we lose a patient, so knowing one was set up here has her a little skittish."

"I don't think it was something everyone knew about. I know I certainly didn't."

"My wife cares so much." Phil sighed. "And the dogs we have seen do have considerable scars."

"I know the MC club shut it down."

"I hope so." Phil raised his mug. "Thanks for this."

He stepped out of the staff room and she went back to her desk to see there were already people waiting. She always liked to keep a fresh bowl of treats for the human and for the dog, so they could be put at ease on each trip. She let the clients know, and then got back to her morning's work.

The phone kept ringing, and she continued to answer calls, dealing with stock supplies. Andy and Phil always left a list of items to order. She had to work through each order for them to finish it off at the end of the day. There was always a lot of work to do, which she preferred. She hated being idle.

By lunchtime, the aches in her body had faded, as she was learning to live with them, but she was also hungry. Andy and Phil were still busy, but she was told to head out for her lunch break.

She looked at her car and decided to walk the small journey into town. It took her fifteen minutes to get to the diner, which was already busy.

Beatrice, as ever, was welcoming with a smile. There were no booths, so she ordered her salad, minus the dressing and the meat, and was about to take a seat at the counter when someone called her name. She turned to see Grant in one of the booths. She also noticed the dog, Wanda, by his feet.

"Go, I'll deliver your salad in a moment," Beatrice said.

Walking over to Grant, she paused at his booth.

"Have a seat," he said.

Aria slid into the booth opposite him. "Er, thank you."

"There's no reason you should be sitting all alone while Wanda and I would love the company."

"You know, I don't think they allow dogs here," she said.

"Ah, Carl and Beatrice like me. Besides, they're suckers for a dog and this is a medical emergency for Wanda."

Aria chuckled. "I don't think you're going to get away with constantly calling it a medical emergency."

"It is. My doggy is sad, and she needs to stay by me to feel happy. It's perfect. What did you order?"

"A salad."

He wrinkled his nose. "Seriously?"

"It's all I wanted."

"All the good food Carl has to offer and you go with lettuce leaves."

She giggled. She couldn't help it.

"What have you ordered?" she asked.

"Burgers and fries. Let's face it, they're damn good." Grant patted his stomach.

She rolled her eyes.

"I can leave you two in peace," Aria said.

"You don't have to do that. You can sit with us. I didn't call you over here to tease you with a seat. I meant it, sit with me."

Aria tried not to think about what Andy had said, about this man having the hots for her, because let's face it, there was no way Grant wanted her. He was a handsome man and could have any woman he wanted. There was no way she'd be on the list.

"How has Wanda been?" Aria asked, not liking the quiet at the table.

"Fine, so far. I think the vets have this one right. I think she was just feeling a little lonely. I've gotten her to eat and she has even given me a wagging tail."

"Congratulations. That is a good thing." She couldn't help but smile at how proud Grant seemed.

"She's a good girl." He ran his hand down her back.

She watched him with the dog, and knew he was a kind man. There was something about him that just told her he was good. Sure, he was part of a feared MC club, but she had never seen them do anything wrong.

"Andy was asking about the … dogfights," Aria said.

"Ah, I get that. It did make news." He shrugged. "It makes sense for her to be asking about it."

By news, meaning there had been a small snippet in the local newspaper. Nothing big to report. She had to wonder if that was the club's involvement. Not allowing anyone to divulge what they had done.

"You guys put a stop to it, right?"

"That we did. Evil fucking bastards using dogs to do their dirty work." He shook his head. "They're out of it now and those people have been dealt with."

A shiver ran down her spine wondering what he meant. She wasn't a fool. She had heard what her parents had said about them over the years, and how it was a little unnerving. Aria ignored the spike of fear. Those men, whoever they were, had been using dogs to fight one another.

"I saw you at the gym," Grant said.

She opened her mouth to speak, a little surprised as she hadn't seen him there. Beatrice interrupted by putting her and Grant's food down at the table.

"Enjoy," Beatrice said.

"Thank you," Aria said.

"You're a doll," Grant said.

Aria couldn't deny that the food on his plate looked good. Looked so good, her mouth watered. Her salad looked great but Grant's food looked even better.

You will get even fatter with that.

Don't forget the calories.

The fat.

The carbs.

Just enjoy your salad.

It's what you need.

"Do you want a fry?" he asked, holding up a nice chunky piece of fried potato.

It looked so good. So tempting. She shook her head. That was the old Aria—the Aria who enjoyed food. The new Aria was going to enjoy the right kind of food.

"I've got my salad."

"Don't worry, I won't ask for any."

She laughed. "It's good."

"Yeah, because crunching on lettuce is fun."

She rolled her eyes. "It truly is."

He wrinkled his nose. "Nah, it's not." He shoved three fries into his mouth and closed his eyes, moaning. "So good."

Her mouth watered, but that didn't matter. She was on her diet. No, not *diet*. They never freaking worked. This was her new healthy eating plan. She shoved more leaves into her mouth, chewing. This was tasty.

"Aria, there you are."

She turned her head to see her best friend, Lidia, walking toward her table. There was no sign of Sean around, and she quickly chewed through her food.

"Why haven't you answered any of my calls?" Lidia asked.

"I'm so sorry. I was busy."

"Where were you Halloween? I waited. Sean said you didn't show."

"I was … busy."

"But you would have looked so—"

"I'm sorry," Aria said. "I'll call you, okay. How about that?"

Lidia frowned and then turned to see Grant sitting there, perfectly happy to be silent.

"Oh, are you…"

"No," Aria said.

"Yes," Grant said.

They spoke at the same time.

Lidia chuckled. "Don't mind me. I'm so sorry for interrupting."

Her friend stepped away with her eyes wide and a big smile on her face.

Aria didn't know what that meant. Lidia had left her several messages, texts, and even emails. She felt bad for ignoring her friend, but what was she supposed to do? Sean had said Lidia didn't want her around. Why force herself on someone who didn't want her around?

Why was Lidia determined to lie to her? To pretend they were friends? None of it made sense to her. Stabbing at her salad, she wished she knew all the freaking answers, but she didn't speak in riddles. If people didn't want her around or couldn't stand the sight of her, then they should tell her. She wouldn't force anyone to deal with the pleasure of her company.

****

Aria was lost in whatever world or train of thought she was in. Grant couldn't think of a single thing to say to draw her back to him. She looked so upset.

He also didn't like that she was eating salad. Sure, it was a good salad. Anything cooked by Carl was good. The man knew what he was doing. But she didn't have any meat or any dressing. It was just a bunch of leafy greens with a few other vegetable and salad ingredients and none of them looked appealing to him. His food was damn good. Burgers and fries were always a hit.

He wanted to ask Aria more. Is this why she was going to the gym? There were so many questions he wanted to ask, but none of them came as he didn't want to spoil the moment. Aria was finally sitting with him. He'd been asking her out for the past six months, and each time she laughed or brushed it off as if he was joking. He wasn't joking. He truly wanted to go out with Aria.

"What were you supposed to dress up as on Halloween?" he asked.

She lifted her head and he watched her chew. "It doesn't matter. It's over now."

Grant frowned. "Come on, you can tell me. I don't do much dressing up for Halloween, but you've got to tell me what you were going to be."

"Why?"

"Because I'd like to know."

"And you always get what you want?" she asked.

"Hell, no."

"I was supposed to be a sexy witch, and I did go to the party, but it didn't work out."

"You went to a Halloween party?" he asked.

"Yes."

"I find that hard to believe."

"Why?"

"Well, I invited you to several parties and you never took me up on the offers."

"You were joking around."

"I wasn't."

She shook her head. "You were."

"Trust me, I'd know if I was joking around. Each time I asked you out on a date it was very much real."

"Huh," she said.

He laughed. "Huh. That's all you're going to say."

"I didn't realize you were asking me out. I'm sorry. I figured it was just a joke."

He frowned. "I don't think guys make jokes of asking women out."

"Isn't there like a rule or something, that guys from your club can't date women outside of the club?"

He threw his head back and laughed. Damn. It was so fucking sad. He wasn't about to tell Aria that he was suspended from the club.

"You know my brother, right, he married Maddie?" he asked.

"Yeah, I do."

"She's not club either. We don't keep it in the club. It's not like that."

"Ah," Aria said.

"So, what do you say to a date?" he asked.

She nibbled her lip and he waited. It wasn't a no straight out of her lips, so he would call this a success.

"I'm not sure, Grant."

"Dinner tomorrow night. How about I cook?" he asked.

"Do you know how to cook?"

"Yes."

"I don't think that's a good idea."

He winked at her. "I think it *is* a very good idea. How about it? You and me, have dinner tomorrow night."

She tilted her head to the side and her gaze moved past his. He glanced behind him and didn't see anything that would sway her.

"You're right. Okay, yes, dinner tomorrow night, but you will need to pick me up from my home. I have to go to the gym after work."

"I'll be at the gym myself. I've got a job there."

"Oh."

"So, how about I walk you to my place?"

"Sure. Sure." She got to her feet and picked up her plate. "I better head back to work. It was lovely seeing you, Grant."

He wanted to touch her, but she was already stepping away from him. Grant hadn't finished his dinner and he frowned as he realized Aria hadn't finished hers either.

He wondered if it was busy at the vet's.

Finishing his meal, he picked up his plate, winked at Beatrice, and headed out of the diner. He went back to the shelter the club had built.

When he arrived, he saw a couple of bikes parked out front. Was Bull sending club brothers to remove him from helping at the kennels? He stepped into the main reception and saw Rusty, Pat, and Stacks there.

"Hello, gentlemen," he said.

"Hey, Grant," Rusty said.

Wanda wandered over to her bed and Grant shook his head.

"What brings you boys out here?" Grant asked.

It was rare for more than two club brothers to be at the kennels. There were three of them and him, so that made four. Not that he could count himself as part of the team. Nope. He was suspended.

"Bull wanted us to check stuff," Pat said. "Anything going on?"

"Not really."

"Nothing?" Stacks asked.

Grant looked between the men. Something had happened. He knew it, but they were not allowed to tell him.

"There was no break in security. I've checked the perimeter. Nothing new has happened. I walked the dogs this morning. They had their morning dump. I cleaned up the morning dumps. Fed them their morning food, and I even straightened up the place a little. Does that give you a rundown?"

"Where were you?" Pat asked.

"What the fuck is this? Is this Bull making my life shit? Is this what he wants, just because I called Maddie once?"

That was a stretch. He had called Maddie a few times, but she understood what was happening here. She cared about the fucking dogs. Of course, his brother cared about the fucking dogs as well. He knew that, but even still, this was pissing him off. All it would take was for Bull to call him.

Pat nodded at Stacks and Rusty. Both men left the reception desk and headed outside.

Grant looked toward Pat, and then he saw it, the VP patch attached to his Sergeant at Arms title.

He laughed. "Ah, I see. Does my brother want my leather cut now?"

"No, he doesn't. You're suspended, Grant. You know what that means."

Grant knew Bull had taken the patch from his jacket without him realizing it. Fucking asshole. His brother had stripped him of his title.

"Tell him to keep the title and shove it up his fucking ass."

"You're angry."

"Fuck off," Grant said. "What are you here for? To fire me? To remove my ass from the premises? I'm the only one fucking taking care of it. I'm sure Maddie would love to see that."

"A couple of dogs have gone missing," Pat said.

Grant froze. "What?"

"A couple of dogs from the shelter. Not here. They've gone missing, and there was a reported break-in two nights ago."

"There was nothing here," Grant said. He frowned. "Two nights ago. My brother suspended me last night. Why wasn't I made aware of this?"

"It was a club decision," Pat said.

Grant hated how much that fucking hurt. "A club decision. I see."

"Grant—"

"Don't fucking Grant me! I get it. My loyalty to the club means nothing. Is that it?" he asked. He shook his head as the anger started to build. "What do I need to do? Do I need to die? Was my loyalty not shown with fucking Maddie? Is my brother too much of a coward to come and tell me himself?"

Pat sighed. "Bull didn't come because he knew you'd be upset and seeing as you're brothers, shit escalates."

"You know, I liked you more when you were fucking silent and had all that damage shit going on in your head." Pat had been in the military. He never talked about his time, but when he returned on his last service of duty, the man had changed.

Grant was being cruel. He knew that. And even as

he hated himself for what he was saying, he couldn't stop himself. Every single part of him was telling him to shut the fuck up, to stop, but he couldn't. The club had voted to suspend him. This was the first time he had ever heard of it, and he fucking hated it.

Pat didn't say anything. He turned on his heel and left.

Grant ran fingers through his hair. Anger rushed through his body, as well as pain. The club had turned their back on him. Why wasn't he surprised? *You are surprised.*

"You're worthless to me. You'll never be half the man Bull is. He is a real man. You're a fucking pussy. You're no good for the club. Fat-loving bastard that you are."

Grant closed his eyes and gritted his teeth. He wanted to scream. No, he wanted to hurt something, but instead, he took several deep breaths. Wanda was with him. The dogs were back in the kennels, and he couldn't take his anger out in front of them. They hadn't done anything wrong. No one had done anything wrong. Calm once again.

He cut off the angry words of his father ringing in his head, and got to work. He took the dogs out for a walk one final time, before closing the kennel.

Wanda was still with him, but instead of going back to his apartment, he drove out of town. He kept driving, heading toward the secure warehouse location that had been texted to him earlier. Grant didn't always respond to these texts. It was rare for him to do so. Bull had no idea what he did. Nor did the club. Why did it matter? They had pushed him to the side, so their thoughts no longer mattered.

He parked his car and left Wanda in the back seat. He locked the doors and headed into the warehouse.

Grant heard the commotion the moment he entered the building. He didn't know how the man, Pierce, ran the show or how he was able to get rich people to pay money to watch men pummel each other. It wasn't something he'd pay money to see. This anger wasn't good. He had to get it out, and the only way he'd been able to do that over the past few years was to come to these events. It was rare for him to do so, but it also stopped him from going to Bull and beating the shit out of him. Not because he was his prez, but because he was his brother. And at times, he fucking hated his brother. Bull was an asshole.

Pierce spotted him the moment he entered the warehouse and moved toward him. Pierce was a large man, heavily inked, but also dressed in an expensive suit. Grant stayed perfectly still as Pierce approached him.

"You want in on the action?"

"I want the next fight. Your biggest fighter, and I don't want him to hold back."

"No one holds back here, Grant."

"Good." Because that's exactly what he wanted. He wanted to fight. To feel the burn.

Grant removed his leather cut as he stood at the edge of the fighting ring. He handed the useless leather cut to Pierce and waited.

The fight that was happening when he entered finished a couple of minutes later. The men shook hands as if they were best friends. Pierce liked to put on a show as well.

"All right, all right, ladies and gentlemen. I promised you a spectacle and today you are going to get one. Tonight, we have one of a kind. He's a small-town boy, but he's got fists of steel, and he's looking to do some damage tonight. I give you guys the fucking Eagle!"

His named changed all the time. Pierce never remembered what he called his fighters. It was fucking laughable.

"And tonight, he's going to be checking on our champion, our steed, our fucking gold box. Let's hear it for Monster."

Grant watched as a large, heavily muscled man entered the ring. He was huge and looked like he could take a beating, which was all Grant wanted. Cracking his knuckles, he stepped up close. Pierce was firing up the crowd, getting them to spend money on placing their bets. Grant stared at his opponent and hoped by the end of it, it would hurt.

"You're a fucking disappointment."

"Get out of my fucking face."

"If I wanted a fucking pussy, I'd have brought a woman back."

"What are you, Grant, you're a fucking loser. A waste of time. Do you think I want a son who loves fatties? You're going to be a laughingstock."

He heard the words running through his head.

"Bull will get rid of you. You're a pain in the ass and no one wants you around. You're useless and Bull will see it. All of them will see it, and then you will have nothing. You're just like your old man."

Hands clenched into fists, and he struck out at Monster. It wasn't his fucking name, but Grant didn't care. He was so focused on the shit inside his head that he didn't see the blows coming. Grant was able to block them, getting the upper hand.

Everything faded away.

All he could focus on was the man in front of him. As he did so, Monster changed, looking like Bull, and for a second he hesitated. He hated his brother and loved his brother with equal measure. Then he turned, becoming the scared face of his father. And that angered him. He never told Bull how bad it got. He never told anyone of the beatings he endured while his father was trying to retrain his mind to be normal.

Grant attacked the man in front of him, relishing the blows that struck him. Back then, he'd not hit back. He had never thought to hit back. Feeling his dad's fists, he had thought it was a good thing, that his father was showing him love and affection. But it wasn't. He'd been the punching bag for his dad, because he'd been too much of a coward to take on Bull. Even back then, Bull had been bigger, older, more terrifying. Grant hadn't seen it until it was too late. Everything he had known had been a fucking lie and there was nothing he could do about it.

He hated his father. Whenever he had started to achieve something, to see a future, his dad had been there to knock him down. There was nothing for him to focus on because it was always, without fail, taken away from him. Stripped away.

Monster got in a blow, then another. Grant would have a black eye, but he didn't care. He'd take the bruises any day of the week as it helped him deal with the shit going on inside his head.

Chapter Four

Aria was nervous as she sat in Jase's office. Grant was working at the gym, or so he said. She'd not seen his truck or his bike anywhere near the gym when she arrived.

Stepping foot inside the gym had also made her nervous. Her body ached, but not in a bad way. In a good way. At least, that's what she kept telling herself.

"So, you've told me that you would like to be healthier and reach your goal weight. This is all achievable. You have no food allergies, so I've set out a meal plan for you," Jase said. "We're going to go through all the details now, and then we'll go out to the gym. Is that okay?"

"Yes, yes, that's fine." She didn't want to talk to him about her eating habits, but all of this would be worth it.

Her mother would stop judging her. People would stop assuming bad stuff about her. They would eventually see more than the fat girl. Hopefully, they'd see a person beneath everything else.

Jase handed her the meal plan. Aria opened it up and saw the abundance of vegetable dinners.

"I have also portioned them out, so you know how much to have of any one item. There's also a list of good and bad foods for you to enjoy. This will help reduce your weight in addition to exercise. This is all about having a healthy balance."

Jase kept talking but Aria just stared at it. Another diet, like her mother put her on. There was no chocolate. No fried foods.

I want this.

Forcing a smile to her lips, she nodded. "Yes, this is perfect."

"Right. I want to get into the habit of weighing you weekly so you can see the benefits of our new lifestyle change. Every two weeks, we'll take your measurements as well. We'll keep a progress chart and it will—"

The door to his office opened and Aria turned to see Grant stepping inside. He didn't even bother to knock. His rudeness wasn't what surprised her, but the state of his face. He was heavily bruised. One eye even looked swollen shut, and there was a cut across his lip.

"What the .... er, excuse me, Aria," Jase said, getting to his feet.

She watched as he grabbed Grant's arm. She didn't think that was the best of ideas seeing as Grant looked ready to ... she wasn't sure ... fall or start a fight.

Jase pulled Grant out of his office but he didn't shut the door completely, so she was able to hear everything.

"What the hell is this?" he asked.

"I'm reporting for duty."

"No, you're not. I mean, seriously, Grant, I think it was a joke you coming here wanting to work and become a personal trainer, but the state of you ... this is just ridiculous."

She didn't like the way Jase was talking to Grant. Clearly, Grant was going through some things. Whatever they were, it was upsetting him. He'd been in a fight, that had to account for something. Who would beat him like that? She had also noticed he wasn't wearing his leather jacket, which was a first. He always had on the Chaos and Carnage MC leather jacket, even in the summer.

"I can still work. I'm here, reporting for duty."

"I'm working with a new client today."

"Aria won't mind," Grant said. "Just fucking ask her."

She wanted to take care of Grant, to ask him how he was doing, to see if he was fine.

"Ugh, strike one, Grant. Fucking strike one."

She had never heard Jase swear before, not that she knew the man, but he didn't seem the kind to curse freely. Maybe Grant had that effect on people.

They stepped into the office.

"Miss Taylor, I need to ask if you have a problem with Grant being present today?" Jase asked.

She wasn't comfortable with her date being there during her weight loss journey, but she didn't want to upset Grant either. He'd clearly had a bad couple of … hours? Days? Weeks? Either way, she wasn't going to add to them.

"I don't mind." She forced a smile to her lips and noticed Jase's eye twitch. He wasn't happy with her answer.

She wanted to apologize, but she kept her lips shut.

Jase rounded the desk and took a seat. "As I was saying, we'll be taking your measurements, and your weight. At first, with such a radical change, you'll see instant success. As we continue with this journey, it will slow down. When we approach that, I want you to be open and honest with me. Some people will stop their new plan as they no longer feel it's working, but it is. What we want is to reach your goal weight, find the right structure for you, and then keep working to stay on the right track."

Grant took her meal plan from her and opened it up.

She clenched her hands into fists and then placed them on her knees. Jase wasn't happy with the interruption, even though Grant hadn't said anything. His actions spoke so freaking loud. Aria was tempted to ask him what he was thinking, but instead, she kept her thoughts to herself and smiled at Jase to continue.

"Also, we know this journey can be intense, and if at any time you feel the need to—"

"You're starving her," Grant said.

Jase's nostrils flared. "Grant, could you please save all of your questions for the end?"

"I would, but rather than you starving our client, and you know, giving her a reason to not live, why not come up with a better plan, like telling her she doesn't need to be here?" Grant asked.

Aria looked from Jase to Grant. This was not what she expected.

"Grant, please leave," Jase said.

"You did the same fucking thing to Maddie and now you're doing it to Aria. Do you just have a fetish with starving women?"

"Stop!" Aria had heard enough. "I asked him to do this. I came here for help. He's not forcing me. No one is forcing me." She wasn't going to point out the obvious, which was that her mother, to a point, was forcing her hand. "Now, if you can't let Jase do as I've asked, then please leave."

There was silence after her outburst, but one look at Jase and she knew he was grateful to her for shutting Grant up. She had to wonder if she did anything at all, or if he was sitting there thinking about something else to say to her. Either way, she took a deep breath and turned toward Jase, waiting.

He started to talk to her about his plan. For the next half-hour, he spoke of small goals, and then about her routine. She was to return to the gym every Monday, Wednesday, and Friday. Weekends she was to rest, as the last day would be an intense workout.

She was a little afraid as he continued to talk

about what was going to happen on those days. After they were finished, Jase checked the time, and it would seem after Grant's outburst, there was no chance of him taking her to the main gym and getting set up. With a glare at Grant, he brought the meeting to an end.

Shaking Jase's hand, she made her way outside, surprised that Grant followed her.

She stopped several feet outside of the gym. "Don't you have to work?" she asked.

"Jase told me to leave." He shrugged. "I'm not going to argue with him."

"Why are you working at the gym? Doesn't your club own a gym?"

Another shrug.

She wanted to ask him about his leather jacket, but there was something within his demeanor that told her to steer clear of that conversation.

"You know, we can take a rain check on our date," she said.

"You're trying to get out of dating me?" he asked.

She rolled her eyes. "I'm not trying to get out of dating you. I'm just..." She wanted to give him space so he could work out whatever issues he was dealing with.

Grant stared at her.

"What happened?"

"I ran into a fist," he answered.

She frowned. "That couldn't have been fun."

"You'd be surprised what I find fun."

She chuckled. "Okay. Fine. If you're ... fine. Then I don't see a reason why we can't go on this date."

He winked at her and then reached out, taking her hand. "Come on. I'm freezing my ass off."

"Do you take advice?" Aria asked.

"No."

"Oh."

"What advice you got?"

"Don't work at the gym. Find somewhere that won't get on your nerves."

"I've got an issue with Jase, but I can handle the work. It's fine."

"I thought you worked at your brother's garage?" she asked.

He tensed up. "That fucking asshole can do without me."

"Okay," she said.

"Sorry. Me and my brother are not a topic of conversation. He's an asshole and I'm perfect."

"Ah, the perfect sibling thing."

"You know about siblings?"

She frowned. "I have a sister."

"You do?"

"Yeah, Isabella, considered the most beautiful woman in town."

Grant frowned and then wrinkled his nose. Isabella, right. The one that just got married. "Yeah, okay. Whatever."

That shouldn't make her feel happy. She loved Isabella. She just got tired of constantly being compared to her, and all the time coming up lacking. None of this was Isabella's fault. Their mother always took over with things. Even when they were younger and Isabella just wanted to hang out, their mother was there to put a stop to it.

"Yeah, I don't believe you."

Grant sighed. "I don't care for her. Besides, I'm here with you, and that's all that counts."

She smiled. They arrived at his apartment, and he made her walk ahead of him, which caused her to be very aware of her prominent behind. Was there a way to walk that didn't highlight how big her ass was?

Aria wished she wore a longer jacket, or even a shirt. But instead, she had no choice but to rush upstairs and imagine him grossed out at how big her rump was. At the top of the stairs, she dreaded looking at him, but forced herself to turn toward him and wait for the response.

He pulled out his keys and flicked the lock.

"Wanda's home, just so you know. Don't freak out. She won't … you know, run to the door or anything, but she might growl as you're the first person I've brought home."

"How is Wanda doing?"

"Better, but I still don't like how she's behaving."

They stepped into his apartment, and as soon as Aria joined Grant's side, she heard a growl.

He reached out, flicking on the light, and there was Wanda sitting near the door, but the moment the light was on, the growl stopped, and Aria smiled at the large dog.

Wanda was huge, but the kind of dog you just loved. At least, she loved.

Grant petted her head. "It's nice to know you care, girl."

Aria touched her head afterward and smiled. "Thank you for not going for me." She wanted to sink her face into the fur on Wanda's head, but instead she settled for a stroke.

She loved dogs. Always had. She had to wonder if it was time for her to get a dog since she loved them so much.

Following Grant into his kitchen, she stayed perfectly still as he put the kettle on top of the stove.

"Here, let me take your coat," he said.

She turned and handed him her coat. Aria

watched him as he threw it over the sofa, and then returned to the kitchen.

"You can take a seat if you like," he said.

He pulled out a chair and she thanked him, lowering down into one of the chairs and then waiting. Nibbling her lip, she glanced around the room, as Grant started to move. He went to the fridge and then to his stove.

"You said you're not allergic to anything, didn't you?" Grant asked.

"No, I'm not."

"Good."

She didn't have a clue what he was doing.

"So, do you have plans to stick around with Jase?" Aria asked. She didn't know if she was going to be able to handle working out with Grant around watching her every move. She might call Jase and ask if they could arrange for another time or even other days.

"I have no idea. I'll see if it sticks, and if it doesn't, I'll move on."

"You know, I did hear you were a damn fine mechanic. That you can fix any problem."

"I do what I need to do," Grant said. "Why are you working out?"

Aria opened her mouth, closed it, not exactly sure how she should answer that. "It's good. It was a Christmas present."

"A Christmas present?"

"Yeah. From my mother."

"Fucking bitch," Grant said.

Aria chuckled. "Wow, okay."

"No, seriously. That is a shit gift and you know it. There's more to life than visiting the gym."

"Says the guy who is currently working at one."

"Nothing sticks, Aria. Gym today, diner

tomorrow, and I don't know what I'll be doing the day or days after."

He put something on a plate and then moved toward her, placing it in front of her.

"A fried peanut butter sandwich."

Aria smiled, but in the back of her mind she had to wonder just how many calories this had. She wanted to ask him but didn't want to be rude, so she picked it up and took a bite. Grant had joined her on the other side of the table. She enjoyed peanut butter. She had never had it fried, though, so this was a whole new experience for her.

"It's good," she said.

Grant winked at her. "Trust me, whenever you have a shitty day, nothing beats a peanut butter sandwich."

"Have you had a shitty day?"

"I've had better days."

She wanted to ask him about them, but at the same time, not pry. This was her very first date. She wasn't sure of the protocol or what was expected.

Grant had cooked for her, and in an odd way he'd shared what he considered his comfort food, and that just meant so much to her. She took another bite, and the peanut butter melted in her mouth. It had been months since she allowed herself a taste, and it was so freaking good.

****

The following morning, Grant felt restless. The dinner date last night had gone well, but he'd fucked up with Jase at the gym. He didn't like the man after he had taken Maddie on as a client. Now he was trying to change Aria, and he didn't agree with that.

Their fried peanut butter sandwiches had been a hit, but it hadn't been the date he wanted. After the food, he had no choice but to walk her home. She had surprised him by suggesting she walk home on her own. That shit wasn't happening on his watch.

He'd walked her home, and once at the door, he'd debated whether to kiss her. Aria had answered that for him by quickly escaping into her home. There hadn't been any time for a kiss. Which fucking sucked. He would love to feel those plump lips pressed against his.

Anyway, he didn't get his wish, and now he'd gone to the kennels, took care of the dogs, but Pat's warning the other day didn't sit well with him.

All the bullshit at the club didn't matter. Yes, he was pissed that Pat was wearing the VP patch. He didn't realize how much it bothered him, until he actually saw it, but now that he did, he had a big issue. That patch was his. Besides that, two dogs were missing. They didn't come from his kennels, so the only place that left was the animal shelter.

Locking up the kennels for a few hours, he took Wanda with him to his truck, and they drove out toward the animal shelter.

After Bull got involved with Maddie and they uncovered what was happening at the shelter, the club had invested a lot of money. All the brothers were huge dog lovers.

He arrived at the main parking. There weren't many cars parked, nor did he see any bikes. Climbing out of his truck, he looked toward Wanda. Her ears were down and she didn't look happy to be back at the shelter. He could imagine it had bad memories for her.

"You stay here, girl. Bark if you see anything. Kill whatever motherfucker comes near you."

He closed his truck and locked it. There was no way he was letting anything happen to the dogs on his watch.

Stepping into the main reception, he saw Hellen on the front desk. She was one of many volunteers, but he did believe the club now paid her.

"Hey, beautiful," he said, moving up to the counter.

"Grant, hey," she said.

His charm never worked on her, but it was worth a shot.

"How are you doing?" he asked.

"Fine. Fine. Yourself?"

"I heard about the dogs. Any luck finding them?"

She shook her head and he saw the worry in her eyes. "No. None."

"Do you mind if I take a look at the security system?" Grant asked. Ever since they had uncovered the dogfighting as well as Maddie's attack, they had put in security cameras.

"Yes, of course. The club has already been by to see it."

"I'm sure they have, but I'm thinking a fresh new set of eyes…" He winked at her. "You know, just for the sake of it."

"Sure. Sure."

Hellen handed him the keys and he winked at her again, but this time he made his way toward the security room. The club could suspend his ass all the wanted but it didn't stop him remembering shit, like where the security room was. Stepping inside, he looked at all the cameras, the angles, the screens.

"Okay, so how the fuck do I do this?" He sat at the main desk and then at the main board, reminding himself where to click.

There was a small computer on the desk, and with a few keys pressed, he was able to remember and see where they stored the old security footage that had been taken over the course of the past few days. He drew it back to the day Pat came to see him, and then moved toward the day before. He was able to speed it up a little, to watch the dogs being walked and to see people coming and going. For two hours, he watched the same segment of the security footage, on and off, being clear. Pretty much playing "spot the fucking difference."

"You know Bull is going to be pissed at you," Maddie said, making him jump.

He spun around to see her standing in the doorway, with a baby strapped to her chest.

"Fucking grass," Grant said, glancing past Maddie's shoulder, but Hellen was nowhere to be seen.

"I'm glad she told me." Maddie moved into the room, keeping the main door shut. "How have you been?"

"Peachy." He clicked on the screen and turned toward her. "What do you expect?"

"I expect you to talk to me, Grant."

He shrugged. "I take it, you know Bull's suspended me. Should you even be talking to me?"

"Yes, I know what Bull did, and he says it's a club decision and trust me, I had nothing to do with it. It's why I'm here. I want to see how you're holding up."

"Still here."

"Grant, cut the crap. I get it. You're an asshole when you feel threatened and all the crap that leads up to it. But this is me we're talking about." Maddie moved beside him and took a seat. "And I'm with your niece."

He looked at his niece and she was wide awake. Love bloomed in his chest.

"She's gorgeous," he said. "I'll sharpen my hunting knives. She is going to have men drooling after her."

Maddie laughed. "She is, isn't she?" She stroked

her daughter's head.

"You heard about the missing dogs?"

"Yes. I know the club is out there, searching for them. They've already checked the security cameras," said Maddie.

"Did they?" Grant asked. "Did they see something?"

"No, nothing."

"Huh."

He looked at Maddie, and she squinted at him. "You saw something."

"Just watch," he said.

He played the video and waited for Maddie to catch on to something. She didn't see it. He played it again. She didn't see it.

"Look at the time stamp," Grant said.

It had taken him a few moments to realize what he was missing.

Maddie frowned and looked closely. "There's ten minutes. It's a jump."

"Yeah, whoever it was had access to this security room. They turned off the main cameras on the path that would lead them out. The two dogs taken were big German shepherds."

"Wow," Maddie said.

Grant got to his feet.

"What are you going to do?" Maddie asked.

"Talk to the only person in this building who has the key, and that's Hellen."

"She doesn't know anything." Maddie reached out to grab his arm.

"She must know something. She was under strict instructions not to give that key to anyone except a club brother."

"Then according to you, she has already broken

the rules." Maddie immediately winced. "Shit, I'm sorry."

"No, you're right, but that is the point, isn't it? There are two dogs missing." Grant shook his head.

"Let me call Bull. He can handle this."

"Fuck that, Maddie. I'm suspended from the club, but that doesn't mean I can't do my job. I know what I'm fucking doing." He stepped out of the room and moved toward Hellen.

"We need to talk," Grant said.

He grabbed Hellen's arm and then pulled her into her office.

Maddie had joined him, and she had a glare on her face. He had no doubt she'd already called Bull and his brother would be arriving in a matter of time. The club had missed that little clue. He didn't have time.

What he didn't know was if this was Vito Crew, which it shouldn't be because most of those members were dead, unless the Vito Crew were working for another part of the Cartel.

"Who did you give the key to?" Grant said.

He was fast losing his temper.

"I didn't give the key to anyone. I have no idea what's going on," Hellen said, looking from him to Maddie. "What's going on, Maddie?"

"There's a ... there's a time difference on the security footage, Hellen. At least ten minutes where it had been turned off while the dogs were taken, and then put back on."

"So, I ask again, who did you give the key to? Who are you working for?" He took a step toward her.

He'd never beaten a woman before. The idea never appealed, but this woman had manipulated the club.

"No one, I swear. I only gave it to that guy you

sent over."

Now, Grant was stumped. "Guy?"

"Yes, the one that was here to … er … ugh, what is it called, update the systems or something. I don't remember who he was, but he said he'd been sent by the Chaos and Carnage MC, and he looked very scary."

Grant gritted his teeth. He'd been so out of the loop when it came to club business that he didn't have a fucking clue what she was talking about. Turning toward Maddie, he waited, and she shrugged.

"How long until Bull gets here?" Grant asked.

"About five more minutes, maybe ten."

Grant pressed his lips together. Did he want to have this out with his brother in front of Maddie and Hellen? He didn't have much choice as he heard the sound of bikes roaring closer. He folded his arms and waited.

"It's going to be okay," Maddie said.

She looked worried. He was happy she did. The last person he wanted to see right now was his brother or any of the club.

Seconds later, Bull, Pat, and Rusty joined them. Once again, his gaze was drawn to the VP patch decorating Pat's chest. When he'd been voted as VP it meant everything to him. He'd known the club wanted the Reynolds blood to stay at the top, seeing as they had led the club for many decades through their father and his father, and now Bull. The brothers always got the VP patch. The younger, insignificant brother. Like him.

Bull was changing the rules, though. Pat now had his patch.

"What is going on here?"

"Did you send a guy over here to update the computer systems?" Grant asked, while he glared at his brother.

Bull looked toward Maddie and then Hellen.

"Grant, I think you should leave."

"He's the one that found the problem," Maddie said.

"Yeah, I should leave. That seems to be the easiest option for you, doesn't it? Kick me out. Suspend my ass," Grant said. His hands were clenched into fists.

"What did you do to your face?" Bull asked.

"None of your fucking business."

"Was it the club?" Maddie asked.

"No!" Bull snapped out the word.

"Trust me, darling, I wouldn't allow them to fucking beat me," Grant said.

Bull ran a hand down his face. "You should leave before I show you're fucking wrong, or is this what you want? Another shot at leadership?"

"I don't want your fucking patch." He'd gladly beat the shit out of Bull, but for the patch, never. He didn't fucking want it. Whenever he'd made a previous claim to the patch, it had been bullshit. He didn't want it. All he wanted was for Bull to get the fuck out of his face.

"We're all getting off track here," Maddie said.

She raised her voice and as she did, Lindsey, his beautiful niece, began to whimper, and Grant immediately backed down. There was a baby in the room. His blood. He and Bull both stepped back, and Grant took a deep breath.

"According to Hellen, the club sent a guy to update the computer system. That's who she gave access to. During that time, there's a ten-minute delay in the footage. One moment the dogs are in the cage, the next moment it's like they vanished."

And seeing as he didn't know anything the club was doing, he moved past Bull and left the shelter. He walked over to his truck and pulled out his keys.

"Grant," Bull said.

He stopped. Should he ignore his brother? Turn? Should he do anything? Taking a deep breath, he turned toward his brother and looked at him.

Bull's hands were open at his sides. "That was good work."

"Did the club send a guy over?" Grant asked.

Bull shook his head.

"Then someone knows how we work and they know how to get into the shelter. Start with Ranford. He's been the closest suspect we have."

"He's not into dogfighting."

"Then someone close to him," Grant said. "I don't know, but if they've taken two dogs, they're going to take more. You know it. I know it." It was only a matter of time before they had a problem.

"Do you need some more guys at the kennels?" Bull asked.

"No, I've got that shit covered." He opened his truck and climbed inside.

Grant was tempted to leave it like that, but he just couldn't do it. Winding down his window, he stuck his head out. "Be careful," he said.

He didn't know who it was that could be threatening the club, but either way, he didn't like it.

Pulling out of the animal shelter, Grant drove back to the kennels owned by the club. This time, Wanda was more than happy to get out of the truck. He opened the doors for her to go into the bed he'd purchased. He walked to the back of his truck, opened it, and pulled out some of the tools he stored.

He closed his truck and then went from door to door, changing all the locks, as well as the security codes. He worked throughout the day, until every single lock and code was changed. Once that was done, he sent a simple word to Bull. It was the one word they had agreed on years ago. The word Grant would send to Bull to warn him of the warpath his father was on—*Carnage*. Grant hadn't used it in a long time, and he had to wonder if Bull would remember it. After all, it had been a long time ago.

He tapped his fingers against his leg as he waited for a response. One came in a few moments later and he picked up his cell phone, clicking on his brother's name. A simple icon of a thumbs-up was shown.

Bull remembered their code. At least he had remembered fucking something. It didn't make Grant any happier with him, but it was a start. Now, all he needed to do was figure out who would claim to be sent by the club.

Chapter Five

"Sweetheart, you shouldn't eat that. It's got way too much butter. Here, have some sprouts."

Aria didn't dare look across the table at her sister and her new husband. Ignoring the mashed potato, she picked up the sprouts and placed a few on her plate. Her mother looked at her with a smile.

Sunday lunch was a nightmare. She'd been able to avoid it for the past couple of weeks, but her parents had been insistent she attend today. Her sister was back from her honeymoon, so of course everything was now much better, and even more important. Her sister did look so happy and tanned.

Aria looked at the table and wondered what else she'd be able to eat. The roast potatoes were a no. Her mother would slap her hand away. There were carrots, so she picked them up. The stuffing was a no. There was not a lot of food. Her mother placed a few slices of beef on her plate and then a drizzle of gravy. That was all she was allowed. Beef, sprouts, and carrots.

Aria sighed. She didn't even have to look at everyone else's plate to know they had a good serving of mashed potatoes, roast potatoes, maple roast parsnips, stuffing, and then the few vegetables. Oh, well. The sooner she ate everything on her plate, the faster she could make her escape.

Aria cut into the beef and shoved it in her mouth. Her mother was a good cook. She chopped the sprouts and took bites of them, followed by the carrots. Isabella was talking animatedly about her honeymoon and the journey they had. Aria was more than happy for her. Delighted, in fact.

"Go ahead, honey, tell them," her husband said.

She already had an idea as to why she'd been

called to her parents' house.

"We're pregnant," Isabella said.

There was a squeal from their mother, and Aria smiled, looking over at her sister. "Congratulations."

"Thank you," Isabella said.

That was all they got to say to one another before their mother cupped Isabella's face and started to kiss her. Aria sipped her water as their father shook Michael's hand. With her parents happy, Aria made her escape and headed toward the kitchen to grab the wine as a celebration.

"Hey, Aria," Isabella said.

She looked up at her sister.

"Hey, so congratulations. Wow, you're going to be a mother."

Isabella put a hand on her still-flat stomach. "I know. It's crazy, isn't it?"

Aria shook her head. "No, not at all."

Her sister moved closer and pulled her in for a hug. "I've missed you."

She laughed. "There's nothing to miss. You know that. I am so happy for you, and trust me, I can't wait to meet my niece or nephew."

"I'm terrified of this pregnancy. What if it's a girl and I screw up?"

"You're a girl, so you know how you want a mother to be." Aria had no choice but to keep a smile on her face. She didn't want to advise Isabella not to be like their mother. "We better get back." She wanted to bring this conversation to a close and very fast.

Stepping into the dining room, her mother was already there with a piece of paper.

"Now, I know your figure is important to you, Isabella. Don't you worry. I was able to have two girls and still stay in shape."

Aria felt sick to her stomach. Isabella wasn't even showing and already their mother was putting her on a pregnancy diet.

"With all due respect, Mrs. Taylor," Michael said. "We have an appointment booked with a doctor. The last thing on our minds is a diet."

"Trust me, Michael, you will want me to keep on top of this. No man wants a woman who looks like Aria."

Aria stood there and put the wine down on the table. This was not unheard of. Of course it wasn't. No man wanted Aria. It was why at twenty-five years old, she hadn't been on a single date, nor had a boyfriend, nor had sex. What kind of man would want to see her repulsive body?

You went on a date. With Grant.

Aria didn't even know if that counted or if Grant was just being nice to her because of them knowing each other at work. Either way, she wasn't going to stick around here.

"I've got to go," Aria said. "Congratulations, you two. I'm so happy for you. Mom, dinner was delicious. See you, Dad."

Aria made her escape quickly.

"Aria, please don't go." Isabella had stepped outside to follow her.

Aria pulled her jacket on as she hadn't lingered inside to risk the jibes from her mother. "I have to go. I've got work and other stuff to do. It's nothing personal."

"I know it's not. Mom is wrong, you know. You're beautiful and you will find a man."

"Who can put up with my ugly fat ass?" Aria asked.

"Don't."

"Did you see the wedding photos?" She looked

toward her sister, who was frowning. "Ah, I see you haven't. Trust me, it's best if you go back inside with Mom. This is what she wants."

"What about what I want?" Isabella asked.

"What do you want, Isabella?" Aria was struggling to keep it together. She was so used to these personal attacks from her mother, all of them verbal about how she looked, how much she weighed, but they still hurt. Normally, she could contain her tears until she was alone, but today that was a real struggle. Isabella wasn't allowing her to escape fast enough.

"I wanted my sister to be with me. You know, to help me through."

"I will be. I'm only a phone call away. We both know Mom would prefer you to call her."

"You do know she's wrong, don't you?"

Aria shook her head. "Mom is always right."

She turned on her heel and walked away from her parents' house. It was Sunday, so going to work wasn't ideal. Phil and Andy preferred her to have one day off. Her only day off, and her presence had been demanded by their parents. If she was a child, she'd have stamped her foot on the ground and declared the world wasn't fair.

She was happy for her sister and wished she could be part of that process, but hearing her mother saddened her. All she ever did was tell her how bad she was, how horrible she looked. The last thing she needed now was to constantly be reminded by her mother just how much she had failed at everything.

Tears filled her eyes, and as she headed toward her home, she came to a stop when she caught sight of Grant walking with Wanda. Swiping at her tears, hoping they didn't fall, she forced a smile to her lips as she looked at him.

"Grant, hi," she said.

"Aria, is everything okay?"

The smile on his lips faded as soon as he looked at her.

"Yeah, yeah, everything is fine. Of course it's fine." She laughed. "Why wouldn't it be?" He cupped her cheek and she looked up at him. "You're upset."

"I've had a really shit day, and I … I just want to…"

"Drink?" he asked.

"Huh?"

"You know, drink? Lose your head."

"I have no idea?" Aria asked.

He held out his arm. "Care for me to help you with whatever demons you're fighting?"

In the back of her mind, she knew she should tell him no, but after thinking about her mother and what just happened, she didn't want to go home alone. Putting her arm through Grant's, they made their way back toward his apartment. It was already warm and she removed her coat. Grant once again threw it across the back of his chair.

"I don't have anything classy, but when I need a moment, I think nothing beats whiskey," he said.

He returned from the kitchen with a bottle of dark amber liquid and two glasses. She watched as he poured two generous shots. Aria had already taken a seat on the sofa, and she leaned forward, picked up the glass, and took a drink. She couldn't help but wrinkle her nose at the taste. It was nasty.

Grant swigged his back in one gulp and took a breath after.

She giggled. "It's disgusting."

"But it will get the job done."

Aria finished the whiskey and it burned on the

way down. She wrinkled her nose at the taste. The fire was welcome in the pit of her stomach.

"How is Wanda doing?" she asked.

"Wanda's doing great. Why don't we talk about you?" he asked.

She giggled. "Me?"

"Yeah, why you looked close to crying? Do I need to go and kick the crap out of someone?" he asked.

Aria thought this was the funniest thing she had ever heard. She also snorted, which was a gross sound.

She covered her face. "Sorry. You would kick the crap out of someone because they had upset me?" she asked. "Isn't that a little extreme?" The words seemed to roll off her tongue.

Should she warn him that she'd never drunk anything before in her life? Never drank at a party, not even with Lidia. She'd always been the designated driver and she took her role seriously.

Grant had poured her a second glass of whiskey. "What is extreme?" he asked. "Protecting you from the evils of the world?"

"The world cannot be that evil." She sipped the whiskey and the fire in her stomach was building.

"There is evil in the world. Fucking monsters that would kidnap dogs and have them kill other dogs. Rapists, murderers, all that shit. You know the drill."

Aria sighed. "Wow, now I do feel like utter shit."

Grant laughed. "Why?"

"With everything going on in the world and how bad it can be, my problems are not that bad."

"Everyone has bad shit. Don't compare yours to others, but whatever it was, it made you cry."

"I didn't cry."

"I saw you wipe at your tears. You can't argue with me."

She wanted to stick her tongue out at him but she stopped herself. Grant was … she didn't exactly know what he was, but it didn't seem right to stick her tongue out at him.

Grant swallowed back his third whiskey while she was still drinking her way through her second. She finished her second and he immediately poured her a third.

"Are you starting to feel better?"

"Yep. You're right, but it could just be you."

"I'm the best medicine there is."

This made her laugh and snort.

"You know, my sister is pregnant."

"Is this good news or bad?"

"Good news. I'm happy for her."

"But?"

Aria finished her third whiskey, knocking it back, swallowing it, and then trying not to cough.

"Brave woman," he said.

She had lost count of the number he drank.

"My mom is already putting my sister on a diet—a pregnancy diet because no man wants a fat woman. No man wants a woman like … me." Aria hated how fucking pitiful she sounded.

"What?" Grant asked.

"That's what I hear all the time I'm near my mom. 'No man wants a fat woman.' No one wants an ugly ass like me." She laughed. "That's why I get gym memberships. That's why I get to eat sprouts, carrots, and a few slices of beef. I have to watch my weight because I'm not good enough for my mom."

There was silence after her soul-baring. Aria looked up at him and he was moving. Wasn't he? She tried to focus on him.

"Fuck her, Aria. She doesn't have a clue what

she's talking about, and you don't need to take shit from women like her."

"She's my mom. She knows best."

"Someone who makes your life a misery doesn't get the job of making you happy. Not anymore."

"Why are you so close?" she asked.

"You're dizzy."

She held her fingers up close together. "A little bit."

He chuckled. "You're drunk."

"Yep, I think I am."

"You're slurring your words."

"They sound right to me."

He chuckled. "Fuck me, Aria, what am I going to do with you?" he asked.

She reached out and it took her a few attempts to cup his face. "You don't have to do anything with me, Grant. I know I'm repulsive. It's why I'm a virgin." She giggled. "I'm twenty-five years old, and you're the only guy I've been on a date with. The peanut butter sandwiches were so good."

"You've never had sex?" he asked.

"Never. Not once. I mean, I've used my hand a couple of times, but I'm not sure if that even counts."

"Fuck me," Grant said.

She giggled. "I'm sure you could have every single woman in town. You probably already have. I don't know if you've screwed my sister. I know she wasn't an angel." She pressed her head against Grant's. "This is nice."

"I don't think you're going to remember much in the morning."

"But I no longer feel like crying, so this is very nice. I think Jase is going to be pissed with me, though. How many calories are in the whiskey?" Her stomach chose that moment to growl. "I'm starving."

"You're going to be so sick tomorrow."

The world was spinning, and she dropped her hands from Grant's face and closed her eyes. "This is nice."

The horrible voices that constantly played in her head were numb. They were not telling her how right her mother was, how she needed to get her fat ass up and start moving. There was simply nothing.

"Aria?" Grant asked.

"Yeah?"

"Let me take care of you."

"Don't you have better things to do?"

She didn't remember his response as the world went dark, but it wasn't scary. No, this was bliss.

****

Grant looked over at Aria in his bed.

He'd carried her to his room last night, and she hadn't moved or shifted once. At one point he had to put a hand on her chest to make sure she was still breathing. She had freaked him out, but she was perfectly fine.

The alcohol was good stuff. The whiskey was one of the best and he always used it on a shitty day. Bumping into Aria, he had seen the pain and desolation in her eyes. He'd wanted to help. He didn't believe the drink was the best idea, but at least it had stopped her from crying. The only problem now was the sickness that no doubt would come.

Getting to his feet, he made his way to the bathroom, took a piss, washed his hands, and brushed his teeth. Aria still hadn't risen.

Wanda was whimpering, so he opened the door and stood, watching as his dog took her morning leak and crap, before letting her back in. He'd clean up the mess in a moment.

The only thing he knew would be good enough for Aria's head was some toast and coffee. He put the kettle on the stove and started to heat it up. He only had instant coffee so he hoped that worked. Spooning a couple of teaspoons into mugs, he waited, and the sound of the kettle whistled. He turned it off, and like an alarm he heard Aria groan.

Grant rushed back into the bedroom and saw her covering her mouth. Here comes the vomit. He guided her to the bathroom and pulled her blonde hair out of the way so she could vomit into the toilet. This happened three more times and he winced.

Aria had mentioned last night, not having a lot of food. Alcohol on an empty stomach was not good. Next time, he'd make sure to feed her.

Once she was done, he helped her to her feet. She quickly covered her mouth.

"There's a spare clean toothbrush in the drawer under the sink. I'll see you in the kitchen."

He returned to the kitchen, put the kettle back on to boil, and he put some bread in the toaster before grabbing some water and painkillers. Aria was going to need them. Her first time with whiskey was not being kind to her. He put everything on the table and paused.

Aria had let slip a whole host of firsts last night and he couldn't help but wonder about them. A virgin. Was she joking about that? He shook his head and made himself some toast, sipping at his coffee.

Aria entered his kitchen. Her hair had been brushed and she'd splashed some water onto her face.

"Morning," she said.

"Morning, beautiful."

"Er, last night, did we … er, did we do anything?" she asked.

"No, you're still very much a virgin."

She covered her face with a gasp. "Oh, God, did I tell you that?"

"Yes."

"I'm sorry."

"Don't worry about it," Grant said. "Is it true?"

She looked at him over the tips of her fingers and nodded her head.

"Wow, okay, er, how?" he asked.

She frowned. "How am I a virgin?"

He nodded.

"Isn't that obvious? I haven't had sex."

"Well, I know that, but I have to wonder, you know, how? I mean, you're gorgeous. Haven't you had boyfriends before?"

"Have you even looked at me?" Aria asked.

"Yes, I am looking at you now."

"Then that's how…"

"Again, I don't see the issue."

"I'm fat, Grant."

He glared at her.

"Trust me. No man wants this." She pointed at her body and Grant had heard enough. He put his mug of coffee down, as well as his toast, and took a step toward her.

"I am looking at you, and I can tell you, I guess I'm not a man, because I fucking want what I see." He was tempted to put her hand on his dick, but he didn't want to push her too far. She was hungover.

He stared into her blue eyes that were open quite wide. Grant wanted to kiss those plump lips, to feel them against his own, but instead he took a step back.

"Water, painkillers for the headache you've got. Toast to settle your stomach, and coffee. I'll drive you home afterward."

"What time is it?" she asked.

"A little after eight."

She gasped and got to her feet. "Crap. Shit. Crap. I was supposed to be at work an hour ago. Where's my cell phone?"

"You left your bag in the sitting room," he said.

She rushed out of the kitchen and he couldn't help but look at her ass. She wore the pair of jeans he'd seen her in yesterday. He had left them on her last night, even though it had upset him to put anything on her body. Aria shouldn't be hidden away. Not from him. Never from him.

Picking up his coffee, he moved to the doorway and listened.

"I'm so sorry, Andy. I was … time got away from me. I'll make it up to you, I promise."

He doubted Andy would care. The other woman was nice and cared about Aria. He also knew that Aria was always at work earlier than needed most mornings, if not all of them. If Andy and Phil caused her any trouble, he'd deal with them. Simple as that.

Aria finished her phone call and returned to the kitchen. Grant had already moved back toward the stove. Picking up his toast, he walked toward the table and sat opposite her.

"What did your bosses say?"

"They're happy that I'm fine." Aria rubbed at her temple. "I'm so sorry for crashing here last night."

"I invited you back, don't you remember that?" he asked.

"There's a lot about last night I don't remember."

"Like telling me you're a virgin?"

She groaned. "Could we stop?"

"Why? It was very sweet."

"I didn't, like, beg you, did I?"

"To what?"

"To … you know?"

He wanted to ask her to say it, but seeing as she looked so embarrassed already, he decided to save her the trouble.

"You didn't beg me to do anything. You told me a statement of fact."

"How is it that I can't remember anything from last night but you do?"

"I can handle my drinks. Last night was your first time and you had three or four shots of whiskey and I have to say it's very powerful stuff. Very, very powerful."

She blew out a breath. "Yep, you're right. I'm sorry."

"Stop saying sorry. I enjoyed the company."

Aria nodded and took a bite of toast, and he watched as she sipped her coffee.

"You know, you're wrong. You're beautiful and there are plenty of men who'd love to have you, myself included," he said.

"Grant, you don't have to say that."

"I know I don't have to say anything. I'm not just saying it, either. I'm serious. I know I want you as mine. I've been asking you to date me for months."

Aria nibbled her lip and he stared at her.

"Is it the patch?" he asked.

"The patch?"

"I'm part of the Chaos and Carnage MC. I know it puts a lot of people off."

"I don't care about that." She sighed. "I … this is … I…"

"Go out with me tonight," he said.

"I've got the gym."

"You don't need it," he said.

"I want to do it. I need to do this, for me."

He wanted to ask if it was really for herself or for her mother. He couldn't even remember what her mother looked like but he fucking hated her.

"As it happens, I'm also working at the gym tonight. I'll be there and then afterward we can go to the diner, or wherever you want to go," he said.

"Er, if you're sure. If you're not too busy."

Fucking hell. He was trying to date this woman and it was impossible to even convince her that was what he was trying to do.

"Aria, babe, I'm trying to go on a date with you, not make an appointment. Tonight, you and me, the diner. How about that? It's a date. A date where at the end of the night, I'm going to take you home and then I'm going to kiss you."

"Oh," Aria said.

"Yeah, oh. Now, I'm going to let you finish your toast, your coffee, I'll drive you home, and if you need it, I'll drive you to work."

"You don't have to do that," she said.

"Trust me, Aria. I want to do that." He didn't know how he was going to convince her of what he wanted to do. She was a stubborn woman.

"Okay," she said.

She ate her toast and he finished his. Wanda was more than ready to go. Stepping out into the cold, Grant remembered the poo and quickly scooped it up, threw it into the trash, then helped Aria into his truck. Wanda was more than happy to climb into the back. She had found a blanket and pulled it over her, which was so freaking cute. He was falling in love with that dog and her crazy ways.

He dropped Aria back at home and she told him she'd drive to work. Grant was tempted to argue with her, but he was already pushing his luck by demanding she go on a date with him.

Before heading to the kennels, he checked in at the diner and brought Beatrice and Carl up to speed on his date. Once that was done, he headed to the kennels, checking all the locks, and then dealing with the dogs, before glancing over the security footage. After he was satisfied, he pulled out his cell phone and dialed Maddie. He needed advice, and fast.

"Grant, I'm pleased you called. I've been worried about you."

"What do you do on a date?"

There was silence on the other end. Grant frowned. "Maddie, you there?"

"Yeah, yeah, I'm here. Dating?"

"Yes, what do you do on a date and I don't mean fucking either. I mean taking someone out on a date?"

"You're going on a date?"

"Yeah."

"Oh."

"What's wrong?" Grant asked.

"It's … I don't know, just you and the whole idea of you dating."

"I can date."

"I'm not disputing that. Of course you can date, and I imagine you'd be very, very good at it."

Grant waited, patting his thigh as he listened to Maddie make a few confused noises over the phone.

"What are you doing?"

"I'm trying to imagine you dating. Who is the lucky woman?" Maddie asked.

He was tempted to keep that part a secret but he didn't see a reason why he should. "Aria Taylor."

"What? You're dating Aria Taylor?"

"Yeah. I've arranged a date with her."

"Are you sure you're not dating her sister? I

mean, no, you wouldn't do that. She just got married recently."

"Why is this so hard for you to comprehend?" he asked.

"Because … well, you used to, I mean, you're not…"

"Damn it, Maddie, just spit it out."

"You hate bigger women, Grant. You bullied me for years because of my weight and I know Aria is similar to my size. You're not, ugh … you're not going to bully her, are you?"

Grant's teeth clenched.

"You fucking pussy. You're not going to fuck a fatty, not on my watch. They're ugly, repulsive, and fucking lazy."

He cut off the memory.

"Look, I like Aria, okay? She's a good woman. I want to go on a date with her and I want to make it good." This was a bad fucking idea. "You know what, forget I said anything."

Before Maddie had a chance to tell him no, he hung up his cell phone and immediately dialed Bull. He hated calling his brother for anything.

"What have you done?" Bull asked.

"I've asked Aria Taylor out on a date, and I wondered what you'd recommend I do on a date. Seeing as you've managed to keep Maddie, you know, with my help, not that it means a lot."

"Are you joking right now?" Bull asked. "When I first got Maddie to come and work for us, I had to kick your ass out of the office because you called her 'Chunk' and some other fucking shit."

"Aria is not fat."

"She's not thin either."

"Are you going to fucking help me?"

"That depends. Are you going to hurt one of the women who helps us out at the fucking veterinary practice?"

"Is that what you're worried about? Me hurting Aria?"

"You hurting the fucking reputation of the club. If you're doing this for one of your bullshit pranks, Grant, then don't bother. Leave the young woman alone."

"It's not a prank," Grant said, but instead of listening to any advice his brother might have, he hung up the phone.

He was done. Finished. Over.

Throwing his cell phone onto the main reception desk, he dropped down onto his seat, and Wanda, clearly sensing his upset, moved toward him, resting her chin on his knee.

"Hey, girl, how are you feeling?" he asked, rubbing at her head. "Don't look at me with those judgey eyes. They're not wrong. Throughout high school I bullied Maddie because of her weight."

He didn't have any excuse for the shit he called her either, and he'd made her life hell. Even when she came to work for Bull, like his brother said, he'd continued to call her "Chunk," as well as tease his brother about his choice in women.

"I'm a fucking asshole."

Aria was … she was … he couldn't get her out of his fucking mind. She was the only person right now that made sense in this world.

He didn't understand why he was suspended, not really.

Running a hand down his face, he kept his other hand on top of his dog's head. Grant leaned back and looked up at the ceiling, thinking about Aria and then about the two missing dogs. The club hadn't called in

Dylan, the local sheriff. They never liked to include Dylan, but what if that in itself was a clue? Someone had been able to get through their security, tell Hellen they were sent by the club, and remove two dogs.

He sat up, still stroking Wanda's head. Sometimes sudden movement startled her, and he didn't want her afraid of him.

Picking up his cell phone, he dialed the sheriff's office and waited. He continued to wait until Grace's gruff voice picked up.

"What the fuck do you want?" she asked.

He couldn't help but smile. Grace was an old woman, and at times had everyone believing she was even alive at the dawn of time, the way she talked. Most people were afraid of her and she had the ability to instill the fear of death into most. Grant found her adorable. Growing up with an asshole as a father made people like Grace seem adorable to him.

"Grace, it's so good to hear your voice."

"Grant Reynolds, what did you do?"

"Ah, it's not what I did this time, but what someone else did. Is Dylan around?" he asked.

"Yeah, he's in his office, causing all kinds of paperwork I'll have to fucking deal with."

Grant snorted. Poor Dylan. The man didn't have the heart to fire her. She was a big help in keeping kids from reoffending, and did more than her reception job. He didn't know if Dylan would willingly listen to him, but it was worth a shot.

Chapter Six

Aria still felt like shit. She couldn't believe she had allowed herself to get so drunk. This was not like her, but being around Grant, at times, made her feel reckless. Why did she try to be nice and perfect all the time? It wasn't like her mother ever cared, not really.

On her way to the gym she thought about Grant, about his lips, about how it would feel going all the way with him.

Stop doing that.

She gritted her teeth and was so focused on the ground, she didn't see who was coming toward her.

"Whoa, Aria, stop."

She crashed into her once best friend, Lidia, sending the other woman to the ground.

"Crap, I'm so sorry," she said, immediately grabbing her hand and helping her to her feet.

Lidia chuckled. "It's okay. I saw you down the street and I've been trying to get your attention. You were so far away."

Staring at her best friend, she couldn't help but think about Sean's words the last time she saw him. *"Yeah, that is not coming to my party. Take your ugly ass away. Lidia is too fucking nice to tell you this, but your fat fucking face is no longer welcome here. She can do so much better than you. Leave."*

Halloween night. Not too long ago.

"Hey," she said. "I, er, I actually have an appointment that I don't want to be late for."

The gym was only a few feet away and as she pointed in the general direction, Lidia turned to see where. "The gym? You're going to the gym?"

"Yeah, it's, yeah, I'm going to the gym now." She forced herself to look at her friend.

Lidia Onslow, perfectly beautiful, slender, and she used to be so nice. At least, Aria had thought she was nice until Sean told her the truth.

"Aria, what the hell is going on?" Lidia asked.

"I don't know what you mean."

"You didn't show up at the party. You're going to the gym now. You don't return my calls and you make excuses to not hang out. What have I done?" she asked.

Aria felt her cheeks heating up at even allowing herself to open up to this woman. Going to the gym, fighting her weight was never an easy battle. In the past, Lidia was there, telling her she was fine, that she was beautiful and sweet, but it had all been lies.

"Why don't you ask Sean?" Aria asked. "You seem to tell him the truth and me, well, you just lie to me to suit yourself."

"What?"

"Leave me alone," Aria said. "If you couldn't stand hanging out with me, you could have just said so. I do listen, and I've got no problem letting this go."

Tears filled her eyes and she forced herself to walk around Lidia and head to the gym. Jase wasn't on the front desk, so she showed the lady who was there her member card and proceeded to go to the changing room. She found a private cubicle to change out of her jeans and sweater, replacing them with a pair of shorts and a very large, oversized shirt.

Once her belongings were packed into a bag, she headed into the main changing room, found a locker, stuffed her bag inside, locked it, and then headed out to find Jase. He was in one of the private gym rooms. There was a member of staff waiting to direct her.

She stepped inside hoping to see Grant, but instead she saw Jase sitting on the mat, legs crossed, with his palms flat together. He opened his eyes and smiled.

"I didn't mean to interrupt." She had swiped at her eyes and she quickly sniffed up, trying to ignore the signs of impending tears.

"Aria, what's wrong?" Jase asked.

"It's nothing." Grant wasn't there, and she was somewhat relieved. "Can we just get started?" She wanted to lose the weight, not spend time fawning over a guy who'd just shown her the smallest amount of attention.

"Of course." Jase got to his feet smoothly, and she watched him as he advanced toward her. "Before we start any physical training, the key is to warm up, so let's see how much you've retained from our previous meetings."

They hadn't done much, but Aria started with her legs, stretching them out, working her muscles, getting her body into the right condition to work out.

Jase moved around her, touching her and changing her posture a couple of times.

"Very good. I'm impressed."

She couldn't help but smile.

"So, I'd like to get us warmed up first. We're going to head out into the main part of the gym. I'm thinking we start with the treadmill first, get you used to momentum. What do you think?"

"You're the boss."

She followed him out to the main gym. There were a lot of people and Aria tuned them all out. Jase must have known how nervous she was as he chose a treadmill in the far corner, which she was thankful for. He waited for her to climb onto the treadmill and she held onto the side, per his instructions.

"We're going to start with a gentle walk," he said, keying some numbers into the treadmill.

She began to walk as soon as it started to move.

One foot in front of the other. It wasn't a fast walk and she didn't know how long this one took before he pressed the numbers on the button. She wasn't out of breath yet, but it wasn't like they were going fast either.

By the third tempo change, Aria started to feel a little breathless but she kept up with the force of the treadmill. Jase stood, watching her. She couldn't help but wonder what he was thinking. Did he find her disgusting too?

He increased the pace one more time, drawing her into a steady jog. She felt perspiration covering her body as she tried to keep up. There was a pain building in her side, and when she was about to ask him to stop, Jase slowed it down, giving her a chance to catch her breath, until he brought it to a stop.

"Very good. I think we can work on increasing your cardiovascular. How do you feel about using the bike?"

"You're the master," she said.

He chuckled. "I like to make sure my students are happy with their progress. Once we build up your fitness, we will then start to work on different personal stretches."

"Where's Grant, if you don't mind me asking?" Aria asked, straddling the bike.

Jase bent down and helped her place her feet into the strap. This bike didn't have a mechanism to start riding, so all she had to do was push and she was away, which is exactly what she did. She held onto the handles of the bike and started to work her legs. They already felt like jelly, but she pushed her body, forcing it to go forward.

"He's not here, as you know. From what I've learned, Grant flits through life, going from job to job. There's a good chance he won't be here again."

"Oh," Aria said.

"It's not my business to pry—"

"Then don't," she said with a smile.

He hoped she wasn't upset. "Grant is not the kind—"

"Jase, I'd appreciate it if we didn't go down that road." She had no way of knowing what she and Grant were. They had gotten drunk, kissed, but other than that, nothing. He was everywhere she seemed to be, but it had been that way for the past couple of months. Grant always arrived at the veterinary practice, in passing, and then she'd go days without seeing him.

It was strange, but she had come to accept it. It was probably one of the reasons why she didn't believe Grant was attracted to her.

Jase held his hands up. "Not my business."

"It's not that, it's just, er, I don't know what it is. We're friends, I think, so there's no reason to, you know, worry. Well, not worry, but…" She had no idea what to say or do.

"Aria, it's fine, and you are my business. You're my client here, and I take this process seriously. Trust me, I've seen men and women on this path, and I believe it's more important to know you. This is going to build into a friendship. I need you to learn to trust me."

"I don't know you."

Jase smiled. "In time, you will. We're going to take it slow."

She nodded.

After working on the bike, Jase called time, and they headed back to the private room where she did her cool-down stretches. Just as she was about to leave for the changing room, he called her over. He held a tablet in his hands.

"I have a standard routine during a weight loss

and fitness regime. I like to take my time. I believe working with a lifestyle change is much more effective to the person. It helps keep your weight at a manageable level as it fits this process with your life." A small presentation video of an animated man showed him through the process. The screen was split in two halves. One showed Jase's recommendation, while the other showed implementing it short term, that didn't necessarily equate to the same results. Over time, the one who was using extreme dieting for weight loss soon changed their methods.

"I don't need to see this," Aria said.

He tapped the screen. "In time, I want to be able to show you techniques you can implement in your own life as well. Stretches you can do when you get out of bed. Stuff like that."

"Sounds like fun."

Jase chuckled. "It can be."

Aria wanted to ask him what it was like to be fit and perfect, but instead she forced a smile to her lips. "See you soon."

"Yes, don't forget your swimsuit next time."

She cringed but as she was walking away, he didn't see.

Aria didn't bother to take the shower. It was getting late, she was tired, and the last thing she wanted to do was get naked and take a long soak in their showers, even if they did look amazing. She didn't bother changing, grabbing her bag from her locker, and heading out.

It was freezing outside, so she pulled her bag onto her shoulder and immediately sped up her pace to make it home. By the time she made it to the front door, her teeth chattered and her hands shook. It took her three attempts to get the key into the lock. Flicking the catch, she stepped inside, closing and locking the door.

She didn't waste any time dumping her bag on the floor and rushing upstairs to the bathroom. She turned on the faucet, stripped off her clothes, and then stepped beneath the hot water. Slowly, she stopped shaking and the heat was a welcoming relief. Tilting her head back, she breathed a sigh of relief. It felt so good.

She had worked up a sweat in the gym. Her body felt good. This was an odd feeling for her. She wasn't used to feeling so … she couldn't even think of what it felt like. Yes, she was tired, but she felt happy.

She took time to wash her hair, lathering the soap into her scalp, before rinsing it out. By the end of her shower, she felt giddy, happy, and exhilarated. It was a good workout at the gym.

She realized she was hungry. Wrapping her body in a bathrobe and her hair in a towel, she headed downstairs toward the kitchen. She'd already gone through the necessary transition in her kitchen. There were a lot of vegetables in the fridge. Right now, she could use a burger, but she frowned. No. No burger. No processed foods. She was going to do this the right way.

Just as she was about to grab some vegetables out of the fridge, her doorbell rang. She was tempted to ignore it, but then it rang again. Closing the fridge, she walked toward the door, checking the peephole to see who was on the other side. It was Grant.

She opened the door with a frown and gritted her teeth as a gust of wind swept through. Opening the door wider, Grant stepped forward, and then a large German shepherd.

"You have a dog."

"Yes, I have a dog. Don't you remember?"

"Oh, right, Wanda, yes, of course," she said.

"You don't mind?"

"No, of course not."

Wanda stared at her and Aria didn't know if she should reach out and pet the giant dog, but instead she turned to Grant.

"What are you doing here?"

"Our date," he said.

"Grant, it's late and I'm tired. You didn't show up at the gym. We don't need to go on this date."

"I want to."

"Seriously. I'm about to cook myself something. You ... this..." What did she say to him that would make him realize she didn't hold him to anything?

He stepped toward her. "I was doing some shit and time ran away from me, but I want this date."

"Grant, you're confusing me. You really are." She rubbed at her temple. "I don't know anything about you."

He shrugged. "Isn't that the whole point of dating?"

She pressed her lips together and then glanced down at herself. "I'm not exactly dressed for date night."

He took a step toward her and wrapped an arm around her waist. "You don't need to be dressed like anything. You're beautiful, Aria. Let me cook."

She was so tempted. Would it be wrong to give in? Wanda chose that moment to step up toward her and whimper.

Grant chuckled. "Even Wanda wants to stay. Let me cook for you. You've gotten out of the shower, and trust me, I'm having a hard time even thinking about you stepping out of that shower all hot and wet." He growled.

There were times Grant seemed like two different people.

"Fine. Fine."

Grant walked straight ahead, going toward her

kitchen. Wanda didn't move.

Aria couldn't help but smile and then crouched down to pet the dog. "He can't be so bad with how much he loves you guys, can he?"

She stared into Wanda's eyes, and an instant hit of love bloomed within her chest. This dog was so beautiful.

****

Grant knew how to fend for himself. Bull was twelve years older than him, and when their old man was alive, he wasn't exactly paternal in his affection. More often, he had to cook and take care of himself. He'd never told Bull the full extent of their dad's shit parenting.

He wasn't the kind of guy to moan, at least not about stuff that mattered. He wasn't going to cry to his big brother because their daddy decided to use him as a human punching bag. That was just the shitty aspect of life. Nothing could change that.

Opening the fridge, he saw a bunch of colorful bell peppers and he grabbed them out immediately. Nothing else appealed, so he opened cupboards. He'd already spotted the onions and garlic on the counter. He found a can of tomatoes and some pasta.

He'd lied to Maddie about being able to cook. After Bull had tried to protect Maddie from the Vito Crew Cartel, Grant had offered to protect her. To do that, without giving away the fact he was still part of the club, he and Bull had come up with a plan to pretend that he had approached the Cartel for a peace offering. That shit never happened. Grant would never turn his back on the club, even if the club had turned their back on him. Sure, he hadn't been the greatest VP, but he'd done his fucking best. Regardless of whether Bull pissed him off, he was still his brother and he wouldn't see the man dead. He'd kill anyone who tried to harm Bull or the club. Even now.

"Are you okay?" Aria asked, stepping into the kitchen with Wanda beside her.

He forced a smile to his lips. "Yeah, fine."

Grant quickly found the frying pans along with the pasta, cooking knives, and got to finely chopping the onion.

Aria took a seat at the kitchen counter. "It's kind of weird having you cook for me."

He chuckled. "Don't you worry. You can cook for me next time." He winked at her and she rolled her eyes. "How was the gym?" he asked.

"Hard but … good, I think."

"You don't sound so convinced there."

"I don't know. I'm just getting used to everything and it's hard to have a guy helping me with all of this."

"You know you could quit," Grant said. "There's nothing wrong with you. Not one bit."

She began to laugh. "You don't have to lie."

"I don't lie."

"Grant, please. All my life I've been told, by my own parents, that I'm unfit and that I'm fat and unhealthy. Trust me, when you're pushed out of your sister's wedding photos because of the way you look—"

"Wait, what the fuck?" Grant asked.

She shrugged. "My mom didn't like the way I looked, so she made sure I wasn't part of them."

"Fucking show me."

He couldn't believe the shit he was hearing and it was pissing him off. Who did that kind of shit?

Grant watched as she left but then it came to him. Of course, parents did that kind of shit. His own father was a piece of work. He stared around her kitchen and had to wonder about her life, about her.

Aria returned seconds later with a small photo in her hands and held it out to him. He took the picture and nearly fucking froze up. Shit. Fuck. Bastard. Cock. Cunt.

One look at the bride and he recognized her. He glanced up at Aria and then frowned. "This is your sister?"

"Yeah, her name's Isabella," she said.

He'd not gotten any names when they had fucked around several months ago. He didn't know exactly when, but it was before he saw Aria at the veterinary clinic.

"Everyone loves her. She had men lining up wanting to marry her, but she fell in love with Michael."

"How long were they seeing each other?" Grant asked.

"Not long."

He nodded. But it still meant he fucked Aria's sister while she was probably already engaged. Shit. This wasn't good.

Staring at the photo, though, he saw what Aria meant. Her arm wasn't even in the frame. No part of her was, and just seeing that pissed him off.

"Your mom sent you these photos?" he asked.

"Yeah." She shrugged. "Please don't worry about it."

"And this is why you're going to the gym."

"Grant, stop it. Stop trying to pretend there's nothing wrong with me. Trust me. I've always been told that I don't quite measure up. Actually, that has always been the problem. My measurements. I've been on every single diet known to man, and I'm ... I'm doing this for me. I *want* to do it."

He didn't believe that.

"Your mom's a piece of shit," Grant said. "You're gorgeous and I'd have loved to see what you looked like in that bridesmaid's outfit. Weren't you the, er, shit, what is it called?"

"Maid of honor?"

"Yeah?"

"No. One of Isabella's friends was. The one our mom decided would look best for the cameras."

She didn't show any sign of tears or anger, or even upset. Nothing. Aria was fucking used to this shit. He ran a hand down his face.

Like you're one to talk. You used to bully Maddie. Still did until you got your head out of your ass and realized you didn't need to put on a shit show anymore.

Grant closed his eyes. There was no way he could judge Aria for what she was doing. He did it all the time growing up. His father didn't want him falling for a fatty.

Bull wasn't the only one who was attracted to curves. Grant had been for the longest time, but once you get a beating that leaves you in bad shape, you learn not to go after what you crave. You start to lash out, like he did with Maddie.

He was never attracted to Maddie, but he did like her. Even in high school he did. Pushing those thoughts aside, he got back to making their dinner. Aria came to join him as he was adding tomatoes to the pot, bringing the heat up to a boil, and then simmering it down.

He found her seasonings and quickly added some salt and pepper. He took the leaves off the basil plant and placed them on the chopping board. The water for the pasta had come to a boil, and he quickly threw in a packet of pasta. He was starving.

This was not what he planned for their first official date, but it would have to do. He'd spent most of the afternoon with Dylan, trying to see if there was a connection to the missing dogs, any strangers in town, anything. They had come up with nothing. He knew he didn't have a choice. He would have to go to his brother, and that idea pissed him off more than he liked. Dylan had been useless.

He knew the arrangement Bull kept, and it was only in rare circumstances that they crossed paths.

Stirring the pasta, he had to wonder if this had anything to with the Vito Crew Cartel, or if it was something else. Was this a greedy person trying to start up the dogfights again? He wouldn't have that, but he thought they had killed everyone involved, or at least pushed them out of town.

Unless there was a different play going on.

Grant paused and looked at Aria.

For all of his and Bull's bad blood, they were still brothers. Was there a threat to the club that had forced him to suspend him? Is that what this was about?

"Are you okay?"

He pulled out of his thoughts to smile at Aria. There would be time to solve his bullshit, but first he wanted to enjoy his date with Aria. He'd been the reason there was a shitty start to the evening, but he'd more than make up for it.

"Yeah, everything is fine."

"Good. That's good."

"You've never been on a date before, have you?" he asked.

"Yeah, I have. I've been on a couple of dates." She shrugged. "Why? Does it show?"

Grant laughed. "I've never been on a date."

"I find that hard to believe."

"I've never dated women, Aria. With my connection to the club, they just throw themselves at my feet."

"Oh," Aria said. "Is this supposed to make me feel better?"

"I want to get this crap out of the way first. I didn't live like a saint. I fucked around and I did so at a young age. I've never had a girlfriend. Never been on a date. With you I'm kind of winging it and just hoping I get it right." He stared at her while he waited for their meal to finish cooking. "The club is part of me, and even though I'm not wearing my patch right now, I will soon. I promise. We're ... I can't tell you what we do or any of that."

She held up her hands. "Grant, please stop. If you want us to be all honest with each other, then fine, my parents won't be able to stand you. And no, that's not why I agreed to this date with you. We're not ... this isn't ... I don't know what this is. I only know that when I'm with you, the world doesn't seem so horrible."

"You like my company?"

"Yeah, I do. It's kind of refreshing. You're the first person in my life, apart from my friend Lidia, who hasn't told me I need to lose weight. That if only I did, I'd be prettier. You haven't judged me for eating or driving my car to work."

"That shit happens."

"It can. I like you, Grant. I don't know if this means anything or if it will go anywhere, but I do like you, like a lot."

"Good, because I quite like you, like a lot."

She giggled. "Can we just take it slow? I know you don't want to. You've got all those women throwing themselves at you."

"Shut up," he said.

He'd never taken it slow with anyone, but with Aria, for some strange reason, he was willing to take it any way she wanted.

Grant returned his attention to the pasta, and he did so just in time. It wasn't quite ruined, but edible. He quickly drained the pasta, saved some water, and then joined the sauce and pasta together, along with the cooking water.

"You don't have any cheese," he said.

"I got rid of it," Aria said.

"Seriously, you got rid of cheese?"

"Don't ask."

"Oh, I know why. It's delicious, full of fat and calories, but will take this dish into the next dimension."

Aria chuckled. "Stop it, please, I'll pretend it has cheese on it."

"And while you do, judge yourself for getting rid of perfectly good cheese." He shook his head. "You know you don't have to go to the gym."

"You really don't like Jase, do you?"

"He's fine."

"Oh, my God, you twitched. You just lied to me."

"Look, I don't like him, okay? So far there are two women in my life, and each one has gone to him for weight loss and all that. It pisses me off." He looked at Aria and sighed. "Maddie French. She was a girl I knew in high school. Anyway, she's married to my brother now, and they have a child, but when things got bad for her, she figured it was because of her size." He didn't want to go into the whole story of what his brother did.

She didn't need to know that in order to protect her, Bull had no choice but to push her away. To keep her out of harm's way, he hit her where it hurt the most—her weight. His brother had been besotted with Maddie for the longest time. But with the danger posed to Maddie, he had pushed her away, humiliating her in front of the whole town. Grant had been there. He'd known the game his brother played and he had a feeling he was playing a similar one now. Bull never trusted anyone, so he always did what he thought was best, and it often included the people he loved.

"I just don't like him."

She giggled. "You do know he's just doing what I asked him to do."

"You went to the gym and you're paying for his company?"

She nibbled her lip.

"Who?" he asked.

"Don't you remember I told you this? My mom purchased it as a Christmas present last year. I'm just seeing it through."

Fucking bitch. He hated her mother already. If he ever met her, he was going to give that woman shit, no doubt about it. And knowing her parents wouldn't be able to stand him, well, that just made his life a whole lot better. In fact, it was fucking joyous.

"Let's not talk about the stuff that's going to make us mad," she said. "Let's just focus on what we're going to enjoy. This food. The pleasure of each other's company. You know, that kind of stuff." She forced a smile to her lips and he could see her doing it.

He wanted to tell her that she didn't need to go to the gym and change her life like that, but instead he picked up their food.

"Let's eat."

He carried it to the dining room, took a seat at the head of the table, and put Aria's chair beside him. Aria sat down. She had already removed the towel from her long blonde hair, which looked slightly damp.

He had to wonder if she was completely naked underneath her bathrobe, or if she was dressed in pajamas or even a negligee. His cock thickened at the thought of her being naked, within touching distance. Those full tits, her juicy ass. Since he had stopped living up to the role he played, he found he enjoyed being himself far more. And Aria's curves were making him want to explore, so fucking much.

He wanted to touch her.

To love her.

To fuck her.

To be with her.

To just have her.

But he also knew Aria needed time. She wasn't used to the kind of attention he wanted to give her. He could be patient, to a point, but he didn't know how long he would be able to wait before he made his move.

Chapter Seven

Aria stroked the dog's neck. She couldn't believe anyone could be so cruel as to steal these two gorgeous dogs, only to tie them up and abandon them near the fucking park, in the woodland. That just pissed her off.

If it hadn't been for Jase going for his run, he wouldn't have seen them. He found them and brought them straight to the shelter. Phil and Andy had already done the checks on them. They were hungry, a little dehydrated, but other than that, they were healthy.

Aria had recognized them instantly as two of the dogs in the care of Chaos and Carnage MC. They had taken over running the main animal shelter. She was aware the one Grant dealt with was like an offshoot of the main shelter.

Andy had called Bull and she had called Grant, just in case. She knew how quickly the shelters filled up. If there was no room at one, there might be room at another.

"So how did your date go?" Andy asked.

She chuckled. "It was fine." There was no need to go into specifics, like the fact he'd arrived late, and instead of taking her out, he had cooked for her. At the end of their night, she had seen him to the front door, and she had really wanted him to kiss her. Instead, Grant had grazed his lips against her cheek. That was it. No mind-blowing kiss, no shocking revelation. Nothing.

So, she had gone to bed and thought of him constantly. She hadn't gotten much sleep, and today she was exhausted and looked forward to seeing Grant. She knew how much he loved dogs, not that she could blame him.

Wanda was so gorgeous and adorable. She had stayed with them in the kitchen, moved to the dining room, and found a comfy spot. Before Grant left, they stayed in the sitting room and talked for nearly an hour, while Wanda sat down on her sofa between them. Aria didn't mind. In fact, she loved the company. She pressed kisses to the dog's head and got a nice long tongue lick, making her giggle.

At the sound of a motorbike, she got to her feet and moved to the main window. She watched as Bull, complete with his leather cut, as well as a couple of other bikers she wasn't quite familiar with, parked outside. She spotted the truck Grant often used pull up seconds later.

He no longer wore his patch and she couldn't help but wonder why. She had meant what she said to him last night, about not caring if her parents would like him or not. Her mother would have a fit regardless. No matter who she dated, her mother would find some reason to bring up her weight.

She watched as Grant looked toward his brother. She couldn't tell if they were talking. Bull shook his head and then moved toward the practice.

Aria went back to her seat as Andy came out of one of the rooms.

"Mr. Reynolds," Andy said.

Bull entered first.

"You called me about two dogs."

Aria got to her feet, holding both of their leads. Grant got down on one knee and she let go as both dogs rushed toward him.

"Where have you two boys been, huh? Where have you been?" Grant asked, talking in a rather husky voice.

She couldn't help but smile as he stroked the dogs.

"Are you good boys?"

"What do I need to know?" Bull asked.

They didn't have any clients at present. It had been a slow couple of hours for the couple.

Andy went into the details of where the dogs were found. She refused to divulge who found them, but simply referred to him as a concerned citizen.

Aria moved toward Grant and crouched down. "Do you know them?" she asked.

"Yeah, a little bit. These boys were rescues, but they had already been in the thick of it. They're going to need someone who ... doesn't mind them together as a team."

"So, they are together?" Aria asked, reaching out to stroke down the backs of both dogs. She had come to love them instantly these past couple of hours being alone with them. They were simply gorgeous.

"Yeah. We think they helped to protect one another, you know, that kind of shit," he said.

She had come to notice he liked to curse a lot, but she didn't mind at all. It was refreshing being around someone who didn't hold back, who just said and did what he wanted.

Grant reached out and stroked her cheek. "How are you today, beautiful?"

Her face heated up and he chuckled. Realizing they were not alone, she tried to duck her head.

"Don't give a fuck about them. I don't." He shrugged.

"Fuck off, Grant," one of them said.

Grant didn't offer a single introduction. Aria didn't know why but she chose not to push it or him.

Bull cleared his throat and Aria had no choice but to get up and step back. Andy waited at the desk and she took her place at the reception. This was her job.

Grant got to his feet.

"We have no more spaces at the shelter."

"I'll take them."

"Grant, come on, we both know they're going to be difficult to rehome."

"I don't give a shit how complicated it is. They're good dogs and I'm not going to put them down."

Bull ran his hand down his face. "For fuck's sake. Does it sound like I want to put them the fuck down?"

Grant glared at his brother. "I don't know, but I seem to recall when it suits you, you're more than happy to kick out what makes life hard."

"This is just like you, bringing club business here when it doesn't have to be. I'm not going to kill the fucking dogs, Grant."

"We've got a couple of guys down south, they've opened up their own dog shelter," one of the other guys said.

He had been quiet up until now. Aria looked at him closely and saw he wore the VP patch. She was sure up until a few weeks ago that patch had been on Grant's jacket. She had certainly stared at his chest enough times to remember.

Grant went quiet and then he seemed to nod. The dogs were going away. Far away. She wasn't going to see them again.

"I'd like them," Aria said, speaking up.

She didn't have any control over her lips, the words just came out and she couldn't stop them. All the men turned toward her.

"Aria?"

"I mean it, I'd like to … have them. Adopt them. I don't want them to go out of town," Aria said. "What do I have to do? What paperwork do you need?"

With Bull's full attention on her, she had never been more scared.

"You do realize these dogs were once part of an

illegal fighting ring that was based here in this town," he said.

She had heard the report in the local newspaper. The Chaos and Carnage MC were only mentioned in regard to rehoming the dogs and of course taking over the general running of the animal shelter.

"I understand."

"I'll help her," Grant said.

He still held the dog leads in his hands and moved through the men, coming to her. He wrapped an arm around her waist, pulling her in close.

Bull stared at them. "So this crap is true, seriously?"

"Don't start, Bull," Grant said.

The one with the VP patch put a hand on Bull's chest. Aria had no idea what was going on and was a little unnerved about it. The VP whispered to Bull who then nodded.

"We're going to take the dogs," Bull said. "And you're going to have to visit the shelter, multiple times. We need to make sure you're ready to deal with these dogs and that they're happy with you."

"Come on, Bull, what the fuck?" Grant asked.

"Rehoming is fucking serious, Grant. Just because you're … none of that changes things," Bull said.

"It's fine. I'll do it." She pulled out of Grant's arms, rushing behind the desk and grabbing her cell phone. "Just tell me what I need to do and I'll do it."

****

"What the fuck was that?" Grant asked.

He had pulled up into the Chaos and Carnage MC parking lot. It had been a couple of weeks since he had come back to the clubhouse, since he had been told he'd been stripped of his patch.

"You know the rules, Grant, and just because you're fucking her doesn't mean she gets special privileges. How do I know she's not going to dump those dogs once you've had whatever fun you've been playing?" he asked.

"First of all, don't ever talk about her like that. Do you fucking hear me? I'm not fucking her, and second, Aria would never do that." He took a step toward his brother, then another, until he was close to Bull's face. "Unlike you, who tosses people aside when you think you're making the right choice."

"I don't know what's gotten into your fucking skull—"

Grant shoved his brother hard. He couldn't help it. Bull just pushed and pushed and pushed and he was getting tired of it. Pat wore his VP patch. He'd been kicked out of the club, for what? For not doing his job? There was more to the club than fucking fixing cars, and seeing as Bull had stopped him from doing that and moved him into dealing with the dogs, his time at the clubhouse had lessened, and now he was out on his fucking ass.

Bull stepped forward, raised his fist, and Grant didn't even bother to block it. He took the fist to the face. Bull was strong and his fist stung. Grant went to the floor but got up quite quickly and glared at his brother. He wanted to hurt him.

"What the hell are you two doing?" Maddie asked, coming out of the clubhouse with his niece on her hip.

The guys who'd kept their distance suddenly disappeared. This was no longer club business. This was family business.

"Hey, Maddie," Grant said.

"What is with you two?" She closed the distance

between them all.

"He's out and that's it. I'm not having his useless ass in my club. He's only here because he's my brother."

Grant didn't show how much that stung.

Maddie shook her head.

"He won't let Aria have the two dogs that were stolen."

Maddie looked between the two of them.

"Give me strength. You two are brothers. I never had a sibling. I don't know what it's like. What I do know is that you two have put up with each other for the longest time. You are family. You're the only family you have left. I know the club is your family but you have each other. Now, you are not coming into this damn clubhouse until you both fix this."

Bull shook his head. "No, I'm the damn Prez of this club and what I say goes. Get the fuck off my property before I call Dylan and have you thrown out. You're trespassing."

"You've got to be fucking kidding me right now," Grant said.

"Bull, what the hell is going on?" Maddie asked.

It didn't matter. Grant heard the unmistakable sound of the siren. Someone had called Dylan, the sheriff, and he was just pulling into the clubhouse parking lot.

"You piece of shit," Grant said.

Bull had stabbed him in the back.

****

Aria had just finished for the day and was heading out of the veterinary clinic when she saw Lidia pulling up in her car. She hadn't seen her friend since yesterday. Glancing around the parking lot, she had to wonder what brought Lidia here. They hadn't exactly parted ways on good terms, but Lidia parked her car and climbed out.

It was already dark, and the only light came from the streetlights as well as the two on the sides of the building.

Lidia paused as she caught sight of her.

"What are you doing here?" Aria asked.

She stayed perfectly still as Lidia stepped toward her. "I dumped Sean."

"What?"

"Yeah, I dumped his ass. He didn't tell me what he said Halloween night but one of his friends was there. Told me exactly how it played out. How you arrived at the party but Sean was there, and he said those horrible things."

"Oh," Aria said.

"First of all, Sean was an asshole. I never actually liked him. I dated him to shut him up and he was pissed at me because I wouldn't sleep with him," Lidia said. "Second, he didn't like the fact that you and I are besties. That I would always put us first. Not him. And third, seriously, we have known each other since kindergarten. We've been inseparable. I have never turned my back on you. I have never hated you. I love you, Aria Taylor, like my sister, okay? I don't have a sister, but you are my sister as far as I'm concerned."

"You don't have to—"

"Am I finished? Do I even look finished?"

Aria smiled. There was no stopping Lidia once she was on a rant.

"Go on," Aria said.

"I have put up with your mother treating you like shit. Telling you all the time about what you should eat and what you should be doing. I've had to watch you deal with all of that and still put a smile on your face, and help others. Trust me, Aria, I don't find you fat or ugly, and in fact, Halloween fucking sucked because you weren't there. We've hung out every single Halloween, Thanksgiving, Christmas, New Year, you name it, and I'm not going to be the one to screw this friendship. That will be you. Also, I'm hearing in the rumor mill that you're dating a horndog, Grant Reynolds. I mean, seriously?"

Aria couldn't control the tears, especially as Lidia finished off with throwing her arms around her, and holding her close.

"I'm sorry," Aria said.

"Don't ever do that shit again. The next guy who tells you that kind of shit, you punch him in the balls. That's the only respectable thing you should do," Lidia said. "Sean is a dimwit and a fucking asshole. I can't believe him. I can't believe you would even believe that."

"I don't know what was wrong with me."

"I know what was wrong. Your damn mother. She's always a problem. Always claiming you're not as good as Isabella. Well, I can tell you now Isabella is not as innocent as she claims."

"Don't. You know Isabella doesn't ask for that."

Lidia growled. "There you go, protecting her."

She hugged her best friend.

"Now that we have all that crap out of the way," Lidia said. "Are you going to tell me what's going on with Grant Reynolds?"

"It's … we should go. It's getting late."

"Oh, no, you don't. We're going to the diner. You and me. We're getting some of Carl's makeup burgers, and you're going to tell me what the hell is going on." Lidia gave her hand a squeeze.

Aria sighed. She didn't see a reason to not go with her friend. Lidia was very … she was always herself. She climbed into her car and followed Lidia to the diner, which wasn't too far. There were a couple of parking spaces.

Lidia waited for her and they entered the diner together. It was busy and Lidia found them a table. The diner was always busy, but that was the way Carl and Beatrice preferred it. They had the best food in town.

Aria's mouth watered but then she thought about her strict regimen. No burgers for her. Just the large salad that she would extend to the dressing.

One of the waitresses came over to take their order. It wasn't Beatrice, but she spotted the other woman behind the counter, helping with organizing meals for the waitresses.

When she ordered the salad Lidia growled.

"Seriously? A salad over a makeup burger?"

"Don't start," Aria said.

Lidia shook her head. "So it's true. You're caving into your mom's demands? The whole gym membership. Personal trainer. That kind of thing."

"Come on, Lidia, don't you think it's time I give it a try?"

"No," Lidia said. "There is nothing wrong with you."

"I'm fat."

"Don't use that word, Aria."

She sighed. "I'm just seeing if it will work. If something new would work. You're ... slender and beautiful."

"Aria, you're beautiful, okay? You are, but you don't see it. Everyone around you keeps telling you that you have to lose weight to be beautiful, why? Fucking why? I'm sick of it. Has Grant put you up to this? I heard some rumors that he can't stand curvy women or something like that." She wrinkled her nose.

"What?"

Lidia shrugged. "It's town gossip, Aria. Come on, who believes all that stuff?"

But what if it was true? If Grant couldn't stand curvy women then why was he attempting to date her? It made no sense.

"But you're happy to believe some town gossip?" Aria asked, changing the subject.

Lidia sighed. "Come on. We both know it's about working your way through the bullshit and all that. When it comes to Grant, it's hard to know what to believe. Last year he was working in this diner and hanging out with Maddie French, and she's now married to his brother, with a kid. So who knows what was going on with that."

"I don't know what's going on with Grant and me, but it's, we're just, you know, having some fun. That's all."

"Fun?"

"Yeah, some fun. Nothing too serious."

Lidia folded her arms. "Have you guys had sex?"

Aria rolled her eyes. "What? We're not in high school anymore. I don't need to tell you when I've had sex, and no, we haven't."

"Aria, you have never had sex. Grant is a horndog."

She covered her cheeks. "Can we not do this?"

Lidia laughed and then reached out. "I've missed this, so much."

She held onto her friend's hand. "Me too."

"Let's not allow any dick to come between us."

Aria couldn't help but laugh. "Deal."

"Megadeal." Lidia winked at her.

"So, Sean, huh, how did he take it?"

****

Dylan didn't allow him to have a phone call.

Grant sat in his prison cell, pissed off. What the fuck was going on? Bull was always there to bail him out whenever he'd gotten caught up in a bar fight or anything that landed him in a cell. This time, his brother was the one to put his ass here.

He rubbed at his temples. He'd not been able to call Aria, which pissed him off. The silence was driving him crazy. He got to his feet and walked around the small cell.

Grant was just about to grab the bars of the cell and start to yell when the main door opened. Dylan didn't come through but a man in a hood and when he pulled it down, he saw Bull standing on the opposite side of the bar.

"You've got about ten minutes," Dylan said.

The door closed, leaving him alone with his brother.

"I need you to shut the fuck up and I need you to trust me," Bull said.

It was on the tip of his tongue to complain and make his brother's life difficult, but instead he opted for silence. There was no point in pissing Bull off any more than necessary.

"There's been Cartel movement. They've requested our presence less and less and William Ranford has the feds on his ass. Drugs were smuggled into one of his bars and just at the right moment, the cops showed up. He's been busted, but so far, he's got a good lawyer, but we both believe this is blowback from taking out Julio and the current leader of the Vito Crew Cartel. I had a package delivered to me a month ago. It had every single image of you in the past six weeks. You're a target, Grant. You are under the protection of the club, but I need them to look away from you."

"You can't do that."

"Shut your fucking mouth and let me speak. The Cartel in the past week have gone quiet. The dogs down south have been taken, as well as the two we've recovered. We believe someone is in operation and testing our borders. Testing our ability to protect. Ranford has had no choice but to go into hiding. There was an attempt on his life. I don't know where he is or what he's doing, but he gave me a clear warning—protect who I hold dear. I know you won't allow me to put you in the clubhouse. Maddie is currently living in the clubhouse, surrounded by our men. I need people to see you as useless to me, Grant. That's why Pat is wearing the VP patch. Your life is in danger, but I can lessen the threat by showing them you mean nothing."

"For fuck's sake, Bull. This shit didn't work the last time. They still figured out you were in love with Maddie."

"You're not my woman, Grant. You're my pain in the ass brother."

"And they know you won't throw me to the curb," Grant said. "That's what this is all about? Protecting me? What the fuck is this? I'm not a child."

"You are still my brother."

"And have you ever considered that I might be able to protect myself? Someone was able to get into the shelter, Bull. They knew how we worked, which is why they were able to take the dogs. You know what that means."

Bull frowned.

"Someone was able to get past Hellen. It's someone close."

"No one new is around."

"Then someone is feeding this information to the enemy, Bull. You as well as I know that it's hard to infiltrate the club. Someone is."

Bull ran a finger across his lips. "Or someone who knows how we run things."

Grant looked toward the door. "Dylan?"

"No, he wouldn't do that. He loves this town too much."

"Look, I don't know who it is but what I do know is this shit isn't good, Bull. You can't kick me out now."

"And what about Aria?" Bull asked. "Do you think our enemy is going to give a shit about going after women? They kill dogs."

"I'll handle it, but you can't take my fucking patch from me."

"Your patch, for now, is taken. There's nothing I can do. You're going to have to live with that. I can't put your life at risk. I promised our old man that I would take care of you."

Grant slammed his palm against the gate. "Don't give me that shit. You and I both know our old man didn't give a crap about me. You were his firstborn son. You were the one he wanted to take care of. Not me. Never fucking me."

He gritted his teeth as he felt the anger rising.

"I'm doing what I know to be best." Bull had already started walking toward the door.

"If you do this, I swear you're going to regret it because I'm not going to stop being your fucking VP. That patch is mine."

Chapter Eight

"Do you think this is the right thing to do?" Pat asked.

Bull stood in his office and for the first time in a while, he thought about his old man. That bastard had at one point been like a fucking hero to him. This was a long, long, way fucking long time ago. The man had been dead for years, killed at his own hands, and yet he was still causing him trouble.

Grant spent a lot more time with their old man toward the later years. Bull had been tired of his shit, and even though he knew he was a little unstable, he figured as his flesh and blood, Grant would have in some way been safe.

Was he wrong?

Over the years Grant changed. He knew that. Bull also knew to a certain extent that Grant's bullying ways weren't even down to his own views. Their dad had a standard of how he felt men should be. Women were trophies. They were meant to look good on your arm, warm your bed, and keep fucking silent. Their dad would have hated Maddie.

Was there a lot of shit that happened that he didn't know about?

"I've got to protect Grant."

"Putting him in a cell is not going to help."

"I'm not going to receive him as body parts in the mail. That kind of shit I can't do." He ran a hand down his face.

There were times he hated Grant and he'd even thought about killing him once or twice, but he'd never actually do it. Last year, seeing William get parts of his dead brother had cut a little too close to home.

He figured the Vito Crew Cartel was the end of

this shit. Yes, he still had business to deal with for the main Cartel, but in the past few months, they'd gone quiet. No gun runs. No drugs. No nothing. Bull wasn't a fool. He knew shit was going down. What he needed to know was where, how, and when.

Maddie hated living at the club, but until he got rid of this new threat, there was nothing else he could do.

"Grant's not a fool," Pat said.

"But he's hotheaded and I can't risk him." There was no way he'd be able to forgive himself. "What do we have on the ground?"

"According to our contacts, no movement. We've not had anything from Ranford either. He'd gone into hiding."

Bull snorted. "And to think he thought he had the answers." Ranford had once told him that the key to getting the Cartel out of his life was to be willing to sacrifice it all. That wasn't how he worked. He had the club, Grant, now Maddie and his daughter. He couldn't just go after the Cartel.

With Ranford now in hiding, it seemed neither could he. The truth was, Ranford's brother brought the Cartel back into his world. It started in the dogfighting ring, but when they kidnapped Ranford Junior, they tortured him and he clearly ended up giving away too much information that came to bite William in the ass.

"I want the club on high alert. We're going hunting. I want to check out all the areas around Carnage. I'm not going to give those bastards any chance to hide."

He knew something was going on, and it was either in his town, or traveling through it. He'd need to talk to Dylan. Bull didn't like how often he had to talk to Dylan in the past few months. He much preferred to keep a distance between him and law enforcement.

****

"I can't believe your brother threw you in jail," Aria said, as she poured the hot water out of the kettle. She had already put the food down for Wanda. After a short hesitation, the dog started to eat.

"Yeah, well, my brother is a real piece of work." Grant was lying on the bed, looking annoyed.

She noticed his jaw kept clenching. Carrying the coffee over to him, she offered him the mug.

"Do you have anything to make this stronger?"

"A spoonful of espresso?" she asked.

He wrinkled his nose.

"Sorry, I don't keep whiskey or anything in the house. I don't drink."

He chuckled. "I noticed." He took a sip of the coffee.

Aria blew across the surface of hers. She'd been surprised to get the phone call from the sheriff, asking her to come and bail out Grant.

"How are you feeling?" she asked.

"Fine."

"I got there as soon as I could."

"What were you doing?" Grant asked.

"I was having lunch with Lidia."

"Your friend?"

"Yeah."

"I bet she hates my guts."

Aria laughed. "Actually, I think you might be her favorite person right now. Probably her only favorite person."

Grant smirked. He reached out and cupped her cheek. "I love it when you laugh." He ran his thumb down and across her lip.

She couldn't help but lick her lips, and he groaned.

"Aria, baby, I'm trying to be good here, to take it slow, but I really want to fucking kiss you right now. You're making it hard for me to be good."

She wanted him to kiss her. Biting her lip, she leaned close and slowly brushed her lips across his. It was quick and swift, and she pulled away fast.

"You think that was a kiss?" he asked.

"It was a start."

He chuckled. The sound was deep, rough, and seemed to spark a response within her body. Grant leaned forward and put his coffee on the table. He took her drink from her, and then both of his hands were on her face.

"No, this is how I want to kiss you." He took possession of her lips, and Aria couldn't think.

She'd never been kissed like this before. In fact, if she was honest with herself, she'd never been kissed, period.

Unlike her friend Lidia, who'd constantly been surrounded by guys, Aria hadn't. She didn't mind, though. The last thing she wanted to do was date. Her parents were already humiliating enough when her sister brought boyfriends home. She had no doubt her mother wouldn't have a problem bringing up her weight if she brought someone home with her. Even Lidia hadn't been immune to hearing her mother moan about what she did or didn't do. It was exhausting.

But this … were all kisses like this? She loved the way he held onto her face, tilted her head to the side, and the way his mouth just moved over hers. It was a dream. Aria expected him to stop, but then she felt the wet slide of his tongue across her lips, and the truth was she was in Heaven.

She couldn't help but gasp and as she did so, he plundered her lips. An answering spark of arousal flooded her pussy. She pressed her thighs together in the hope of trying to keep herself together, but nothing would do. Nothing.

She moaned.

He growled.

And when he broke the kiss, she missed the feel of his lips.

Staring into his eyes, Aria couldn't help but take a quick glance at his lips, just to be sure he was here and this was really happening. She reached out, putting her hand on his leg.

"I knew those lips would be fucking amazing," he said.

She smiled. "I … er … it was good."

He frowned.

"Aria, have you kissed anyone before?"

She licked her lips. "Yeah, of course I have. Like all the time." She felt her cheeks heating up. "No, I haven't. I've never been…" She pulled away from him. Could this have gotten any more embarrassing? "I've never done … anything. I'm…"

"You're a virgin."

Aria nodded her head.

"I'm not a virgin," he said.

She chuckled. "Seriously? You're not? Wow, call me surprised."

He snorted.

"I know you're not a virgin, Grant. I don't even know why I've told you this." She shrugged. This was not exactly how she wanted to see him tonight, or any night for that matter. This was so embarrassing.

She went to stand up, but he grabbed her arm. "Aria, baby. Don't go, okay? You already told me this."

"It's fine. Let's be honest, okay? It's not like you want me. Look at me. I'm nothing like those women that hang out in the—"

He silenced her by grabbing her, pinning her down to the sofa, and then kissing her. Aria didn't fight him. There was no way for her to do that. He had her hands pinned above her head, and he held her in place.

She had her legs wide open, giving him plenty of room between, and she felt the hard ridge of his cock pressing against her core. Aria was so shocked. Grant was aroused by her.

He pulled away from the kiss. "I'm going to start spanking your ass if you keep saying that nasty shit about yourself."

"Grant?"

"I do want you." He pressed his pelvis forward. "You feel that? That's not because I don't want you, it's because I do. I very much want to fuck you, and after the day I've had, I'm holding on by a fucking thread here, Aria. Kissing you is enough for now, but trust me, I want more."

He lifted just a little and his gaze roamed down her body. "I want to look at these tits. I want to see you completely naked, and I want to explore every inch of you."

"Why?" she asked.

Grant chuckled. "Someone has really done a number on you."

"I don't know what you mean."

"That's fine. I have an idea who it might be. I'm guessing a parent, right? Only someone like that can get in our fucking head and screw us up so much that we start to forget who we are. I'm not a good man, Aria. In fact, I've been a total bastard at times, but I promise you, I am not lying to you about this. I want you." He thrust his pelvis against her again. "And so does he."

"But, doesn't he like … isn't he like used to

responding to what you want?"

He laughed. "Trust me, babe, if I wasn't attracted to you, I wouldn't be hard. We've got to work on your confidence."

She didn't want to talk about the way she looked.

"You always spoil everything. No man wants to see a woman shoveling food into her face."

"You would be so pretty if you would just stop eating."

"Aria, seriously, would it kill you to just try the diets I've put you on?"

"You're so ugly and fat. Why did I have to be cursed with you?"

Her mother's bitter comments over the years. Admittedly, the last one was said to her while her mother was drunk. It was rare for her to see her mother drunk, but it had happened once.

The experience had been cruel. Aria had thought her mother didn't have a filter, but it had turned out to be the opposite. Her mother had been holding back for a long, long time. If she believed her drunk mother, then she was disgusted by having a fat daughter. She hated it, was humiliated by it.

She tried to push those thoughts out of her mind as she stared at Grant. "Parents can be cruel."

"Tell me about it. My old man knew how to fuck with my head all the time," Grant said.

It was the first time he had ever admitted to something so personal. Aria couldn't remember his father or the way the Chaos and Carnage MC crew were before Bull took over. According to her parents, it had been a horrible group of men. Despicable, cruel, and dangerous. She knew if she ever took Grant to see her parents, it wouldn't be pretty.

"Aria, I want to kiss you," he said.

"Then kiss me."

She wanted him to chase the bad memories away, so she would never think about them again. She was tired of constantly hating herself and of always feeling like she didn't measure up.

Grant didn't need a second invitation. He let go of her hands and she expected him to stop kissing her, but then his hands began to slide down her arms. A whimper escaped her lips as he broke the kiss this time, but he didn't stop. No, his lips trailed down toward her neck and when his teeth nibbled on her pulse, she gasped, arching up.

Instant pleasure shot through her body. She closed her eyes, sinking her teeth into her lips to keep herself contained but it didn't work. Nothing worked.

"Tell me to stop," Grant said.

Stop what?

Why?

Who would want to stop this?

He moved down and began to open the buttons of her shirt, spreading it open. Aria opened her eyes and looked down as he exposed her breasts.

He groaned. "They're just as big as I imagined." He cupped them in his palm. "Fucking beautiful." He pressed his face against them and she couldn't help but gasp. "Perfection."

No one had ever used that word to describe her.

"Fucking tell me to stop," he said.

Why would she tell him to stop? There was no way she wanted him to stop.

"Please," she said.

"Baby, there's only so much control I have." He pressed kisses to the curves of her breasts and as he reached behind her back, Aria realized he was trying to flick the catch of her bra. He did so and much to her surprise, he had her bra as well as her shirt off within seconds.

"Tell me to stop."

There was no way she was going to tell him anything. Pleasure rushed through her whole body. There was no stopping it. However, she was top naked, while he was still fully dressed. She placed a hand on his chest and bunched up the fabric of his shirt.

"Is this what you want, baby?" he asked.

Her lips were so dry. Words were impossible, so she nodded her head with a single jerk.

He chuckled, the sound deep, hard, masculine. He made her so damn wet. Aria didn't know what was happening. She was never like this. Never. Not for anyone. Why was Grant so different?

There had been guys in the past. Stupid guys. The kind of men who'd approached her and said they'd give her a pity fuck, or they'd screw her if she paid them. Horrible stuff. Cruel and mean. She had always turned them down.

Lidia had always told her that she was beautiful and that guys were jerks.

Grant once again removed all those thoughts from her mind as he pulled the shirt he wore up and over his head, showing off his heavily inked chest.

Wow. She didn't say the words out loud. Grant was ... wow. There was no other word for it. Heavily muscled, which was surprising as she had never seen him lift weights. He had lots of ink. She caught sight of a lot of chains, all with different loops that decorated his body.

He took her hand and placed it on his chest. "Do you not like it?"

"Er, yeah, I do. Do they mean something?"

She felt some ridges on his chest, as if they had once been scars, but with the ink, it was too hard to make out.

"I guess. We're all trapped to a certain degree, right? Chained by the harshness of life. By the secrets we keep. The lies we keep telling."

She looked at him, a little astounded.

"Or, they're just hours sitting in an artist's chair."

"What is it for you?" she asked.

Aria was starting to see two sides to Grant. The playful boy he portrayed, the one who had no worries or cares in the world. Then there was the kind of man who made statements about life, about secrets and chains. What was in Grant's life, besides the club, that kept him locked up?

He slammed his lips down on hers once again, throwing her whole body into chaos as he shut her mind down to everything else but the pleasure of his mouth. She had no idea how he did it, but he was a master at control. A manipulator. And in that moment, she didn't care.

The kiss stopped but the pleasure didn't, as he once again traveled toward her breasts, but this time he didn't stop. There was no talking. Just his lips on her tits, sucking at her nipples. He pressed them together and teased the hard buds.

"I could suck these all day long." Grant pressed his face against the mounds.

Aria moaned as he pinched one nipple, then the other, only to cover them afterward with his lips, sucking each hard bud. She couldn't think nor focus, nor did she want to. He'd taken over her mind and she didn't want to fight. Giving into Grant felt like a freedom she had never experienced. There was no stopping it.

Another moan escaped and then his hands started to move down between her thighs. He hesitated and she knew he was waiting for her to tell him to stop or do something, but Aria didn't say a word. This was different. Grant was different. She had never felt this way with anyone else, and she trusted him.

Staring into his eyes, she felt him flick the button of her jeans. The sound of the zipper echoed around the room, and then his palm pressed against her pussy.

****

Grant ran a hand down his face as he walked Wanda past his brother's garage, and then headed toward the outskirts of town. Pulling out his cell phone, he found Maddie's number and dialed. For several rings he waited, and then, when it went to voicemail, he hung up, only to dial again.

He wasn't going to give up that easily. He waited. Finally, after the third time attempting to call her, Maddie picked up.

"Grant, how are you doing?" she asked.

"What's it like taking things slow?"

"What?"

"You know, dating."

"Is this about Aria?" Maddie asked.

"Yeah."

"Why are you asking me for dating advice?"

"You're my friend. That's what friends do, right? They ask shit like this."

"Yeah, but I'm a woman. Why would you ask me about taking things slow? I'm assuming you mean sex."

"I mean everything."

He heard her sigh. "Why don't you just call Bull?"

"Not happening. I'm not asking that son of a bitch for anything."

"Grant, I don't know what's going on, but—"

He was about to tell her about the danger she was in. To ask her a whole bunch of questions for her to see the obvious. Bull was protecting his family.

This was Maddie. She'd already been hurt. He couldn't do that to her, even though he and Maddie didn't exactly see eye to eye about a lot of things. The fact he bullied her for years when they were growing up was a big problem, but they had managed to form a friendship. At least he believed they had, and he was very protective of that.

"I'm not asking Bull for relationship advice," he said instead of scaring her. "I'm asking you. Why do I have to ask my brother?"

"Because you're talking about sex."

"And you're trying to tell me you don't like sex?" Grant asked. "You've got a kid, and I know you guys didn't bump hips once to make little Lindsey."

"I'm not talking to you about this."

He sensed she was close to hanging up.

"Wait, okay, just wait." He sighed. "Do you think … do you think I'm a good catch?"

"I'm not following."

"Do you think Aria would go for me?"

Maddie was quiet. Too quiet.

"Maddie?"

"Grant, ugh, this is … yes, I think Aria would go for you, but you've got to not be a dick, like you were to me all those years."

"I won't be." He'd never hurt Aria. He was no longer a dick to prove himself. That shit had ended along with risking his life at the club to save Maddie.

His old man had been dead a long fucking time, and he didn't have to impress that asshole. Habits were hard to end, but this was one he was determined to get rid of.

"Look, I know I hurt you all through high school and the shit I said was wrong, and I can understand why you never, ever want to see me again, but I am a changed man. I'm not that guy. I was never that guy. Shit happened, and I'm so sorry."

"Grant, you don't have to keep apologizing, I forgive you."

"You do?"

"Yeah, of course. I think I made that clear when that guy, er, Julio was beating the crap out of you and I thought you were unconscious. I realized then that you were my friend and I cared. Besides, you're also my brother-in-law."

Grant snorted.

"Will you and Bull ... be okay?" Maddie asked.

"I don't know what we'll fucking be. I've got to go."

"Grant, wait, if you and Aria want to take things slow, then just ... it should be easy. You know. If you're with someone you care about, then everything comes naturally."

"It does?"

"Yeah, it does. I promise."

"Thanks."

"No problem."

Grant pulled his cell phone away from his ear and hung up. He didn't know what it was but chatting with Maddie always relaxed him. He felt calmer than ever before.

Stopping near the Carnage sign, he stared out at the main road. As a kid, he had often come here. Most of the time after taking a beating. It was only rare that his dad forgot about not attacking the face. When that happened, Grant would lie and say he got into a fight with some out-of-town asshole or something. No one questioned him.

Most of the time his dad was clever, though. He

knew not to pummel the face. There was always a risk Bull would come around.

Grant hadn't realized it back then, but as Bull got older, their old man got meaner. But the truth was—and this was what he hadn't realized—their dad had become afraid of Bull. Where he was happy to beat the shit out of Grant, he'd kept his distance for the most part from Bull.

When it came down to Bull taking over from the club, it hadn't been a challenge. Their dad had run the club close to the ground, nearly wiping Chaos and Carnage off the face off the earth. Bull had pulled them through, although there had been challenges.

Grant remembered when Bull had presented him with the VP patch, and how the club had voted for it. Deep down, Grant had known that patch never meant anything to Bull. His brother had wanted someone else— Pat. He'd ignored that and instead saw it as a chance to prove himself. His brother, though, rarely gave him the tasks of a VP. Rarely trusted him.

Taking care of Maddie had been the first real test he'd passed. Now he was out on his ass because Bull was protecting him. No, that shit didn't make sense. Bull wanted rid of him for years.

If he left Carnage for good, he wouldn't see Aria again. As much as he hated this fucking town and wanted a fresh start, he wasn't going to step out on Aria, nor would he step out on his brother. Running fingers through his hair, he clicked his tongue and Wanda walked beside him, heading back to town.

He decided to take the back way. There was nothing he needed in town. He had to go and talk to Jase but speaking to the gym owner only served to piss him off, and he wasn't interested in that shit. Not right now. He wasn't going to the mechanic shop either, even though Rusty had given him a call, as well as Pat.

Over the years he'd had many jobs. He wasn't lazy, he just found work so easily, and he flitted from one to the other, never staying too long. For a short time, he ended up working as a waiter in the diner while he'd been protecting Maddie. That had been fun. Some of the guys, not club but locals, had thought they could take the piss out of him. Meeting with his fists had soon dissuaded them from saying shit.

Making his way toward the trailer park, he came to a stop when he saw a couple of men he didn't recognize. They had pulled a woman from a trailer. Her hair was a mess. She had blood running down her face. He clicked for Wanda to hide.

Grant didn't have any weapon on him. He'd stopped carrying his fucking gun after removing his leather cut, and he refused to wear the fucking thing while he'd been supposedly suspended from the club. Fucking Bull.

He was too far away to make out any of the words they were saying, but Grant saw the symbols on the back of the men's necks. They were Cartel. What the fuck were the Cartel doing in Carnage? This was not the deal. This was why killing Julio had been important.

The deal Bull made with the Cartel was simple— they would do all the drug and gun runs, and escort the products through Carnage while rarely stopping in town. If they had to, the product had to be shipped within the next ten hours. That was Bull's agreement. He didn't want guns or drugs on his turf. This deal stopped the Cartel from using them as a pit stop, or using its residents.

Grant didn't recognize the woman, but he kept himself still as the man who was clearly in charge fired his gun, shooting her through the skull and ending her life. He didn't recognize the fucker either.

Pulling out his cell phone, he dialed Bull's number. This went against everything he had told himself he would do.

Fucking … ugh!

He didn't scream. Didn't make a single sound. His heart raced, but not out of fear for himself. No, he feared for fucking Wanda.

"For fuck's sake, Grant, what do you want now?" Bull asked.

"I wondered if you knew about the Cartel being in Carnage?" Grant asked.

"What? Grant, is this some kind of joke?"

"No fucking joke. I'm serious. I just saw the Cartel and I don't know if it's one of ours, but he just put a bullet in a woman's head. I'm at the trailer park."

"Shit. Get the fuck out of there, Grant."

He hung up his cell phone and then held it up in front of him, zooming in on his camera to take the image of the ink on the back of the man's neck. All the Cartel they had dealt with had the ink on the back of the neck.

Grant was tempted to call this in to Dylan, but he had a horrible feeling the sheriff would end up dead, and he kind of liked the old guy. Sure, he was pissed off for getting thrown in the cells for a day, but he was just doing his job.

For the most part, Dylan left the club to deal with business. They had a joint goal in mind—to protect the town of Carnage, as well as its residents.

Grant touched Wanda's collar and urged her around the back.

The men were already dragging the woman into the trailer and within seconds it was burning. With his cell phone out once again, he took a picture of the man, and then waited. Grant kept to the shadows, not allowing his presence to be known.

"Little shits like you get on my fucking nerves. Always crouching down like the cowards you are. Thinking you know shit when you know nothing. But I'm going to teach you."

Grant pulled out of the memory.

The shit his father would say and do was enough to mess with any kid's mind. His father had started at a young age. Scaring him, then beating him for pissing himself. As far as his father was concerned, all he was trying to do was make a man out of his youngest son.

"You're nothing. Bull will be fucking king and then when he realizes what a piece of shit you are, you'll be six feet under."

He was always saying that shit. Always telling him he wouldn't be good enough for Bull. How his brother would end his life.

Grant waited, holding onto Wanda so she didn't expose them. His girl seemed to know there was danger. He would fucking kill them if they hurt his dog.

He waited. Patiently waited.

And then, they climbed into a big black truck with blacked-out windows and took off. Grant didn't move. This was one of those times he knew he had no choice but to stay down or risk getting caught. He'd made this mistake himself, once before with his father. Hiding so he didn't know he'd snuck into the club and headed to the basement.

The basement had been the only place that was off limits to the boys of the Prez. Grant had watched Bull go down to the basement and he'd seen every single member of the club go down as well. Most of the time, they came back up laughing at something, so Grant had figured there was something fun down there. Seeing as his father was already a bastard to him, he figured his dad just didn't want him to have any fun.

It wasn't that.

No, it had been where the Chaos and Carnage MC had taken their enemies. Grant had watched them torture a man until he was close to death. His dad must have known he was there, because he pretended to leave, and Grant attempted to make his escape, only he'd been there, waiting. That day, his father had said it was time for him to become a man.

At ten years old, Grant had never told another living soul. This had stayed between him and his old man, but that day he'd ended another man's life. He wasn't allowed to leave the basement, and even though he'd been scared and terrified, he had held that knife and at his father's enraged instruction, he'd slit the guy's throat.

Later that week, his dad had informed him that he'd killed an innocent man, and from that day forward, he had to do whatever his dad told him. Otherwise, he'd hand his son over to the cops. The memory was so clear. Even though that was over twenty years ago, Grant recalled the fear.

Every time he picked him up from school, Grant had to wonder if his dad had told anyone. The fear had eaten him up, threatened to kill him with it, and then, when he couldn't stand it any longer, he'd found it easier to be mean—to hurt Maddie, to be cruel to everyone around him.

Some kids had gravitated toward him. They liked to think he'd been cool. The truth was, Grant had needed to survive.

His own father had fucked with his head. Messed him up. And now it was up to him to get himself out of the shit.

Minutes passed, maybe even hours, before he got

to his feet and started to head toward the garage. That was where his brother would be. He still had to keep functioning, even if he had his woman in lockdown.

Grant thought about Aria. She was safe for now. He had to protect her.

Rather than think about what he'd just seen, he thought about last night, feeling her pussy against his palm. She'd been so tense as he touched her. He couldn't believe no one else had touched her. No one had taken the time to explore her precious body. She was untouched and he couldn't believe how fucking aroused he was at that knowledge. Aria was all his. And he wanted to give her the fucking world.

He wanted to show her how good it could be between them. To feel him. To feel them. She'd been so wet, and even though he'd wanted to take her jeans down, expose her pussy, and lick her fucking clean, he hadn't. No, he'd rubbed her clit, staring into her eyes, watching every reaction, learning her responses as he touched her. She drove him wild.

It hadn't taken much to make her come. A few strokes of his fingers, but when he was more than happy to just hold her, Aria had asked him to come. To show her what he liked. That was hot as fuck.

He'd worked his dick, staring at her, wanting to be balls-deep inside her, but he'd taken his sweet time, sliding up and down his length, and when he'd gotten close to release, he'd warned her seconds before flooding her tits with his cum. It had been one of the hottest nights of his life.

He had fucked so many women, but none of them had meant anything to him. Aria did, and he knew everything he shared with her would have meaning.

Chapter Nine

"What the fuck were you thinking?" Bull asked, shoving him across the room. The door to his office was already closed.

Grant wasn't interested in fighting his brother. If he needed that kind of shit, he went to the ring. There were times he wanted to hurt his brother and even goaded him, but rarely did he actually hit Bull.

"I was fucking walking in town with my dog."

They had left Wanda outside by the door. He didn't know if she would have tried to go for his brother.

"Prez, you need to calm down," Pat said.

"Why are you even here?" Grant asked. "Is your head so far up his fucking ass you don't know what you're supposed to be doing?"

Pat never showed any sign of his words insulting him. Not once. He just stood and took it. All the freaking time. It was so annoying. Pat was ex-military, and he knew the man was deadly. He also knew he kept a lot of secrets. He never talked about his time serving his country.

"Enough, Grant."

There was so much more he wanted to say but now wasn't the time. He wasn't in the mood to fight with his brother, the first time ever, but this was serious.

He grabbed his cell phone and pulled up the two pictures he'd been able to take. "Do you recognize these symbols? I wasn't looking for trouble. This was happening in our trailer park, Bull. In Carnage. They shot her in the face." And as if right on time, they heard the sound of sirens. The fire engine passed by the garage. "And they dragged her inside and set fire to the trailer." Grant shrugged.

"No one saw you?" Pat asked.

"No, not that I know of. They could have, but no one pursued me, and I waited some time. They got into black cars, windows tinted. The works. They drove off and headed out of town." He shrugged.

Bull took the cell phone from him and scanned over the image. "I don't recognize these symbols." He handed the cell phone to Pat. "I don't know how you manage to find yourself in impossible situations like these, Grant, but it's not funny."

Grant smirked. "It's a gift."

Bull shook his head.

"That's the Vito mark," Pat said. "Julio had one exactly like it, as did several of the crew, but this looks like it has also been added to."

Bull took the cell phone back.

"Do you recognize the guy?" Grant asked.

"Not a clue, but he does look vaguely familiar." Bull frowned.

"Is it possible he was in cahoots with Dad?"

Bull's nostrils flared. "I dealt with every single fucker that Dad dealt with."

"Come on, Bull. You and I both know his reach was far and wide." Grant didn't need to point out the obvious—that their old man was a greedy son of a bitch and was known for doing what it took to get money. Once he got hooked on dope, there was no controlling the man. He was a law unto himself. Dangerous, deadly, and cruel.

Bull shook his head. "Why now? Why wait?"

Pat took the cell phone and stared at it. And kept staring at it.

"It's not going to speak to you," Grant said.

"What do we know about Julio?" Pat asked.

"He was the one who took over the Vito Crew Cartel and did a whole bunch of dogfighting and shit."

Grant hated to point out the obvious but it was pissing him off seeing Pat with his fucking VP badge.

"We all know I'm talking about family. There's a striking resemblance, wouldn't you say?" Pat asked.

"I didn't spend a lot of time talking with Julio or staring lovingly into his eyes," Grant said.

Bull and Pat were now ignoring him and instead passing his cell phone between themselves.

"You think it's a brother."

"The Vito sign would explain part of it, but he has always spread his wings, maybe. I've got some contacts. I can find what I need. See if he's a wanted man, find out what he's into."

"Do it," Bull said.

"I'm getting fucking tired of these pieces of shit in my town."

Pat took his cell phone and Grant held up his hands, as the man just left the office. Wanda walked in the door and sat by his side.

"Is Aria going to come to the clubhouse to see about the dogs?" Bull asked.

Grant was tempted to walk right out of the office, but when it came to Aria, she was important to him. He held onto the back of the chair and stared at his brother. "Why are you doing this to Aria?"

"Grant, they're two aggressive dogs. We both know they've killed—"

"Other fucking dogs. We don't know if they've killed people, and can you blame them? The shit the dogs go through." Grant shook his head.

"You're … defensive."

"Aria is willing to take those two dogs. That's a good thing."

"And don't you see how reckless that is? She doesn't know their history. We have to make sure people are prepared in case of triggers. I'm not being a dick here."

"You could have fooled me."

Bull rolled his eyes. "Why does everything have to be a fight with you?"

"Because you do everything to make my life hard, that's why."

Bull slammed his chair back. "For once in your life, if you would stop acting like everything is a joke or a game, you might see that this is serious. Those dogs were trained to kill."

"Each other."

"And you don't think that same aggression can be used to turn against a person? Trust me, it can. I'm protecting her because with how you're doing, you don't fucking get it."

"I would never put Aria in danger. She's a good person and I know she can help those dogs. You don't know her. Don't you ever fucking accuse me of trying to hurt her." He wanted to kill Bull. He had to get away.

"Always the fucking same, Grant. Walking away, running away, hiding. What is it? Responsibility so fucking hard for you?"

Grant spun around, shoving the chair into the desk. He heard it crack but he didn't care. "Don't assume to know shit about me, Bull. We may be brothers, bound together by fucking blood, but you don't know me. You, or the club."

"What is there to know?" Bull asked. "Come on, tell me what I'm supposed to know. You never come to work. You always do whatever the fuck you want. Do you want me to forget that you wanted to get in with the Cartel over a year ago? How you wanted me to make the club more deeply involved?"

Yes, he did remember. Grant hadn't thought

about the shit he was saying. He'd just spoken, without thought.

"If it was left to you, Grant, the whole club would be swallowed up by the Cartel. They would be deep in the roots of this town, and your precious Aria would probably be a whore for them, or possibly even dead."

Grant stared at his brother.

"Have you never fucked up in your life, Bull?" he asked.

Bull frowned.

He'd surprised him. Good. Grant liked that. Usually, he would have charged at Bull, started a fight, been the same old fighting brothers, but not this time. Something was different for Grant. He didn't know if it was Aria or the shit he'd just seen, but he looked at his brother and shook his head.

"What the fuck are you talking about?" Bull asked.

"Forget about it. It doesn't matter." He never told Bull about anything that happened. He headed toward the door and Wanda followed him, stopping as he did. "I will be there with Aria. I'm not trespassing on club land, but I won't allow you to scare her either."

"Grant!"

His brother started to call his name, but Grant had heard enough. He kept walking.

****

"I will not take no for an answer, Aria. You will come to family Thanksgiving. Your brother has arranged it all."

"Mom, he's not my brother, and have you ever thought that I might have stuff to do?"

"Honey, you never have stuff to do. Stop being a horrible person. You will come to the restaurant. You will not embarrass us, and you will be part of this

family."

Aria kept playing the same conversation over in her mind. She'd been on break, sitting in her car eating her salad when her mother had called. She lifted up and panted, aware of Jase putting pressure on her feet as she did the sit-ups. They were killing her sides but she did a rep of ten more before collapsing to the mat.

"Good work." Jase patted her knee and got to his feet. Unlike the last two visits, this time he held a clipboard in his hands. "I want to take some measurements from you before we continue."

She wrinkled her nose but didn't complain. Perspiration covered her whole body and she moved over to the weighing scales and stepped on. Nibbling her lip, Jase took note and jotted it down in his book.

"Is that good?"

"You've lost three pounds," Jase said.

"So that is not good."

Jase frowned and looked up from his clipboard. "Why wouldn't that be good?"

"It's only three pounds. Shouldn't I show a dramatic weight loss to start?" Wasn't that what he said? With her changing every element of her life, she should start losing weight fast and then plateau. Not start out sucking at this.

Why am I surprised? Losing weight has never come easy to me. I am so fat and ugly. Everyone tells me all the time.

"Aria, everyone's fitness journey is different. Weight loss and weight gain are pesky little devils. You don't want to lose weight too fast, because in my experience, it's so easy to put it back on. My plan is about a lifestyle change, which in turn will benefit you. I'm writing these down as you have goals, but for me, I don't like to become obsessed with numbers."

"Is that your long-winded way of telling me to stop worrying?"

Jase chuckled. "I guess it is. Look, Aria, I don't believe in forcing people to come to the gym, which I know is crazy, but I want my place to be a fun experience. Not to battle some desire to please other people. Working out, fitness, this is all a personal goal. If you're happy with who you are, then we can stop this, unless this is what you want."

Before she got a chance to answer, Jase was summoned to a problem.

There were mirrors all around the gym. She hated her reflection. Over the years she had fought hard not to look at herself. She had so many people in her life telling her she didn't match up to what they wanted. She didn't fit their model, and it was easier to not see what they saw.

Aria lifted her head and looked at her reflection. She refused to wear tight-fitting clothes. Why enhance what people told her was gross? She was more interested in hiding every single part of herself, not encouraging people to look. The leggings she wore were large, as was her shirt. It was too big so it fell a little off her shoulder.

"Well, well, well, what do we have here?"

Aria turned to see Sean, Lidia's ex, heading toward her.

Great. Just who she needed to see.

"You're not supposed to be in here," Aria said.

"No? This is a place for people who want to look their best. This is not a place for people like you."

Aria stared at Sean. He hadn't liked her from the moment they met. She tilted her head to the side and stared at him.

"What do you want?" Aria asked.

"Me, I want nothing, but I'm sick and tired of

seeing you. This place is not for fat people. Fucking ugly people. You make me sick." The disgust on his face was real.

Aria stared at him and it was almost funny. Actually, it was really funny. He reminded her so much of her mother.

"Wow," Aria said. "I didn't realize I could be so repulsive by just being here."

"Why don't you just fucking leave?" Sean asked. "I can't believe Lidia picked that over me." He held his hand out and pointed up and down.

"Who the fuck do you think you're talking to?"

Aria gasped and spun around to see Grant heading toward them. He'd changed into a pair of shorts and a polo shirt with the gym's logo. His heavily inked arms were on display and the shirt looked a little too tight on him, but he looked incredible.

He stepped in front of her, reached out, and moved her behind him. He was protecting her. Aria was surprised.

"What the fuck is this?" Sean asked. "Fatty's little army." He laughed to himself.

Grant took a step toward him. She saw that he was a little taller than Sean and scary as well. The smile was soon wiped from Sean's lips.

"Go on, say it again," Grant said. "I dare you."

"Dude, you can do so much—"

Sean never got to finish. Grant landed the first blow and Aria gasped, taken aback by the sheer force of it.

"Do you think it's funny to call her names, you little dickhead fucker!" Grant threw a punch to his gut, then another. "Go ahead, say it again. Say that shit. Come on. Do it."

Sean didn't get the chance to say another word.

He did try to fight back, but he was no match for Grant, who showed absolutely no mercy. Just as Sean fell to the floor, Jase rushed into the room.

"What the hell are you thinking?"

Jase stepped between the two men, but Aria knew Grant was done. If he wasn't, there would be no stopping him.

"You left her alone so this piece of shit could speak shit to her!" Grant yelled.

"What?" Jase asked.

"Yeah, exactly. You don't even know what's going on." Grant shook his head. "Come on, Aria."

"We're not finished," Aria said. She looked toward Jase.

"What did this man do?" Jase asked.

"I walked in on it," Grant said, getting into Jase's face. "Calling her all kinds of fat names. Telling her she doesn't deserve to be here. Is this the kind of operation you're running?"

Jase looked toward Sean.

"Get out," Jase said.

"Jase, come on, man."

"Get the fuck out of my gym, right now." Jase looked like he was shaking, his rage knew no bounds.

He looked toward her. Aria stared at him.

"I will understand if you'd like to leave for tonight, but I promise you, you are always welcome here."

She frowned, looking from Jase toward Grant, then back again.

"I'd like to finish my session, if that's okay?" Aria asked.

Grant cursed.

She rushed toward him, cupping his face. "Please don't be angry," she said.

Grant took hold of her face, tilting her head back. "You don't need to be here. I wish you could see what I see." He pulled her in close and kissed her hard. "But I'm not going anywhere. I'm sticking around."

"He could sue you," Jase said.

Aria gasped.

"Let him."

The rest of the session went by without a hitch. She heard Grant's disapproving grunt from time to time when he wasn't happy with the plans Jase organized. They did some more warm-up exercises. Jase took some measurements, and Grant didn't like that. It was the only time he didn't give them any kind of space. Aria quite liked how jealous he got.

By the end of the session, she was tired, but she also felt quite wired.

Grant took hold of her bag.

"Where's Wanda?" she asked.

"At home. It was way too cold. My place is closer. That's where we're heading," he said, taking hold of her hand.

There was no room for her to argue as they rushed toward his apartment. The moment they stepped through the door, Grant dropped her bag on the floor and showed her toward the shower.

"Wait here," he said.

Aria wrapped her arms around herself. There was a mirror to her side and she caught sight of her stomach. She quickly turned her back, but not before trying to suck in her stomach. It didn't matter what she did, she'd always be too big.

Grant returned holding a pair of sweatpants and a large shirt.

"I'll get dinner ready."

"Grant, make sure it's…"

"Don't," he said.

She licked her lips. "This is important to me."

He stared at her and shook his head. "I'll cook you something, and stop panicking." He stepped out of the bathroom and Aria sighed.

He was the only person who didn't complain about her weight. Who didn't make her feel like a failure for not being stick-thin.

She took a quick shower, not wanting Grant to wait for her, being cautious of the amount of hot water she consumed. Cleaning up after a workout felt so good. Her hair was no longer slick with sweat. She dried her hair on the towel as best she could.

Changing into the clothes he'd brought for her, she was thankful they had fit, and within ten minutes she stepped out of the bathroom.

The scents of onion and garlic filled the air. She walked into the kitchen to find Grant once again cooking.

"Don't say a word," he said.

Aria chuckled.

Wanda came over to say hello.

"I called Bull. I'm heading over to the clubhouse tomorrow to meet the two dogs."

"I'll be coming with you."

"Bull said that. It was kind of a surprise that he told me what you were doing. He's your brother, right?"

"Yep."

"Are you two close?"

"Sometimes."

Aria chuckled. "I'm not too close with my sister either. I don't know if that's because we don't get along or because my mom was always taking her out."

"Your mom sounds like a bitch," Grant said.

Aria smiled and then nibbled her lip. Grant had walked toward her and pointed the knife at her. "I know that face. You want something?"

"Yeah and no." She pursed her lips."

"Now I'm intrigued."

Aria rolled her eyes. "My mom called me today and has ordered me to go to Thanksgiving dinner. My sister's husband has arranged for it to be at a fancy restaurant."

"You've been ordered to go?"

"Yes."

"And you know you're a grown-ass adult."

"I know, but trust me, it's easier if I go and just get this over with. I've been able to avoid all the other family get-togethers the past few weeks. There's no refusing this one. It'll be easier."

"You ever thought about telling this woman to go fuck herself?"

Aria snorted. "It's my mom."

"And you can tell parents this stuff too."

"Did you tell your parents?"

Grant tensed up. "Eventually. Yeah, I told my old man. Not my mom."

"Why not your mom?"

"Didn't know who she was. Never met her."

"Oh," Aria said. She had no idea what to say to that. "I'm so sorry."

"Don't be. I don't care."

It seemed so strange to hear that. She found it rather refreshing.

"Would you like to come with me?" Aria asked.

Grant paused in stirring and turned to look at her. "You're inviting me to a family Thanksgiving?"

"Yes, but you should also know…" Aria paused, wincing. She tried to think of a delicate way to say that her parents hated him and everything he stood for. There were no words.

"What?"

"Er, it doesn't matter."

"Come on, Aria, out with it." He stopped cooking to come and stand in front of her.

"My parents are not exactly big fans of the club, you know."

She avoided looking into his eyes for the longest time and then, once she delivered the bad news, she did. She was a little taken aback to see he was smiling.

"You're smiling," Aria said, pointing out the obvious.

"Yeah, you're so cute when you're nervous. Don't be, babe. Trust me, you haven't upset me. Not in the least." He reached out to stroke her cheek. "Do you think this will be the first woman to be pissed that I'm the guy her daughter brought home to meet her parents?"

Aria's brows rose. "So you've met a lot of parents..."

He shook his head. "Scrap that. Shit, that's not what I meant. Trust me, I've not met a lot of parents."

"Don't worry about it."

Grant cupped her face and tilted her head back. "I look forward to this."

She wrinkled her nose. "I don't."

"Why?"

"Trust me. I know my mom, okay? I know what she's like. It's not going to be fun."

He snorted. "I can imagine."

Aria thought about Sean. "Thank you, for, you know, the gym."

Grant paused and she heard him breathe and visibly count to ten. She couldn't help but giggle.

"He did make you angry, didn't he?"

"He's an asshole. You can't listen to guys like him. Or women."

Aria ran her hands down her thighs.

Grant poured some tomatoes into his onion and garlic. The pot with the water was also boiling. He added the pasta, and had just placed the steaks onto the grill pan.

Rather than watch the food, he came toward her. "Why are you doing this?"

"Why am I doing what?"

"The gym. The exercise?"

"I told you before. I want to." She didn't need to tell him that she was just tired of everyone treating her like crap for the longest time. Just because she wasn't thin. Her mother hated her because of the size of her clothes. She'd never been good enough for them, and it was exhausting.

She wasn't going to tell Grant that while she was on the phone, her mother had already insisted on her picking low-calorie or fat-free items. To avoid meats. If they'd been having Thanksgiving at home, then her plate would have been served by her mother, with the minimal amount of food. That was her mother's way.

Thanksgiving and Christmas sucked.

When she could, Isabella had been able to sneak away some more food. Whenever she was around with Lidia, her mother had always been super nice to her, never once complained about her weight. There had always been treats and love there.

Aria pushed those thoughts out of her mind. There was no point in thinking about them.

Her mother had always been difficult. She always talked about how difficult it was having a large child, how other mothers would laugh at her. Isabella was the perfect child—the firstborn. Aria would forever be the disappointment.

"You want to?" Grant asked.

"Yeah, I do. I think it's time I got fit." She had a desire to poke at her stomach, but not in front of Grant. No, when it came to Grant, she wanted to appear sexy, and talking about her weight was the furthest thing from sexy.

Grant cupped her face again. "You don't need to do this for me," he said. "I like you exactly the way you are. Your big tits, those juicy thighs, that ass. I want to touch every single part of you. The past few months, you're the reason I kept coming to the vet. The dogs needed it, but you ... you were what drew me in."

Before she could say anything, he slammed his lips down and kissed her.

Chapter Ten

"You're frowning," Maddie said.

Bull looked up from his computer screen. It was nearly two in the morning. He'd just gotten the update from Rip that Grant was okay and was in Maddie's old apartment around the back of the diner. He'd also been told about Aria Taylor was there as well. He didn't know much about Aria, but she wasn't his brother's type. All the years he'd known Grant, he'd gone for super-slender women, not the ones with curves, similar to Maddie. Strange.

"Just waiting."

He was hoping Pat would have some answers by now. He'd already been on a call with Dylan. The fire had spread to two other trailers. The first one did have a body. The residents were not in the other two. There had been no security footage in the surrounding area. Nothing to help clue Bull in.

"Does this have anything to do with the reason you got Grant arrested and me and Lindsey are here all the time?" Maddie's arms were folded.

Bull knew he couldn't keep fooling Maddie anymore, if he even did in the first place.

He got up from behind his desk and rounded it to look into her eyes. "You're pissed at me."

"I'm not pissed. I'm confused. I thought you and Grant were good." She shrugged. "I don't know."

Bull rubbed the back of his head. "Grant and I, we're brothers. There will be good days and shit days, and everything in between." He ran a hand down his face and reached out to take her hand, pulling her close.

"I know there's a threat to the club, Bull. You don't have to keep it from me. The guys try to pretend all the time that nothing is happening, but it is. I can tell."

She smiled at him, but it didn't quite reach her eyes. "I get that it's club stuff, but this is starting to bother you."

He had tried to keep club shit away from her for the longest time, but while there was a threat to the whole town, he couldn't do it.

"It's not just a threat to the club. It's to the town. Last year, the dogfighting ring should never have happened. With us here, Carnage is a patched place. It belongs to the Chaos and Carnage MC. It's my turf. My town. By those bastards doing what they did, it made me look weak." He gritted his teeth.

"Bull, you're not weak."

"I'm not? You got attacked at the animal shelter. You were in the hospital. I was afraid you weren't going to wake up because you took a beating so badly."

"Don't think about it."

"I can't stop thinking about it, not now." He held her hand, locking their fingers together. In order to protect Maddie, he had no choice but to push her away, or pretend to push her away. To pretend he no longer cared about her. He'd hurt her in the worst way.

"I love you," he said.

"I love you too." She stepped closer to him and he wrapped his arms around her. "I thought you killed them." She whispered the word "killed" and he couldn't help but laugh. Adapting to the life of being his woman had been quite hard on her. She tried, but it was always difficult for her. He leaned down, pressing a kiss to the top of her head.

"I did."

"So what's the problem?" She lifted her head to look into his eyes. "I don't get it."

He stroked her cheek. He would do anything for this woman. Anything in the world.

"Not all bad people die, babe. Sometimes you kill

someone, and it brings forward someone even worse."

"Carnage is under threat?" she asked.

He nodded, not able to bring himself to say that out loud. It's under threat because he didn't have a clue who would attack them. Who the fuck would dream of taking them on?

****

"You do realize you being here is going to piss people off."

Aria tried not to listen to the scary biker guy who'd gone to stand with Grant. It was so cold, but she didn't care. Bull was there, as were a couple of club members, watching her with the two dogs. They were both male.

There was no distinctive breed, they were a mix of what appeared to be a boxer or possibly a Doberman, maybe even crossed with a German shepherd like Wanda. Speaking of Wanda, she sat perfectly next to Grant. Aria loved how devoted the dog was to Grant. Her heart broke a little as Bull had told her these dogs didn't have names.

She wasn't afraid of the dogs, not even after Bull told her some of their history of dogfighting—how they would be starved, teased, hurt, to do their owners' bidding. She couldn't believe anyone would be that cruel, but then, this was people they were talking about. Of course there was cruelty.

She crouched down and both dogs moved toward her. She stroked one, kissing him on the head, and when she looked into his eyes, it was the strangest thing.

"Ernie," she said.

Maddie, Bull's wife, chuckled and walked toward her.

Aria smiled. "I don't … that is so strange. It's like he told me his name."

"It is like that. Some dogs just speak to us, I guess. I've seen it happen at the shelter a lot."

Did this mean that Ernie wanted to be her dog? Kissing the top of his head again, she looked toward the other and kissed him, staring into his eyes. They were so beautiful, so brown, so full of hope.

"Bruno," she said.

For this, she got a lick on the cheek.

"Come on, Bull, you can see the dogs like her."

Bull held up his hand. He walked toward her. "Are you even ready to house two dogs?" he asked.

"Yes, I'm ready." She and Grant had gone to the pet store during her lunch break. She had all the necessary items to take them home. Grant had also brought his big truck of a car with him. They hadn't attacked Wanda either. They were good dogs. She just knew it.

Bull stood and rubbed at the back of his head.

Was he debating it?

She loved Ernie and Bruno. They were hers. She just knew it. Andy and Phil had already agreed that she could take them into work, especially during this time, when she was getting to learn all about having dogs.

"I'm going to give you two weeks with them," Bull said. "Someone from the club will stop by, check on you and the dogs, see how they're doing, and how they're adapting."

"Seriously, Bull. Don't you think that's overkill?" Grant asked.

"Do you have a problem with that?"

"None at all. I can take them?" she asked.

"Yes, you can take them."

She got to her feet and the truth was, she didn't have a clue how to command or instruct them.

"Come on, Bruno, Ernie, let's go home." She

suddenly stopped. "How do I, ah, pay?"

"A small donation to the animal shelter is all that's required," Maddie said.

Aria smiled. "I'll do that tomorrow."

Bruno and Ernie followed her all the way to Grant's car. She opened the back doors and in they climbed. There was no growling as Wanda took the front seat. There were two front seats in Grant's truck—one for Wanda, and the other for Aria.

"I'm sorry about my brother," Grant said, the moment they pulled away from the clubhouse.

They were heading toward her place. She already had everything set up. Food, beds, toys, the works. She had no idea how this was going to work, but she wanted it to.

"Don't worry about it. He cares about the dogs' well-being. That's a good thing."

She glanced back. Both dogs had lain down on the back seat. She was going to take care of them.

The drive wasn't a long one. Grant turned off the ignition and Aria climbed out of the front seat, rounded the truck, and helped Bruno and Ernie out of it.

Wanda joined them in the house, and Aria stood at the closed front door, and watched.

"Go on, dogs, go and enjoy." She nibbled her lip and winced. "I have no idea what I'm doing."

Grant laughed. "Do you think I've got a clue when it comes to Wanda?"

"You don't?"

"Nope. I just do what comes natural to me."

"Natural?"

Aria rubbed at her temples and then walked into the sitting room. Both beds were set up. She wanted them to be cozy.

"Come on, Ernie. Come on, Bruno. Time for you

to see your new home. That's right. Come on." She patted the bed and at first neither dog moved.

She smiled at the dogs and held up a toy for them to see. That did seem to appeal to them. They both came forward and she couldn't help but laugh as they walked closer.

"I see. They just need a bit of bribing." It took about ten minutes, but both dogs walked onto the bed. They sniffed the area and then started to slightly scratch at it with their paws. It was the cutest thing she had seen and she loved it.

"This is good, right?"

"Yes, it's good. It will take time, but they'll settle. Look at Wanda."

Aria got to her feet and moved toward him. Even though she was nervous, she wrapped her arms around his waist. "Thank you."

"You're thanking me?" he asked.

"Yes. For coming with me. For ... having faith in me."

"Aria, you're helping them out. Trust me. The shelters get full easily and it's not always easy to house previous fighting dogs. It can be difficult."

"It's not just that, you don't tell me that I'm taking on too much. You have confidence in what I'm doing, and you believe in me. That is ... it's nice."

"I'm not going to like your mom, am I?"

She shrugged. "You might love her."

"Anyone who hurts you, I'm going to have a big issue with." He pressed a kiss to her lips. Aria ran her hands up his back, holding him close.

She loved being near him, feeling him. Another moan spilled from her lips and he growled.

"Aria, I better go," he said.

She pulled away and looked up into his eyes.

"Why?"

"Because…"

"What if I wanted you to stay?" she asked, nibbling her lip.

"I could make up a bed."

She pressed a hand to his chest. "No. What if I … wanted you to stay with me?"

"Aria, what are you saying?" Grant asked.

She had been thinking about this a lot in the past couple of weeks. When she was with Grant, he made her believe she could do anything, be anything. There were no limits to what she could achieve, but it wasn't just that. He made her feel so many things—aroused, alive—and she wanted to be with him, even if she was terrified.

"You know what I'm asking."

"I've got a good idea," he said.

She nibbled her lip and stared at his chest. "I want … do you want … to sleep with me?"

This was so hard. Heat flooded her cheeks. She had never been so embarrassed before. Scrap that, she had, but normally that was in front of witnesses. Only Grant got to see the pleasure of her humiliation today.

"You're asking me if I want to have sex with you?" Grant asked.

"Just forget it. It doesn't—"

She was stopped as he took hold of her hand and placed it on his cock. Even through his jeans, she felt how hard he was. She gasped and looked up at him, a little taken aback.

"Aria, I want to fuck you. I want to make love, have sex, whatever you want to call it. I want to be with you." He tilted her head back. "But I also know you've never done this before and I don't want to do anything that you'll regret. For the first time ever, I want to take my time with you."

"I'm ready, Grant. Trust me. I know what I want."

He nodded. He looked at the dogs. They were already snoozing, and so he took her hand, and her heart began to race as he walked upstairs.

They were really doing this. Walking upstairs toward her bedroom. This was going to happen. She was excited and a whole lot of nervous.

Arriving in her bedroom, she turned toward him. Grant closed the door.

"Do you want to turn out the light?" Aria asked.

He shook his head. "No." He removed his jacket. It wasn't the leather cut but a denim one she was starting to get used to.

Aria didn't know what to do as he pulled his shirt off over his head, and then he was topless in front of her.

"I want you naked, Aria. I want to be able to see you. I won't be turning off the light."

"Oh."

This was going to be a huge disaster, there was no doubt about it. How could it be anything but? She had never been naked in front of anyone before.

Pulling off her sweater, she then took her shirt off, tossing it to the floor. She stood before him in her jeans and a bra.

"Aria, look at me."

She lifted her head and Grant had moved even closer.

He stroked a finger across her shoulder, sliding his fingers beneath the catch of her bra. "I'm naked."

"You're wearing jeans."

He chuckled. "I'm part naked. I think it's only fair that you are as well."

"I'm not sure about this."

Aria didn't stop him from pulling down the strap

of her bra. Then the other. He reached behind her and flicked the bra open.

"You're good at this," she said.

His lips brushed against the curve of her shoulder. They were close as he slid the bra off her body. Her heart raced and she felt nerves rushing through her body.

His hands touched the bare skin of her back, and then, within seconds, he had them both chest to chest, and she felt how close he was. She gasped. The hard ridge of his cock pressed against her core. She sunk her teeth into her lip, trying to contain her pleasure, but nothing could stop the way she felt. He felt so amazing.

"I want to see you, Aria. I want to see every single part of you, and if I wasn't attracted to you, I wouldn't be in this room right now excited about the thought of fucking you."

"Okay."

"I need you to trust me."

Tears filled her eyes and she quickly squeezed her eyes closed to stop them from falling. She didn't want to allow the tears to fall.

Grant pulled away and as she opened her eyes, she watched him. The temptation to cover her body was strong, but she kept firm, not moving her hands, just looking at him.

He groaned. "They're fucking beautiful, just as I knew they would be."

Before she could ask him what he meant, he had already cupped her tits and was pressing them together. His face pushed between the mounds and he started to kiss each one. Aria gasped. She didn't know what she was expecting but it certainly wasn't this.

He stroked the tips of her breasts, pinching the hardened nipples as he flicked his tongue against each mound. That was a sensation she wasn't prepared for.

"Fucking perfect."

He kissed each one.

Grant let go of her tits and then, within seconds, he had his jeans down his thighs, followed by his boxer briefs.

And for the first time in her life, Aria stared at a naked man. A completely naked man.

Grant was a dream come true. The inked body, the muscles, and the way he wrapped his fingers around his engorged length sent a tingle rushing through her body. She couldn't think, nor process what she was seeing. He was perfect.

"Aria, I'm naked, baby, it's time for you to join me."

She stared at his body and even though in her mind she was screaming at herself not to go too far, not to let him see all of her naked, she did so. It was better to rip off the Band-Aid than to keep teasing it, tugging it, until it felt even worse, removing layers of hair with it.

She got naked. Stripping her body for him to see. And the moment she stood before him, she clenched her hands into tight fists. She could do this. This was easy. Lifting her head, she prepared to see the disgust that she had seen on the faces of Sean and her mother.

She opened her eyes and looked at Grant, only to find his eyes roaming up and down her body, but he was also working his cock. He'd not gone soft.

Grant let go of his cock and closed the distance between them. His hands went to her ass as he pulled her in close, their bodies flesh to flesh. She gasped.

"Fucking perfect. I always knew you would be." He growled the words against her body.

Aria didn't say a word but then he captured her lips and all thought left her mind. She was so focused on him. His hands. His body. His everything.

The kiss was out of this world, even more possessive than ever. His tongue traced across her lips and as she opened, he plundered her mouth and she gave in to him, wanting everything he gave. Hungry for him. Desperate. In need. Craving everything that was him.

He squeezed the curves of her ass before running up to capture her neck. Grant moved them until she felt her bed at her knees. He broke the kiss long enough to lower her down onto the bed.

Staring up at him, she saw arousal. He reached down tracing a single finger from her neck, going over her tits, and then across her stomach. He didn't touch her pussy, but slid down toward her knee.

Grant knelt before her, gripped her knees, and spread them wide. She gasped.

"Trust me," he said.

She sank her teeth into her lip and nodded her head. Words were not easy, not right now.

He stroked the inside of her thighs, moving up, and when he grazed her pussy, another moan spilled from her lips. It was hard for her to contain the sound, not that she wanted to.

"Fuck me, you're beautiful," he said. "I'm a lucky man."

He touched her clit and Aria gasped, arching up. Grant put his hand on her stomach and pressed down.

"I want you to feel everything," he said.

She wasn't exactly sure what he meant, but then his lips were on her pussy, licking at her clit, making her moan. The pleasure was instant.

Aria felt every little stroke, every little flick. It was out of this world. She had never known pleasure like this. She'd never been with a man. This was all so new.

"You taste so fucking good," Grant said, growling the words against her flesh. She loved it when he talked like this to her. She never wanted him to stop.

Another moan, another whimper, and she felt the hit of her orgasm take her by surprise. It was so fast, so hard, and she was so ready for it.

Grant held her throughout. His hand pressed on her stomach keeping her in place as he licked at her.

Aria didn't know how much more she could take, but he seemed to know when to stop as he slowly brought her back down and soothed out the pleasure by kissing her clit one final time. He didn't move away, but climbed between her spread legs. They moved up the bed, until she was against the pillows and staring at him.

"I would love to suck on your pussy all day long," he said.

She chuckled. "That was incredible."

"Tell me if you want me to stop."

She shook her head. "No, I don't. I'm ready."

"This is … it's going to hurt."

Aria giggled. "Do you want to?"

"Yes, I do. I don't want to hurt you."

"If we can believe the romance books, it'll be over before we know it." She couldn't believe they were talking about this right now, just as she was ready for him to do it.

Grant reached between his thighs and Aria had already spread her legs. The tip of his cock pressed between her slit, stroking over her clit and making her moan. He did this a couple of times. Each touch to her nub made her more aroused with every passing second, until he moved down, and she knew this was it.

Staring into his eyes, Grant looked right back at her, and then he tensed. He slammed balls-deep inside her. It was painful. Aria had no choice but to bite into her lip to try and contain the pain. This was what she'd been wanting.

She was no longer a virgin. She had given that to Grant Reynolds.

****

The following morning, Grant stood in Aria's kitchen. She didn't know he had woken up yet, but now he stood, watching her as she danced in his shirt, in front of the stove. Damn, he loved her ass.

Last night had been a mixture of the best and worst night of his life. She had been so fucking responsive to him. He'd taken her virginity.

Aria was now his. All his.

He'd fucked many women in his time. With every other woman he'd been gone the moment they had woken up. Actually, he'd taken off the moment he had finished fucking them.

Not with Aria. With her, he stayed.

He'd taken her virginity, claimed this woman as his own, and then, he'd seen the evidence of this being her first time. He'd felt it as well. The tightness of her pussy. The giving of her virgin flesh. He hated himself for seeing the pain in her eyes. There had been no way to stop it. It had taken all his strength to not just take, to fuck her, but he'd waited, hoping with time that the pain lessened.

Aria had smiled at him, biting her lip at the same time, telling him that it was all fine. But it wasn't. He'd hurt her.

Grant didn't know how long it had taken for her to get used to the feel of him inside her, but the moment she had, she started to wriggle against his dick. After that, he had fucked her, tried to make love to her, but like a horny teenager on his first time, he'd not been able to contain himself. Not when it came to Aria. He had come hard and fast. It had been over lightning-quick.

Aria had been surprised, and he had told her it

was never like that. He helped to clean up the blood, soothed her pain, and he had every intention of giving her a couple of days, but then she had touched him. She had asked him for more, and they had fucked two more times before they fell asleep. She snuggled in his arms. Grant loved that, feeling her body against his.

He felt her leave him this morning. He watched her leave, pretending to be fast asleep. He loved when she picked up his shirt. Now, standing just outside the kitchen, he watched her, hypnotized by the sway of her hips.

He didn't recognize the song on the radio. The music played and he smiled. Her hair wasn't constrained but fell around her in waves.

Bruno, Ernie, and Wanda had already been taken out and fed. He saw the bowls were dirty on the floor.

This felt like home.

Grant didn't know why it felt that way. Nowhere had ever felt safe to him, nor like home.

"Morning, beautiful," he said, waiting for Aria to step away from the stove.

The moment he spoke she let out a cry and spun around. Her hand pressed against her chest. "Grant, you scared me."

He walked into the kitchen pulling her in close. "And you looked sexy as fuck," he said. He grabbed the curves of her ass in his hands, a little disappointed to see that she wore panties. "I like this. You wearing my clothes."

"I'm making you breakfast."

Grant growled against her neck, flicking his tongue against her skin. "I could eat you for breakfast." He ran his finger across the band of her panties. "How are you feeling today? Are you sore?"

Aria groaned, pressing her face against his neck.

"I'm fine. Everything is fine."

"You don't need to be embarrassed." He gripped the back of her neck and forced her to look at him. "Morning, beautiful."

She smiled. "Morning, yourself."

Her cheeks were bright red.

"I missed you," he said.

He pressed his cock against her stomach. She gasped.

"Breakfast?" she asked.

Grant looked behind her and he stepped forward, keeping hold of Aria as he flicked the heat off the stove and the grill. "Can wait."

He pulled Aria into her dining room and then lifted her up onto the table. Cupping her face, he took possession of her lips. Sliding his hands down, he broke the kiss long enough to pull the shirt off her body. He had to have her again.

Grant couldn't hold back the desire to plunge his cock deep inside her cunt, to fill her womb with his cum. He had to do it.

With the shirt out of the way, he pressed a kiss to her lips and then cupped her tits in his palm. He worked his thumbs across the tight nipples and then took them into his mouth, taking his time with each bead. Flicking his tongue across each peak, he ran his hands down, going to her thighs and spreading her legs, making her open them wide for him. She whimpered as he touched her clit.

Kissing down her stomach, he urged her back and then sat down on the chair, drawing her closer. Aria had no choice but to follow his touch as he pulled her into position. She was open. No other man had been inside her. Aria was all his.

Grant had never had something like this. She had

given him a gift last night—her virginity. Opening the lips of her sex, he stared at her cunt. So precious. So wet.

He pressed a single finger inside her, watching as she took him. She was so tight. He added a second finger, and still marveled at her tightness. Pushing his fingers in and out of her cunt, he drew them back to circle her clit. His mouth watered for a taste of her.

Pushing his fingers back inside her, he took her clit between his teeth. He bit down, just slightly, and then he flicked his tongue back and forth, working her pussy. She tasted so fucking good.

He wanted her to come, to ride out the wave all over his face, and then he wanted to fuck her, to watch her take his dick.

Sucking at her clit, he felt her pussy as she started to build her orgasm. The ripples tightened, building toward a fever pitch. She was so close, and as he thrust her over the edge, he worked his fingers, drawing out every single ripple as he drove her higher and higher.

He waited until he knew it was a little too much, and brought her back down. She panted his name as he did so. Pulling his fingers from her cunt, he licked them, sucking each one in turn before standing up. Her legs were still wide open.

Shoving his pants down to his thighs, his cock sprang forward and he pressed the tip to her clit. His name spilled from her lips and he loved the sound. Sliding back and forth, he worked her pussy until he couldn't take it anymore, and then holding onto his length, he began to pump inside her. He started with the tip first, then gave her more and more of his dick, until he was fucking her. Her tits bounced with every thrust. He held onto her hips, keeping her in place as he worked his shaft inside her. Each time he pulled out, his length glistened with her cream.

Grant pulled out of her and then helped her off the table, long enough to ease her forward, bending her over the table, and then, within seconds, he was back inside her. Holding onto her hips, he fucked her harder, loving the feel of her ass against his pelvis. So soft and juicy.

"You feel so fucking good, Aria. I could fuck you for days." This time, he took his time, working her into another orgasm, and then watching his cock as he took her. Her cunt opened around his length.

He'd not worn any condoms and he had no desire to wear them. He didn't want anything between himself and Aria. She was perfect.

This time as he came, he thought about what his cum could be doing. How it flooded her womb and maybe, just maybe, he could be making a baby with her. Then Aria wouldn't be able to leave him. He'd get to stay in her life. They would be bound together by another person. Their child.

Grant eased out of her and as he did, he saw some of his cum spill from her pussy lips. He pressed his fingers to her hole, and tried to push his creamy cum back inside her. He wanted to get her pregnant.

Aria needed to belong to him in every single way that mattered.

Chapter Eleven

"You've had sex."

Aria looked up to see Lidia waiting for her by her car. It was lunchtime and Grant had already texted her that he was having to deal with the dogs at the shelter.

"What are you doing here?" Aria asked.

It was cold. Snow had fallen. Ernie and Bruno were inside the vet's keeping warm. Phil and Andy had given her their lunch order and she was about to go and get it.

"First, you're my best friend and hanging out with you on your lunch break is a given. I've been doing it for years, Aria. Have you forgotten? Second, I heard about what that fucking piece of crap did, and I wanted to come and see you."

"Ah, Sean," Aria said.

"No, dickwad, evil bastard. Those are acceptable names."

"He's called Sean, and if I remember correctly, you thought he was 'the one' at one point."

Lidia wrinkled her nose. "No, I never did. Trust me, he was never the one. He was a piece of crap. I just didn't realize how much of a piece of crap he was." Lidia stepped toward her. "He nearly cost me my best friend. I can't stand him. It's as simple as that."

Aria smiled. "You'd have found other friends."

Lidia shook her head. "I hate it when you do that. It makes me hate your mother so much. You always think you can be easily replaced and you can't. No one will ever be as good as my Aria. Besides, Sean's a guy. He will not come in the way of our relationship. Now tell me, was it the MC guy?"

She laughed and then looked toward the vet's. "I've got to go and get lunch."

"Then I'll ride with you. Ass-face has already cost us so much time. I'm not going to let him steal another minute."

Before Halloween night, she and Lidia had spent a great deal of time together, including lunch breaks. Sean was the first guy to have ever gotten between them, and Aria knew it was her fault. She had believed his lies, and that was all on her, not Lidia.

Lidia climbed into the passenger seat of Aria's car and hummed to herself as she put on the seat belt.

"So, MC guy. Is he hot in bed?"

"Lidia, come on, I'm not going to tell you that."

"Why not?" Lidia asked. "You didn't have sex until now, and don't even pretend you did, we both know you didn't. This is a big deal. You had sex with a guy and not just any guy, but Grant Reynolds."

"Why does that matter?" Aria asked.

"You do know that Grant has a reputation around town, right?" Lidia asked.

"Yeah, I know." She cringed just thinking about it.

"Do you?"

She turned to Lidia and then looked ahead of her as she pulled out of the parking lot. "Yeah, I know. I know he's been around. A lot of women have used him or whatever."

"He's flighty," Lidia said. "From what I heard, he bangs and runs."

"What?"

"Grant is never there for round two, nor is he there long enough to say if it's good enough. He's a quick fuck master," Lidia said.

"Oh."

"Did he leave you?" Lidia asked.

"No." Grant hadn't just screwed her and left.

He'd stayed. He even was tender with her. Cleaning up the evidence that he had been her first. She had told him not to do it, but he'd run her a bath and cleaned up the bedroom.

They then had round two and three. She had woken up with him. They had sex on her dining room table, then after she insisted on cleaning it, they had eaten breakfast together.

"Oh, my, this is unheard of," Lidia said. "Grant never stays around but he did with you."

"How do you even hear of these things?" she asked.

Lidia chuckled. "I have my ways, baby. I have my ways of hearing everything." She clapped her hands. "This is so good. Tell me more."

"He has agreed to go to Thanksgiving dinner with me. Michael has booked everyone at a restaurant. That should be interesting."

"Oh, my God, I cannot wait for this. Can I come?" Lidia asked.

"You hate my family dinners."

"I know, but I heard what happened with Grant and Sean. He called you all kinds of names and he punched him. I want to see the look on your mom's face as she goes against Grant. Can you imagine it?" Lidia chuckled. "I want to see that old bag get what's coming to her. I bet Isabella did it on purpose."

Aria frowned as she pulled up to the diner. "What do you mean?"

"Come on. Your sister gets so angry with your mother. I'm sure you've seen it."

She thought about it and Lidia rolled her eyes. "Fine, clearly not. You leave the table. When I've been at your family's house before, Isabella has told her to stop, to leave you alone. Even your dad has. They have your back, Aria. They do."

She found that hard to believe. "It's fine. My mom cares in her own way."

Lidia growled. "No, your mom is a vapid woman." Lidia hissed and put her fingers in front of her lips as if she had fangs. "Her mouth shoots out poison."

Aria couldn't help but laugh. Lidia had spent many hours trying to do this whenever her mother's cruel words had gotten to her.

"Stop it."

Closing the door of her car, she headed into the diner, going straight up to the counter. Beatrice told her it would just be a minute.

Lidia sighed. "I wish I could come," Lidia said.

"You have no idea what's going to happen."

"I have an idea." Lidia sighed. "But I already promised my mom I'd be there for Thanksgiving. She did invite you, by the way."

"I'd love to come, believe me."

"Maybe we could have a Friendsgiving."

Aria laughed.

"Come on. You could introduce me to Grant. I want to make sure he only has the best of intentions with my bestie."

"Or we could just wait until Christmas?" Aria asked.

"You don't want me to meet Grant?" Lidia tilted her head to the side.

"It's not that, I just, I don't know … you know…" She didn't want to say that she worried Grant would get bored. Especially now. He had stayed with her overnight, but that was different. She'd been a virgin. Maybe he was being polite and the other women knew the score beforehand. She had no idea.

Rubbing at her temple, Beatrice came over and

Aria placed the order. Lidia tacked on a quick order as well.

Aria sighed.

"I got two dogs," she said, quickly changing the subject.

While they waited she talked about Bruno and Ernie.

"I can't wait to meet them. You always did want a couple of dogs. I figured you would get them eventually."

Beatrice brought out their order and Aria paid. She stopped Lidia from getting her money out. Lunch was on her.

They walked back to her car and Aria froze when she saw her tire was down. She handed the food to Lidia and then crouched down, seeing that it wasn't just air out of her tire, but it looked like it had been cut. It was clear to see there was damage to the outside of the tire.

"Aria, what's the matter?" Lidia asked.

"I think someone has punctured my tire..."

She looked on the ground. She didn't roll over anything. Rubbing at her temple, she groaned. First, she had no choice but to call into work. Andy said she'd be there in a moment.

She turned to Lidia. "Andy's on her way. You're going to have to ride with her."

"Aria, what happened?"

"I must have rolled on something, right?" Aria looked up and down the street. If someone tried to puncture a tire in broad daylight, that was risky.

"You've got to call the tow truck. Reynolds' place. Ah, a certain boyfriend is there, right?"

"Grant doesn't work there," Aria said. "It's his brother Bull's place."

"Huh, I thought Grant did work at the shop."

"He does, I think, I don't know. He works at the gym, at the mechanic shop."

"The diner," Lidia said. "Where does this guy not work?"

Aria put the call through. Someone named Sweets answered. She told them what she thought might have happened. He told her to wait, they'd have the tow truck out to her.

Before the truck arrived, Andy came to pick up the food. Lidia wanted to stay with her, but she insisted on her friend being taken back to collect her car. Andy told her to keep them updated. Finally, the tow truck arrived.

"Aria?" the driver asked.

"Yeah, that's me."

"Rusty. Sweets told me you've got a slashed tire?"

"I think it's slashed or punctured, I'm not sure."

He climbed out of his tow truck and then rounded her car to where the damage was. He whistled. "Sweetheart, did you know this has been done on both tires?"

"What?"

"Yep, front here, and the back one, opposite." Rusty clicked. "Do you want me to take it to Bull's?"

"Er, yeah, of course. Please."

"No problem." He started to whistle as he got everything loaded onto the back of his tow truck.

Someone struck her tire. There was only one person she could think of who would do that—Sean. Why did Sean have it in for her? Was there any way to prove it?

She rubbed at her temple, feeling a headache start to develop. Glancing around town, no one stopped to pay them attention. She didn't see any sign of Sean, not that she'd been looking for him. Sean didn't exactly register on her radar. He'd been her friend's boyfriend, nothing more.

Rusty got the car loaded up and then helped her into the truck.

He was still whistling as they rode down the main street heading toward the garage. She knew it was the best one in town, and even though her parents drove out of town to get their car serviced and fixed whenever they needed to, she always used Bull's. She rarely had any problems with her car as she used it mainly in winter, or when she absolutely had to.

Rusty pulled into the main lot at the same time Grant ran around the main gate inside, with Wanda following behind him.

Aria climbed out of the truck and frowned. "Grant?"

"Rusty texted me. Someone slashed your tires?"

"Huh? I didn't..." Rusty whistled a little louder. "Might have sent him a quick message before I loaded up. Figured he'd want to know what was going on with his woman."

She didn't have time to enjoy being referred to as "his woman."

"You don't have to worry," she said. "It's probably some prank."

Grant stepped up toward her and cupped her face, tilting her head back. "Pranks involve toilet paper and knocking on someone's door and running away. They use eggs, not knives." He pressed a kiss to her lips. "Let me check."

He let her go and she licked her lips looking up to see a couple of the mechanics who were also members of the Chaos and Carnage MC. She felt her cheeks heat. It was the first time, apart from him going a little crazy with Sean, that Grant had shown her affection in public. This was all new to her.

It was a good thing she had invited Grant to Thanksgiving dinner. Her parents were going to find out about them sooner or later.

She looked away from the prying gazes and instead watched Grant. Rusty was unloading the car off the truck.

"Be fucking patient. This shit takes time."

"Grant, you don't even work here," Bull said. "You shouldn't be here."

"Aria's tires were slashed. I'm going to check it out and when it suits you, I work here. Don't give me that shit. We both know I'm a good mechanic."

"You're a good mechanic when you fucking show up," Bull said.

She watched Grant's jaw clench.

"I called him, Boss," Rusty said. "Figured he'd want to know his woman's car got targeted."

"I need to know so I can find the person who did it," Grant said.

Aria didn't know if she should name Sean. What if he didn't do it? What if it was just a bunch of kids messing around and they didn't mean to slash her tires?

"You got any enemies?" This came from the man who often wore the VP patch. She couldn't remember his name, but she'd seen Grant go toe to toe with him a few times.

"Not that I know."

"For fuck's sake, Pat, seriously, you think she has enemies?" Grant asked. "Get your head out of your ass."

"Everyone has enemies. Some of us are aware of them, others are not."

The only person she'd pissed off in the past few weeks was Sean. Her mere presence irritated him. Again, she didn't know if he had it in him to slash her tires. Not after Grant hit him.

"I don't know," Aria said.

Grant growled. "When I find who did this, they're going to fucking regret it." He pulled her in for a hug, holding her close.

She wrapped her arms around his waist and she had to wonder who would think to slash her tires, other than Sean?

****

Thanksgiving

Grant hated wearing suits. They never felt comfortable, but Aria had told him it was a fancy restaurant. He'd left Wanda at Aria's house with Bruno and Ernie. Aria's car was still in the shop. Bull didn't have the brand of tires Aria used, so they had to be ordered, and seeing as Thanksgiving was right around the corner, getting her tires had proven to be a little bit of a chore. The moment they arrived at the shop, Grant intended to fix her car. He wanted to check out the whole vehicle and make sure nothing else had been tampered with.

Grant didn't know who'd slashed her tires. He had a feeling it could have been that prick who'd been bullying her at the gym, but he couldn't be entirely sure. Grant had bullied people before, but he'd never gone out of his way to slash someone's tires. Not in daylight and certainly not a woman.

He wondered if it was because of him and his connections to the club. Even though Bull had suspended him and Pat now wore his fucking patch, to some people that meant nothing.

"Thank you," Aria said.

"For what?"

"For coming with me tonight. I don't know if you

had other plans."

"None." Bull had invited him to the clubhouse, as per Maddie's request, but he'd turned it down as he'd already committed to Aria. He had no intention of letting her down. Also, he wanted to meet the woman who thought it was okay to constantly attack her own daughter for the way she looked.

The night was going to be an eventful one, especially as Aria had already warned him that her parents didn't like the Chaos and Carnage MC at all. They would go out of town to avoid them rather than use the garage, even though it was the best one for miles.

Irritating people was his forté.

He looked forward to being his charming self tonight. He'd never embarrass Aria, but if someone spoke out of turn, then he wasn't going to sit back and take that shit. No. Not on his watch.

"Do you normally have something to do on Thanksgiving?" Aria asked.

"The club usually has a lot of food and a lot of alcohol. They're having the same shit again, but I'm not interested in that. With Maddie there, it'll be scaled back a bit, possibly. I don't know."

"Do you miss being at the club?" she asked.

Grant tapped his fingers on the steering wheel. It would be easy to lie but even the thought of doing that to Aria didn't sit well with him. When it came to her, he didn't want to make anything up. What he had with Aria was real and he wasn't going to taint that.

"Yeah, I do. Being suspended from the club hurt like a son of a bitch. I want my patch back. My brother and I, we've always argued. Always." He chuckled. "It doesn't matter what it is, we've always got the opposing opinion and sometimes I do shit to just wind him up. It's fun, you know."

Aria chuckled. "I'm not exactly sure if I know what you mean."

"You've got a sister, right?"

"Yeah, but we were never close. My mom liked to take Isabella to the shops and spend time with her. My sister was the one who got shown off. Me, I was always left at home."

Grant tightened his grip on the steering wheel.

"Isabella and I were not close. I don't know if we ever will be."

He couldn't help but think about his brother. He and Bull weren't close. Were they? Not really close. He always had his brother's back, but that was it.

"Do you want to be close to her?" Grant asked.

"Sometimes I think it would be nice. Like knowing she's pregnant. I'd love to be an aunt, spoiling her and stuff, but our mom had already started to take control." Aria sighed. "So I guess it will never happen."

"Bull and I don't always see eye to eye. He thinks he knows best because he's older than me. It pisses me off at times."

Aria reached out and put a hand on his knee. "I have Lidia."

Grant took her hand, locking their fingers together, and then bringing her hand to his mouth to kiss her knuckles.

"And now you have me," he said.

"And you have me."

He smiled. He just couldn't help it. It felt good to have her.

After another ten minutes, he found the restaurant. It was a fancy place, even though it appeared to be in the middle of nowhere. The parking lot was close to bursting. Grant found a space, parked the car, and turned off the ignition. There were a lot of small fairy lights illuminating the building.

"Have you been here before?" he asked, hearing Aria's sudden inhale.

"No, have you?"

"Babe, up until a few months ago, I wore the Chaos and Carnage leather cut, and trust me, I wouldn't have come here. This is not my scene." He gave her hand a gentle squeeze. "Come on, we can do this."

She chuckled.

Grant let her go long enough to climb out of the car and round the vehicle to her side. She was already in the process of getting out. Taking her hand within his, he clicked the lock on his keys, and then with Aria at his side, they walked into the restaurant.

The maître d' at the front asked for their name and Aria gave him her sister and her husband's name.

Grant had a quick glance around the restaurant. This was not his kind of place at all. Very quiet. Soft music played.

The maître d' left the main desk and walked them over to a table, with four people sitting there. He also noticed there was only one single chair at the table. No one had set him a place.

Grant spotted the mother instantly. She took one long look at Aria, stared up and down, and he knew instantly she wasn't happy with the figure-hugging dress Grant had convinced her to wear. She'd insisted on wearing a cardigan over her shoulders.

Instantly, he was angry.

The older man was her father, then he spotted the husband that Aria had told him was called Michael. Then his gaze landed on her sister, and fuck, piss, shit, fuck, cock, of all the people in the world, why did it have to be fucking her? He didn't know her name. Hadn't known her name. This was Aria's sister.

Even she looked taken aback to see him. Good. Great. This wasn't going to be a fun fucking Thanksgiving.

"Aria, you made it," her mother said.

"Yeah, I did tell you I was bringing a plus one."

"Your boyfriend?" this came from Michael.

"The only one," Grant said. "Grant Reynolds." He held out his hand and Michael took it. He was impressed that Michael had a firm handshake.

Next he shook hands with Aria's father. When it came to the mother, he took her hand and even as he hated it, he kissed her knuckles. "Charmed," he said.

"Would it be possible to have a chair brought and another placement at the table?" Aria asked.

"Certainly," the maître d' said, offering her a smile.

Grant clocked the bastard eyeing up her ass. He also noticed a couple of other men checking out his woman. Grant stepped behind her. He was the only one who would be checking out his woman's ass. Pulling out the chair, he helped her sit and then thanked the maître d'.

A couple of waitresses had stopped by the table to bring the necessary cutlery.

Well, this wasn't a great first impression from her family.

"I'm so sorry," Michael said. "Joan said that Aria's plus one wouldn't be coming."

Grant could only assume Joan was the fucking mother.

"No problem at all," Aria said. "Easily fixed."

"Reynolds, why do I know that name?" her father asked.

"He owns the mechanic shop in town, honey," Joan said.

"Oh. Oh."

Grant smiled. "Actually, I don't own. My brother does."

Aria was not wrong about her parents. They couldn't stand him just on his name alone. This was going to be fun.

"Are you okay, sweetheart?" Michael asked, rubbing at Isabella's back.

"Yes, I'm fine."

"Are you sticking to that diet like I told you?" Joan asked Isabella.

"Mom, I'm pregnant. Sickness comes and goes."

"As do her cravings," Michael said. "I don't have a problem going out late at night for potato chips and ice cream."

Grant chuckled.

Joan gasped. "Honey, you do not want to give in to those … cravings. Trust me. Fight them. Follow my plan and you'll rid yourself of your baby weight."

"It's fine, Mom."

"So, Grant, what do you do?" Michael asked.

"He's part of the Chaos and Carnage MC," Joan said. "That's what he does."

"Mom," Aria said.

"Actually, I've currently been suspended from the club. At this point, I'm neither in nor out of the club. Let's see, what do I do? Depending on the day, I'm a mechanic, personal trainer, waiter, or currently working at an animal shelter."

"Multiple jobs?"

"It pays the bills," Grant said.

He used to do the necessary work for the club as well. Whatever recon his brother needed, Grant was more than happy to do. In fact, there wasn't a job he'd not been great at. Even during his prospect years, he'd done every single little dirty job Bull could think of. Cleaning shit out of toilets, babysitting brats, standing for long hours holding beers for the guys, being a personal errand boy for the members.

He'd taken everything. Grant had known Bull wanted him to quit, but being part of Chaos and Carnage MC was in his blood. Nothing their father or Bull could say or do would take that thirst away from him.

"How did you two meet?" Michael asked.

He seemed to be the one taking the lead. Grant also noticed he was trying to distract Joan from talking to his wife. Every time the older woman went to speak, and it appeared to be directed at Isabella, he'd ask questions.

Grant smiled at Aria. "At the veterinary practice where she works. I had to go in with a few dogs. She was right there."

"Dogs are filthy animals. They should all be put down," Joan said.

"That's strange, I have the same viewpoint on people," Grant said, staring at Joan. He then laughed. "Dogs are just misunderstood is all. They're amazing companions. Loving. Loyal. They don't want anything from us but love and affection. Sometimes, even people can't give you that. Aria has just adopted two dogs."

Isabella gasped. "You have?"

"Yes, I have. Bruno and Ernie." Aria pulled out her cell phone and held it out for Isabella to take.

"They are so cute." Isabella held the cell phone out to her husband.

"They are cute," Michael agreed, kissing her head.

Isabella tried to show their mother but Joan waved her hand. Her husband, however, had a look at the picture.

"Are they not a handful?" he asked.

"No, they're not. They're wonderful and loving. They were rescued from a dogfighting ring. They needed homes and I just fell in love with them, Dad."

Her father looked happy but Joan, oh, she wasn't happy at all.

"Will you excuse me?" Isabella said, getting up from the table.

"Do you need me to come with you?" Joan asked.

"No, Mom, I just need to use the bathroom."

Grant got to his feet seconds later. "All that coffee, I have to use the men's room." He kissed Aria's cheek and headed in the direction of the bathroom.

He spotted the women's bathroom and waited outside. Isabella only took a few minutes but he'd also noticed no one else had gone in or come out of the men's room. He grabbed Isabella's arm and shoved her into the men's room.

"What are you doing?"

"What happened nine months ago, you never speak a fucking word of it. As far as I'm concerned, I don't know you, you don't know me, got it?"

"I would never … I promise," Isabella said. "It was a moment of weakness."

"It wasn't weakness on my part. I was looking for a quick fuck, and you were there. You meant nothing to me. But Aria, she's the real deal. You say anything to hurt her, and I will end you, got it?"

Isabella nodded. "Michael, he can't know."

Grant knew she'd been wearing an engagement ring. She had told him it was over between her and her boyfriend and the wedding wasn't going to happen.

He'd tuned out. Getting his dick wet at the time had been more important. Now, he was fucking sick of himself. This was before he'd even met Aria.

He didn't want this mistake to ruin what he had

with Aria. "Not a fucking word."

Letting go of Isabella's arm, he headed back out and made his way over to the table, taking a seat beside his woman. The waitress had already been over with the menus.

Running his hands along Aria's back, he cupped her shoulder. Seeing the woman he'd screwed one night around the back of the bar in town, hadn't been ideal. He couldn't believe that woman was Aria's sister. It explained why he recognized her from her picture but it hadn't been quite clear to him who she was.

"Feeling better?" Aria asked.

"Yeah, I am." He kissed her head.

Fuck, he loved this woman. Grant paused. *Where the fuck did that come from?* When it came to Aria, he'd known his feelings for her were strong, but this was a revelation to him.

He was in love with Aria Taylor. They were not just surface-level feelings either. These were deep feelings. The kind that consumed.

From the moment he first met Aria, he'd been completely besotted with her. He found any excuse to go to the vet's just to see her. He'd wanted to talk to her, get to know her. Dating her, being around her, he'd never felt so fucking whole before in his life. Not at all.

Bull had found that woman in Maddie.

Grant had thought it wasn't possible to find a woman that would make you forget your entire being, but now he sat with Aria and her parents at Thanksgiving, and he just knew deep in his soul she was the woman for him.

Isabella joined them at the table.

"Time to eat, I'm starving," Isabella said.

"Now, remember, the calories you count now will reward you when you've given birth. Trust me. I didn't keep my baby weight on for any longer than I had to," Joan said.

He saw Aria's hands grip the menu tightly.

"Aria, I suggest you stick with the vegetables. I've noticed you're not following the diet like I told you," Joan tutted. "You shouldn't have worn that dress."

"Aria will order what she damn well likes," Grant said.

He didn't know if Joan was used to people just listening to her shit, but he wasn't going to sit back and allow her to say that shit to his woman. Aria looked fucking stunning.

"Pardon me?" Joan asked.

"It's Thanksgiving, if Aria wants to order a big giant steak, she'll order the steak. If it's too expensive, I'll fucking pay. If she wants the lobster, she can have the lobster. If she wants the full-works Thanksgiving dinner, followed by pumpkin pie, that's what she's going to eat." Grant stared at Joan. "And as for the dress, I'm the one that told her to wear it and personally, it was a mistake of mine."

Aria gasped.

"Because I've had to sit here and watch several men drool in her direction. Aria's my woman, and she looks fucking gorgeous, so why don't we cut the shit and all the drama, and let the woman—that's right, the woman, not a child—make her decision?" Grant turned toward her. "You look amazing, as I said you would. Your ass is a fucking dream."

He didn't care that her cheeks were bright red.

He'd only been in the mother's company for less than twenty minutes and she had already pissed him off significantly.

"Eat what you want and you can wear what you

want." He gripped the back of Aria's neck and pulled her in for a kiss.

He felt her gasp. The kiss would have to do for now. He wanted to do so much more to her.

Grant turned to look at Joan. "It's fucking Thanksgiving, who really gives a shit about calorie counting? Get over yourself."

Chapter Twelve

Aria couldn't believe it. No one had ever spoken to her mother like that before. For the whole meal, her mother sat, clearly pissed off, but she hadn't once brought up calories or dieting, or anything. It was the first ever meal with her family that had been fun.

After Grant's outburst, Isabella had been the first one to order the full Thanksgiving special, complete with pumpkin pie and extra whipped cream. Michael had the same, as had her father. Aria had also ordered the Thanksgiving meal as well. She didn't like pumpkin pie and instead had a chocolate pecan pie with whipped cream. Grant had the same.

Her mother … ordered the same.

It was the first real meal they'd had. She hadn't said a word, nor complained.

Stepping into her home, she spun around to Grant as he closed her front door and she turned toward him.

"I cannot believe you did that," Aria said.

"What? Tell you how amazing your ass looked?"

Aria giggled. "No, said that stuff to my mom. No one has ever said anything like that."

"Are you guys afraid of her or something?" Grant asked. His hands slid down to her ass. "I meant what I said. This dress is for my personal gaze only."

She rolled her eyes. "Guys were not checking me out."

"Oh, they were. I was surprised I didn't have to throttle the maître d'. If I hadn't been there, he would have been all over you."

She shook her head. "Stop it."

"No, you don't see how amazing you are, but I do. I know you're amazing, wonderful, and everything in between." He cupped her face. "I think you're beautiful."

She stared into his eyes and couldn't look away. From the moment Grant had entered that veterinary practice all those months ago, he had made her heart race. She had never felt such instant attraction before, but she had fought it.

All her life she'd been told how she never measured up, how she was never going to be good enough. She never for a second thought Grant would want her, and yet here he stood.

He cupped her cheek. His thumb stroked across her bottom lip.

"I want to fuck you, Aria," he said.

"Then … fuck me."

Grant groaned. He spun her around and pressed her up against the door. She wrapped her arms around his neck, holding onto him as he kissed her hard. His hands went from her face, down toward her tits. He cupped them, pressing them together through the tight confines of the dress. They both moaned as he ran his hands down toward her ass, gripping the flesh.

"I can't get enough of you," he said.

With his hands all over her, she couldn't get enough of him, didn't want to. He was everywhere, which was exactly what she liked—his hands all over her body, making love to her, heightening her senses.

Grant took hold of the straps of her dress and slid them down her body. He spun her around, taking care of the zip in the back. The sound seemed to echo within the hallway. Each inch that he opened had her pressing her legs together to try and stem the arousal.

He had the dress off her body within seconds, followed by her bra and when it came to the panties, he tore them off. They were not going to be salvageable. She didn't care.

He ran his hands over her ass and he growled.

Aria didn't know where she got the courage, but she reached out and pushed the dinner jacket off his shoulders. From the moment he'd put the suit on, she'd known he was uncomfortable. Grant hadn't complained. He'd done it for her.

She got to the buttons of his shirt and slid each one through, opening the shirt, exposing his chest with the chains over. She ran her hands over his body before going toward his zipper. Sinking to her knees in front of him, she heard him growl.

"Fuck, baby, I knew you were going to look beautiful on your knees in front of me, but I didn't know how much."

Aria smiled up at him, pulling down his pants. Grant had already kicked aside his shoes, and he helped her with the pants. She grabbed the boxers and tugged them down his thighs.

His cock sprang forward and she watched, mesmerized as he wrapped his fingers around the length. He worked from the tip down toward the base, moving up and down. The tip grew slick with his pre-cum and she couldn't help but lick her lips. She wanted to taste him just as he'd tasted her. Sliding her tongue across the tip, she tasted his salty pre-cum.

"Oh, fuck!" He released a hiss, followed by a growl.

She smiled at him. "I wanted to taste you, like you tasted me."

"I've got no problem with you doing that, baby, no problem at all."

She titled her head to the side and smiled at him. "Tell me how."

"Open your lips. Don't use your teeth, just your lips."

She slid her mouth open and made sure her teeth

were not on display.

"If at any time you want me to stop, sink your nails into my thigh." He grabbed her hand and put it on his thigh, splaying out her hand. "Use those nails."

She smiled. Aria didn't think for a second she was going to use her nails on him.

He put the tip of his cock on her tongue. "Close your lips around my dick and suck it, as you would a lollipop."

Following his instructions, she took him to the back of her throat and started to suck on him. Her lips touched his hand and then he gave the order for her to move her head up and down. Aria did as he commanded, sucking on his cock, loving the sounds he made, following everything he told her to do. She loved the feel of him in her mouth, and all too soon he'd pulled away.

He lifted her up off the floor and took her toward the stairs, putting her on her knees, spreading her thighs. His fingers touched between her thighs, finding her core. She cried out as within minutes, his cock was balls-deep inside her. They both moaned as he filled her.

He pulled out of her until only the tip was within her, and then he slammed inside, over and over, fucking her harder than before. The grip he had on her hips was almost bruising, but she didn't care. Grant took her hard and then he buried himself to the hilt, holding still, not moving. One of his hands slid between her thighs and he began to stroke her clit.

"I want to feel you come all over my dick," he said.

He stroked her clit, working her nub. The hit of pleasure was instant and she moaned his name. With his cock deep inside her, the sensation was so different, so new.

He didn't move but his fingers created a dance

between her thighs, drawing her closer to the peak. Another moan escaped. She felt so close. On edge.

Grant was there, as he always was, to catch her. She came hard, screaming his name.

Grant didn't stop until she couldn't take it anymore, and then his hands returned to her hips and he held her in place, taking her pussy. There was nothing sweet or kind. This was cold, hard fucking, and Aria loved it. Grant's grip tightened on her hips as he filled her hard, and then she felt the kick of his cock as he came.

Afterward, he wrapped his arms around her, kissing her neck.

"That was all I've been wanting to do all night. That dress is mine. You can't wear it in front of anyone else."

She chuckled. "Was it really that bad?"

"Babe, men wanted you."

She didn't think that was possible. The only man she ever wanted was the one whose arms were wrapped around her. Grant was the only guy she had ever wanted. He'd been a first for so many things.

He pressed kisses to her shoulder, sliding his tongue across her pulse.

"As much as I love kneeling on the stairs," he said. "I think it best we move to the bedroom."

****

Bull looked toward William Ranford. The man didn't look like he was in control. The clothes he wore were filthy. He had several days' growth of stubble.

"This is what going after the Cartel does to you?" Bull asked.

He'd been tempted to take on the Cartel, which was exactly what William Ranford had done. He'd been the only one to take the Cartel on and win, at least as far as Bull could see.

William laughed. "No, this is what a shitty, younger, weak brother does to you. I should have killed him when I had the chance."

"Why didn't you?" Bull asked.

"Call me sentimental, but I happen to like my brother. He was family."

"Then you shouldn't have taken on the Cartel. They came after him. Your weakest link. They've taken your city," Bull said.

William chuckled. "And you think there's no way back from that? I've dealt with worse problems, trust me. My brother dead, I've got nothing."

"Why did you want this meeting?" Bull asked.

He owed William for saving Maddie's and Grant's lives. Even though he looked like he'd been through a nightmare and back, he still had a great deal of respect for the man.

"Hernandez is dead. His body was discovered in a pit a few days ago," William said.

Bull's contact within the Cartel was Hernandez. They had been the ones to come up with the agreement for the Chaos and Carnage MC to distribute. It meant keeping the Cartel out of Carnage for good. He'd not been able to reach the man for some time and in fact, the whole of the Cartel had been quiet. Bull had noticed it after he took out the rival Julio in the Vito Crew Cartel.

Something didn't add up. Each part of the Cartel had a leader. Hernandez had been the coastal one, who helped to distribute through Carnage.

"Why are you telling me this?" Bull asked.

"Hernandez may have been Cartel, but he was also fair. He saw the benefit of having an MC run product. You guys were good, easy to blend, and able to get their shit out fast. Someone else is running the shots and if the rumor is true, they're already in Carnage."

"If that's so, why are you here?"

"Do you think Julio was the only bastard that took my brother? I'm at war with the whole Cartel. They have a hit out on me, and trust me, I'm going to make every single one of those fuckers pay. I'm not finished. My story isn't finished. I will end all of them."

"And you think it will be over?" Bull asked. "Others will take their place."

William smiled. "And because you never take your eye off the ball, they never get a chance at power. You squash them."

Bull shook his head. "You're risking your life being in my town."

"Bull, I've been in your town for four months and you haven't seen me. Trust me, I know what I'm doing. Shit is about to get real, very fucking quickly. You've got to be prepared for it when it goes down."

William spun on his heel and headed in the opposite direction than he came.

"Do you need money?"

"I've got everything I need." William held his hand in the air as if it were a final salute.

With William gone, Pat took a step toward Bull. "I know who the guy in the picture is," Pat said.

Bull turned to him. Pat had taken the details with him several days ago. He couldn't believe Grant had taken the pictures. His little brother could have been caught or even killed.

When Pat returned to the clubhouse, he had said he didn't have the information, but he knew someone who could get them all the details they needed. They just had to be patient.

It had been a long, very long, couple of days.

"Julio had a stepbrother," Pat said. "His name is

Miguel Vito Carlos. He is one of the most dangerous men, and has been hunting for power, to take away from Hernandez. He wants to control the whole of the States. Julio was a small-timer but he was working on Miguel's orders. Part of the Vito code is to infiltrate the towns with small petty crimes, then flood it. He comes in, takes control. He has the manpower to do it. He's already taken Ranford's territory. He took Hernandez, and now he's coming through here."

"No," Bull said. "He's not coming through. He's already here."

****

Aria giggled and Grant absolutely loved the sound. He couldn't get enough of it.

"Stop. Stop."

"No, I'm tickling you, and you're going to do it."

Aria tried to stop his hands. "Please, stop. Stop. Fine. I'll do it."

Grant instantly stopped tickling her. He climbed off the bed. He was completely naked and he held out his hand for her.

Aria sunk her teeth into her bottom lip.

"Do I need to come and tickle? Did you lie to me?" He went to kneel on the bed but Aria quickly got up. The bed was now between them.

She held her hands up in surrender. "I didn't lie to you. I wouldn't do that." She shook her head. "Seriously, why do you want me to do this?"

"I think it'll be good for you."

Aria shook her head but rounded the bed.

Grant couldn't help but watch her tits as they bounced with every single step she took. She mesmerized him. His dad had beaten him for liking curvy women, but he didn't give a fuck. Aria was a dream. His dream.

She took his hand and he pulled her to him,

wrapping his arms around her and then walking her into the bathroom. He noticed she avoided mirrors. There wasn't even a big one in the bedroom. Just a couple of shitty mirrors in the upstairs bathroom and in the downstairs one.

Stepping in front of the mirror, he stared at her reflection, noticing Aria looked everywhere but at herself. He kissed her neck.

"What's the matter?" he asked.

"Nothing."

"That is not a nothing face. Look at yourself. You promised, or do I get to keep tickling?"

Aria's gaze met his. Tears filled her eyes.

"I've got you, baby. I've always got you. Nothing bad is going to happen. It's just you and me here, right now."

Her lip wobbled and it made him hate her mother once again. He would never like that woman. He fucking despised her. The shit she had said to pollute Aria's mind irritated the fuck out of him. He and Joan should never be alone. Especially if he had a gun. It wouldn't end well.

Her lip wobbled and she looked at herself.

"Now, tell me what you see," he said.

"Grant, please."

"I'll tell you what I see. I see a beautiful woman with gorgeous big tits. They were designed to cushion my head. Those nipples." He groaned. "Perfect for sucking. Then let's talk about those hips." They had bruises on from where he held her in place last night. "They are designed for my hands. Look, my fingers match."

Aria giggled.

He noticed the tears fell down her cheeks.

"Don't even get me started on these thighs. I love

how tight they feel wrapped around my waist." He moved his hands toward her ass. "And this ass, I love spreading it open and seeing my cock sinking into your pussy."

"I don't see any of that," Aria said. "I see an ugly, fat waste of space." She covered her face.

"No." Grant turned her toward him. "They're wrong, Aria. They are so wrong. You're beautiful, you're gorgeous, and you're curvy, exactly how I want you to be. There's nothing wrong with you." He cupped her face and kissed her.

She tried to fight but she was no match for him. Aria wrapped her arms around him.

"Every single day I want you to stand in front of the mirror and I want you to see what I see. I want you to think about how you would treat a child of your own if she looked like you."

"Don't," Aria said.

"Your mother is a fucking terrible person, Aria. Your dad should have stood up for you, or your sister. They didn't." Grant pulled back and forced her to look at him. "I know what it's like, having someone tell you every single day that you're not good enough. That once people realize what a waste of space you are, they'd get rid of you."

Aria frowned. "Who said that to you? Bull?"

"No, my old man. He told me I was a mistake. That he should have killed me when I was born."

Aria whimpered. "No. He's wrong. So very wrong."

Grant smiled at her.

"Exactly, and your mom is so very fucking wrong. You don't have to listen to her vile shit anymore. You're a grown-ass woman. She's nothing. It's time for you to live for yourself, Aria. You don't need to do anything to make her love you. You're perfect the way you are. Everyone else can go fuck themselves."

"Why are you doing this?" she asked.

"Because it is time for you to see the truth. You need to see what I see." Grant ran his hands down to her ass, pulling her closer to him.

"Is this so you'll stop me going to the gym?" she asked.

"No, this is for you to realize you are so fucking worthy. You shouldn't listen to that woman. She pissed me off so much."

Aria rested her head against his chest and Grant kissed the top of her head. Glancing at their reflection, he admired the curve of her back. He ran his fingers up her spine, then back down again.

She pulled away to look into his eyes. "Your dad was wrong about you, Grant."

"Let's not talk about him, Aria. He's not worth my time."

"But he is still living in here, isn't he?" Aria asked, pressing the tips of her fingers against his temple. "When you deal with your brother, he is who you hear, not Bull?"

He took hold of her hands and pressed kisses to the tips of her fingers.

"That's different."

She giggled. "No, it's not. Do you realize my sister and I have never had a real conversation? Yeah, that's right. I've always been there, but my mother has always been this force, this presence, that I don't even know if Isabella likes me."

"I think she does," Grant said. He didn't want to talk about her sister. Not now. Not fucking ever.

She had been a big mistake. One he'd made before Aria, but he knew if she ever found out that he fucked her sister on a meaningless night out, she'd be upset. He didn't want to hurt her. The sex with her sister meant nothing. Was nothing. She had to know that.

Tell her the truth.

Grant opened his mouth about to tell her that he and her sister had a history. Aria rested her head against his chest and even pressed a kiss to his heart. "You are so much more than what your father said, Grant. So much more. I wish you could see what I see."

Damn it. He didn't want to spoil this.

Gripping the back of her neck, he tilted her head back and she looked up at him. Staring into her eyes, he found her so fucking beautiful. He loved her kind blue eyes, her full blonde hair, just everything about her, he craved. From the moment he stepped into the veterinary practice and saw her welcoming smile, he'd been hooked.

"What's the matter?" she asked.

There was so much that was the matter, but he couldn't say a fucking word of it.

Slamming his lips down on hers, he walked her back, step by step, until they were back in her bedroom. He nudged her down to the bed, and stepped between her thighs. She opened them for him and he couldn't help but groan as he glanced at her perfect cunt. His cunt. All his. No one else would ever know the pleasure of her body. He was going to devote his life to this woman, only to her. Cupping her pussy, he slid a single finger inside her, finding her slick and tight.

"Are you ready for my cock, baby?" he asked.

"Yes."

"Good."

He moved her up against the pillows and then gripped the base of his cock. He lined the tip against her pussy, and he couldn't resist a few warming-up strokes, sliding between her wet slit as he bumped her clit. She gasped, arching up. Her mouth opened, a moan about to fill the air.

Grant took her closer to orgasm but he didn't allow her to go over the edge, no, he took his sweet time. When she came, he wanted to be balls-deep inside her. He moved the tip of his dick to her entrance, staring into her eyes as he sunk inside her, inch by slow inch.

She was perfect. Tight. Wet. And she belonged to him.

Grant didn't know what he loved more. He knew he didn't want it to stop.

Taking hold of her hands, he pressed them either side of her head, locking her in place, keeping her captive under his control.

He wasn't that deep inside her yet, but as he pulled back just a little, he didn't give her a chance to get accustomed to the feel of his dick, and then he plundered her hole, going hard and deep within her core. Grant went fast at first fucking her, watching her as she thrust up against him, trying to take every single inch of his cock.

She was so fucking beautiful.

Slowing down, he went every agonizing inch thrusting in and out, working her pussy. He loved being inside her without a condom. He'd not once worn a condom and he knew he should have, but he also wanted to keep this woman. Aria was his. He felt it deep in his soul. She was part of him and he couldn't let her go.

Make her pregnant.

He'd always considered himself to be as close to honest as possible, and staring into Aria's eyes, all he wanted to do was make her his. To stake his claim. In the back of his mind, he knew he had a secret, a big one. One that would hurt her if she ever found out.

Don't hurt her.
Love her.
Show her what everyone else failed to do.
"Grant?"

He slammed his lips down on hers, making love to her, prolonging the pleasure, not wanting to give up for even a moment. He was so close to his peak, but he wanted her to come. Pulling away, he held himself deep within her but reached between them and began to stroke her clit, drawing out her pleasure. She gasped his name.

Aria didn't make him wait long as she came, screaming his name.

Grant followed her seconds later, filling her with more of his cum, hoping soon he'd have an answer if he'd made her pregnant.

****

"Damn, that sounds epic," Lidia said.

Aria chuckled.

Thanksgiving had been a week ago, but between work, the gym, and dividing her time with Grant, she hadn't been able to catch up with Lidia.

She bit into her sandwich and chuckled to herself. "It was pretty great."

"Has the wicked witch been in touch?" Lidia asked.

"No, she hasn't." Aria shrugged. "Let's face it, she never is."

"That's true. Joan Taylor is known for loving the perfect princess of a daughter." Lidia rolled her eyes.

"Enough about my Thanksgiving, what about yours?"

"How about we talk about your slashed tires as well?" Lidia asked.

Aria sighed. "There's nothing to tell. My car is ready to be picked up today. That's where I'm going after work." She shrugged. "Grant called Dylan, but he checked the security cameras in town, and it didn't catch anything. No one saw anything suspicious."

"But they were slashed?"

"Yep." Aria hadn't admitted to anyone that she felt a little uneasy about that piece of information.

"Aria, I see that look in your eye," Lidia said.

"Look? What look?"

"The one that says you're trying to be a big girl. You don't need to be a big girl. You're freaked out, aren't you?"

"No, of course not." She tried to scoff and pretend she was totally fine, but that was a big fat lie.

"Has anyone ever told you you're a terrible liar?"

She stuck her tongue out. "I'm not a terrible liar."

"Are you going to tell Grant that you're freaked out?"

"It's nothing."

"No, Aria, it's not nothing." Lidia slammed her palm down on the counter. "Don't ever for a second think it's nothing. You're scared. Your feelings matter."

"I know they matter."

"Do you?" Lidia asked. "Because you have a way of saying one thing with your lips and your eyes tell another tale. You're not always happy, are you?"

Aria shrugged. "There's nothing that can be done."

"You're dating one of the Chaos and Carnage hotties."

"He's not a member. Well, he is, but he's not. Ugh, it's complicated." The door to the veterinary practice opened and Aria was so thankful for the reprieve when it came to her friend. She smiled only to be a little surprised to see her sister, Isabella, step through the door.

"Wow," Lidia said.

Isabella smiled.

"Hello."

"Did you get a pet?" Lidia asked.

Isabella frowned. "A pet?"

"You know, this is a veterinary practice?"

"Do *you* have a pet here?" Isabella asked.

"No, I don't need one. I have a long-standing friendship with the receptionist."

"And I have a close relationship called 'sister,'" Isabella said.

"What's going on?" Aria asked. Her sister never, ever came to see her. Not during the day, not at work, never.

"I was … I was wondering, I'm going shopping this weekend. I need some new clothes. This baby is growing fast, and I was hoping you'd like to come," Isabella said.

"You're inviting me shopping?"

Isabella nodded.

Aria turned to Lidia with a frown.

Lidia pinched herself. "Nope, we're not dreaming."

"What about Mom?" Aria asked.

"I haven't invited her. I just wanted it to be the two of us."

"I'm sorry about what Grant did at dinner—"

"Don't be," Isabella said. "He was amazing. Do you even know why Michael insisted on us going to a restaurant?"

Aria shook her head but decided to take a guess anyway. "He didn't want to taste Mom's food."

"That was a big problem for him, but he was so tired of her constantly going on about diets. He didn't want me to follow her strict regime. I'm pregnant and we want to enjoy that, but he also hated the way she treated you." Isabella rubbed at her temple. "I have never been so ashamed in my life. I never stood up to her. Never told her to shut up. All those dinners. Even after we left home, I never told her enough was enough. Michael couldn't stand it. He hated having a full plate and seeing you only allowed to eat vegetables and then with limited gravy as well. That's why he arranged the restaurant and Grant, well, he put us all to shame."

"Has Mom been in touch?"

"Yes," Isabella said. "She wanted to form an intervention to remove the criminal from your life. I told her no. I told her I'd never seen you so happy before. You are happy, aren't you?"

"Yes."

"I told her no. I won't come between you and Grant."

Aria was a little taken aback by this. "And now you want to go shopping with me?"

"Yes. You and I have never gotten to hang out, like sisters. I'd like that. I don't know what it was that Grant did, but he opened my eyes. I want to have a relationship with my sister. Not one where I stare at her over the table, hoping I have the guts one day to stand up for her. Mom has been wrong for so long. I hate the wedding photos and I refuse to put them up. Mom has tried to force me to decorate my house. Enough is enough."

"Mom hasn't even visited me in my house," Aria said.

"That's because she's pissed off that you got the house. She was hoping I'd get it, but I'm so pleased our grandparents did what they did."

"As fun as this is, I've got to head out to work." Lidia wrapped up her packages and threw them in the trash bin. "You need to talk to Grant."

Aria got to her feet and hugged her best friend tightly to her. "Love you."

"Love you too, babe."

Lidia left the practice, and now she was alone with her sister.

"So what do you say?" Lidia asked. "You and me, shopping?"

"I guess that would be fun." She didn't want to tell her sister no. "How is the pregnancy?"

"Fine. I mean, the morning sickness has been the worst part of it, but other than that, everything is a breeze." Isabella put her hand to her stomach. "So, er, do you have your dogs with you?"

"Yeah, I do." She reached down, stroking Ernie and Bruno's head. She pushed out her chair and waved her hand for Isabella to come around the counter to see her dogs.

The moment Isabella did, she sighed. "They're so cute."

"Yep, they are."

Just then a horn honked and Isabella chuckled. "I better go. Michael is waiting."

Aria was surprised when her sister suddenly pulled her in for a hug. "I love you, Aria."

"I love you too."

Isabella kissed her cheek and then headed out to her husband. Aria gave a wave and she saw Michael respond with one of his own.

"You two are good dogs, aren't you?"

Andy and Phil came out of their individual rooms. Each held a clipboard. It had been a slow couple of days since Thanksgiving.

"Any new appointments?" Andy asked.

"Tomorrow, we're close to fifteen," Aria said.

"That's good." Andy held out the clipboard.

"Could you please place an order for these?"

"Everything will pick up," Phil said. "Word of mouth will help." He opened his mouth about to say something else, when the door opened.

Aria turned to see a tall man in a designer suit, and even though they were nearing winter, he wore a pair of sunglasses. She saw the ink decorating his neck. There were three other men with him as they stepped through the doorway.

"Can I help you?" Phil asked, moving in front of the desk. He'd positioned himself between the men and his wife.

Aria stood up as well. There was something about the men that made her a little uneasy.

"It has been brought to my attention that two dogs were brought here," he said. His voice was deep and there was an edge of authority to it.

Aria didn't dare look to the floor.

Phil and Andy didn't say a word, waiting for him to speak.

Whoever he was, he smiled. "They are my dogs."

"You'll have to go and check the local animal shelter. The dogs that came into our care several days ago were rescues from them. They were returned there," Phil said.

"I see," the man said.

"You have the wrong veterinary practice," Phil said.

"Right, of course."

Aria had to wonder if he did. If not, then what did this mean? Was this man responsible for the dogfighting ring?

The man in question turned toward her and his gaze lingered a little too long. "Do you know of another veterinary practice?"

"No," Phil said. "The last one closed down after it was discovered the vet was involved in an illegal dogfighting ring."

Aria felt fear root her to the spot. The men had moved their hands down to their waistbands and she just knew they were carrying guns.

"Well, if you hear any news, please get in touch." The man left and she watched as he disappeared into a black van.

"He was talking about Ernie and Bruno," Aria said.

"No, you don't know that," Phil said.

"They're the only two dogs that have been found."

"They didn't respond to him," Andy said. "That could mean anything."

Aria's heart raced.

"Andy, I need you to get on the phone and call Bull for me," Phil said.

"What?" Aria asked.

"Call Bull and tell him Aria is going to need a lift to get her car."

She had no idea what was going on. "This is scaring me."

"I don't mean to scare you but you currently have both of those dogs and I don't like the way he looked at you," Phil said.

"Did you recognize him?" Andy asked.

"No, I'd never seen him before in my life." The fear was there, though, she felt it.

He scared her.

"Call Bull," Phil said.

"You don't think he's going to hurt me, do you?" Aria asked.

"I don't know what's going on, Aria. Bull warned

me to contact him if I saw anything suspicious. A guy with multiple bodyguards and packing weapons, that's something to take note. You don't come to a veterinary practice heavily armed."

"Maybe he's a celebrity."

Phil chuckled.

Andy came back through to the room. "Bull's on his way."

"If you want to call Grant, you should," Phil said.

Aria hesitated. The last thing she wanted to do was upset her man or worry him. It could be for nothing, but a part of her knew this wasn't nothing.

She went for her cell phone and picked it up, waiting for him to answer.

Chapter Thirteen

Bull arrived with Rusty and Pat at his back. He wasn't taking any chances. He'd given Phil the instruction to call him if he ever saw anything suspicious. The brief description of what Andy told him made him so fucking angry.

So Miguel was quite happy to wander into town as well as veterinary practices and frighten his people. This fucker was going to pay.

Bull stepped into the shop to find Aria there looking a little panicked. Phil and Andy were a little more put together.

"Please tell me you have security footage monitoring this place," Bull said.

"Of course we do." Phil pointed in the direction for him to follow.

"Stay here," he said to Pat and Rusty.

He had no doubt his brother would arrive shortly. Once that happened, he was going to have to convince his brother to let him deal with the shit that went down.

Phil took him to the back of the shop where a small room showed the cameras on screen—one in the waiting room as well as a couple in the parking lot. That was it. Very limited on security.

Phil was already rewinding it back to when the man walked into the shop. Bull watched as he stepped inside. There was no sound, but he watched the man speak, how he conducted himself. This was Miguel. It was the same man from Grant's phone.

As if thinking about his brother made him appear, Grant stepped inside. "What's going on?" Grant asked.

"Do you recognize this man?" Bull asked.

"Yes."

"He the one from your pictures?"

"Yes."

"He was asking about two dogs," Phil said. "He mentioned two dogs that were brought here. We told them they belonged to the animal shelter and that was where they were sent."

"I've already got increased security at both shelters," Bull said.

"This the bastard that took the dogs?"

Bull wasn't going to discuss any more while Phil was present. "We need to bring your woman in," Bull said.

Grant shook his head. "Not happening."

"Do you see this?" Bull pointed at the paused screen that showed Miguel looking at Aria. "He knows her, which means he's been watching you this whole time."

"There were several seconds that passed where he just stared at her," Phil said.

Bull wanted to tell the vet to shut up, but without him, he wouldn't have this information. He stepped out of the room and headed down the hall to where Aria was sitting, rubbing both dogs behind the ears.

"Did the dogs respond to his voice?" Bull asked.

"No."

Bull nodded. "I need you to come with me."

"This is not happening," Grant said.

He'd heard enough. He grabbed Grant by the arm and pulled him outside. Pat and Rusty stayed inside, where he wanted them to be.

"Do you have a fucking death wish?" Bull asked. "Do you want to see her dead?"

"She is not part of the club."

"This isn't about being part of the club and whenever she's with you, her life is in danger. This bastard is already here, Grant. Don't you get that? He has already killed. He has hunted on our land. This man is not playing games. He is serious and if you want to get your woman killed, then fine. Just tell me that is your end goal."

"No, it's not. I fucking love her, Bull."

This surprised him.

"You what?"

"I love her. I can't let anything happen to her, but look at her. She's scared and taking her to the clubhouse…"

"Is what I'm going to have to do," Bull said. "This threat is real. It's worse than Julio." Bull ran a hand down his face. This was his brother. "Hernandez is dead."

Grant stopped. "What?"

"Yeah, Hernandez is dead. Body was discovered a few days ago."

"But he's the one that controls—"

"Not anymore," Bull said. "Miguel Vito Carlos killed him. That same man was in that practice, staring at Aria, Grant. He's in town. He's here to destroy the club."

Grant shook his head. "Then why haven't they done it already?"

"Because he likes to destroy slowly. He's Julio's brother, Grant. Stepbrother. And I don't think I need to remind you what brothers do for one another."

Grant ran a hand down his face. "That is so fucked."

"He's the one that pushed Ranford into hiding. He's here as well. It would seem we've got a lot of fucking hiding places in Carnage." Bull growled.

"I need my leather cut back," Grant said.

"You can have it back and the patch. I was only trying to fucking protect you, Grant. That's all."

"Yeah, and how has that worked out for you?"

Bull burst out laughing. "Maddie's going to be happy to see you."

Grant sighed. "What do I tell Aria?"

"The truth, or as close to the truth as possible. That's all you can do and hope that she's as understanding as Maddie."

****

Aria stared up at the clubhouse. Grant hadn't said a word on the ride over to the Chaos and Carnage MC clubhouse. He'd asked for her to wait and now he faced her and kept opening and closing his lips.

"Is everything okay?" Aria asked.

"It … Aria, I'm back in the club. My suspension has been lifted," Grant said.

"I kind of gathered that with the fact we're here and you haven't been arrested." She forced a smile to her lips even though she was very nervous.

She had watched Bull and Grant as they took their conversation outside, and she knew deep in her gut something wasn't right. Grant looked pissed, as did his brother.

"Yeah, my brother is not exactly bright."

She smiled.

"Look, I don't know how to say this, but the shit that's going down with that guy is real."

"Is he responsible for the dogfighting rings?" she asked.

"We believe so, well, not directly. We're not sure where he comes in, he's related to the son of a bitch that set them up."

Aria nodded. "Grant, just tell me. I knew when we started this everything wasn't going to be so smooth sailing, you know."

Grant chuckled. "The way he looked at you, he's a threat, Aria. I've seen him hurt someone before and I don't want to see you hurt. I need you to trust me and to do that, to protect you, I need for us to stay here."

"You want me to stay at the clubhouse?"

He took hold of her hands and she watched as he kissed one then the other.

"Yes. We're going to have to stay here. The brothers will protect you."

"Grant, I have a job and commitments."

"I know, and I'll get you back to them, I promise, but for now, I need you to trust me, do you think you can do that?"

She smiled. "Of course. I do trust you, Grant."

He cupped her cheek and then kissed her, hard. "Thank you." He sighed. "Now, the guys at the club are—"

She pressed a finger to his lips. "Stop panicking. I was a virgin at sex, but I'm not new to this. Trust me. I can handle it."

Grant laughed.

"That doesn't exactly fill me with confidence," she said.

He climbed out of the car. She opened her door and got out, went to the back seat, and let Bruno out. Grant had already let out Ernie, and Wanda was once again beside Grant. Their three dogs had formed a bond of sorts.

"I don't have any clothes," Aria said.

"Don't worry about it. I'll handle that." He took hold of her hand and they headed inside.

Bull and the two men he'd been with at the veterinary practice were already there. They had pulled into the parking lot before her and Grant. She recognized most of the people there, including Maddie French, who had a child on her hip.

"Maddie, I'd like you to finally meet Aria. Aria,

this is my bestie, Maddie."

"I wouldn't say we're besties. I just can't seem to get rid of him," Maddie said.

Aria was a little surprised as the other woman pulled her in for a hug.

"It's nice to meet you."

"This is my little niece, Lindsey." Grant took the baby from Maddie's arms and held her close.

Aria had never thought of Grant as a paternal type, but she saw how much love he had for the little girl.

"You've met my brother, Bull. That there is Rusty. Stay away from him. Pat is there. Don't get too close, the dude's a vegan."

Aria laughed but gave him a wave as she had no idea what to do. She'd never been to the clubhouse before. Lidia had never wanted to go to one of the parties held at the clubhouse. She was going to have to talk to her best friend, let her know what was going on.

"Then you've got Sweets, Rip, Stacks, Bud…" He kept naming people and she knew it would take some time to remember their names. She had no idea how long she was going to be here.

Everyone smiled at her, nodded in her direction, and then Grant held her hand tightly and moved her away, heading toward the door in the back. Grant didn't stop holding her hand as he took her up several flights of stairs.

"Where are we going?"

"To my room."

"You live at the clubhouse?"

"I used to live at the clubhouse, then I took Maddie's home from her."

Aria giggled.

"I'm not joking."

"I didn't think you were."

They stepped inside a small room. There was a small bed, a couple of chests of drawers, and she noticed there was nothing on his walls, no posters or pictures.

Grant closed the door.

"I don't have a bathroom. We have to share one but there is a lock on the door."

Aria nodded. "Do you know how long this is going to be?"

"No," he said.

"The guy I saw, he's bad news, isn't he?"

"Yeah, he is." Grant sat down and waved her over, patting the bed beside him.

She laughed and moved closer to him, but Grant took hold of her hands and then pulled her down so that she straddled his waist. His hands went to the curve of her waist as he drew her down against his cock. She gasped.

"Do you feel that?"

"How can you be thinking about sex right now?" Aria asked, laughing.

"Simple, my woman is alone with me in my bedroom. This is not hard for me to think about." He winked at her.

Aria cupped his face. "Are you in danger?"

"Nah, danger laughs at me."

She rolled her eyes. "I'm serious, Grant. That guy looked scary."

"And you don't think I am?"

"I do. I think you're very scary."

"But I don't scare you?"

"No, you don't."

"Good."

He slid his hands toward her ass, squeezing the cheeks. She moaned his name and he thrust up against her.

"Fuck, you feel good," he said.

His face pressed against her neck and she arched up, moaning.

Sex should be the last thing on her mind but as he pushed her skirt out of the way, he cupped her pussy. He slid his fingers beneath the fabric of her panties and he plunged them deep inside her. Aria gasped, gripping his shoulders tightly.

"I love watching you, Aria."

"Do you think we should be having sex?"

"Yeah, I do." He pulled out of her pussy and stroked his fingers against her clit. "All day I've been thinking about this pussy. Wondering if it was missing my cock. Is it missing my cock, baby?"

"Yes." Her cheeks were on fire. She couldn't believe what she was saying, but then she couldn't bring herself to stop either. Why would she want to? The pleasure he gave her was out of this world. Feeling a little bold, she reached between them and started to stroke the hard ridge of his cock. He growled.

"That's right, baby, touch me. Put those hands on me."

She flicked the button of his jeans and drew down the zipper, tugging it until it was free. She slid her hand inside, finding his cock and he wrapped an arm around her, lifting just slightly to adjust himself. He pulled his jeans off his body, moving them down.

Within seconds, he'd torn her panties. Aria had lost count of the number of panties he'd destroyed. There was no limit to what he'd do to get her naked.

He moved her hand out of the way and Aria settled into position, holding up her skirt so that he could find her entrance, and then she sat on his dick. They both moaned as she slammed down on him, seating him to the hilt within her pussy.

"Oh, fuck, that feels good. So fucking good."

His hands were on her ass.

Dropping the skirt, she held onto his shoulders and began to rock up and down his length, staring into his eyes as she did so, not wanting to let go. He grabbed her ass, working her over his dick. She loved feeling him.

"I want you to come," he said.

"No, I want you to come, Grant," she said.

This time, she was on top. She was in charge. He wasn't going to stop her. Not now. Grant groaned and she took possession of his mouth, kissing him.

He let go of her ass to sink his fingers into her hair, drawing her close. Even though she was in charge, it wasn't hard for him to take over. When he tried to grab her in a way to change positions, she wouldn't let him. Grant growled against her lips.

"I'm going to come."

And she wasn't going to stop. Aria broke the kiss and watched him as she drove down on his length, sending him over the edge, watching him come. She loved how his face changed, the pleasure as he filled her.

Before he had even finished, he wrapped his arms around her back, taking her to the bed. He pulled out and then his fingers moved between her spread thighs, touching her clit, stroking her. Aria was so sensitive that all it took was a few gentle touches and she came, screaming his name.

Grant kissed her, swallowing the sound.

****

Later that night, Grant stared at a sleeping Aria. She was curled up against him. He didn't want to wake her but he was thirsty as hell and needed a drink. Sliding out of bed, he was careful not to wake her.

Wanda, Ernie, and Bruno had made their way into the bedroom before they had fallen asleep. Wanda lifted her head, sniffed the air, and then settled back down to sleep.

He pulled on a pair of sweatpants and left the bedroom, making sure he closed the door as he did so. Rubbing at the back of his head, he made his way down toward the kitchen. Bull sat at the main table, and Grant was tempted to step back and to just go thirsty.

He and his brother didn't have the best relationship. There were times it was great, and then others it sucked big time.

Grant wasn't going to run away. He'd gotten his patch back. He expected he'd have to fight Pat for the patch, but nope, the man had given it to him without batting an eye. Pat was a strange man, quiet.

"You're up late," Grant said. "I thought when you had a kid, you took advantage of sleeping when you could."

"Lindsey's not a bad kid. She sleeps through the night. We got lucky with her."

"That's good."

Bull ran a hand down his face. It was a trait Grant recognized, as he did it himself, as did their father, on multiple occasions. What he had just learned, though, was his brother had lied to him about Lindsey keeping Maddie up. Oh well, his brother was an asshole dickhead.

"We got to flush him out," Grant said.

"I know."

Grant poured himself a glass of water. He was tempted to just leave it at that, but instead he took a seat at the table.

"It's not going to be easy," Bull said. "We can't allow anybody in town to get hurt."

"And we can't bring too much heat," Grant said.

Bull nodded.

"What's Ranford's position?"

"He's been in town and again, I don't know where."

"Carnage is a big place. It has a lot of old abandoned farms and shit like that. It's not hard to get lost," Grant said.

Bull blew out a breath.

"What is it?"

"I keep thinking about our old man," Bull said. "What he'd do in a situation like this?"

"Why are you thinking about him? He got us into this mess."

"Did he?" Bull asked.

This was new. Other than Maddie, Grant couldn't remember a time Bull doubted himself, and certainly not his leadership.

"Am I dreaming right now? Seriously, we both know Dad did this. He got us into this mess and you got us out."

Bull snorted. "I didn't get us out. We've still been making the fucking runs." Bull shook his head. "We've been nothing but fucking messengers, keeping the vultures at bay, and now they're coming to pick us off."

"Dude, even vultures can be shot down. Sure, they're scary fucking birds, but last time I checked, a bullet still killed them."

Bull laughed. "When was the last time you killed a bird?"

"Never have, but I've seen those wildlife documentaries. Trust me, everything can be killed." Grant took a long swig of his water. "We just need to know when to strike."

"We've got to draw them out."

"Well, I know we've got at least two draws," Grant said. "Actually, make that three."

"What?" Bull asked.

"We've got the dogs, Ranford, and Julio's resting place."

"All three of them are risky," Bull said.

"I guess we're going to have to take risks to protect everyone in the club," Grant said. "And you've got me, so four. I'm your brother, so you can offer me up as bait. You know I'd be awesome."

Bull shook his head. "I'm not going to do that." Bull ran a hand down his face.

"Don't go doubting yourself, Bull. You're better than our old man, and you can't forget that."

"What has gotten into you to be so nice?" Bull asked.

"I guess I'm in better company."

Bull laughed. "Aria. She was never your type before."

Grant looked at his brother and it was on the tip of his tongue to tell him to go fuck himself. "When I was nine years old, I ran home and told Dad about an amazing girl at school. She was smart and nice and kind. Dad knew her name. It was Maddie French. I never had the guts to actually talk to this girl, but when I told him about her, not that I liked her or anything, he removed his belt and whipped me real good. Told me that under no circumstances would a son of his ever be with a fat whore."

"Grant?"

"That wasn't the only time that happened. Whenever he thought I was staring at a woman he believed to be a little on the large side, I'd get a beating. I'm no fucking coward, Bull, but at nine years old, I didn't think to hit back. I learned how to survive. It was easier to bully women like Maddie, look away from what I wanted, and screw who I thought would impress Dad."

Grant shook his head. He'd never gotten real with his brother. This was a first. "I could lose Aria."

"No, you won't."

"Before I met her, I had a one-night stand with a woman I met. Turns out, it was her sister. I've already lied to her, Bull. If she finds out the truth, she won't forgive me." Grant had done enough soul-searching for the night. He got to his feet. "We'll figure out the Cartel problem. We have ways to do it that won't harm the town."

"Grant, I had no idea."

"We both know our old man is a piece of work. Knowing it doesn't change."

"I should have been there."

"Bull, you couldn't always be there, and Dad knew what he was doing. It just took me a little too long to realize I didn't need to pretend anymore. I love Aria, I would do anything for her."

"Then tell her the truth," Bull said. "Tell Aria what you just told me. Don't let someone else tell her."

"No one else knows. Just her, you, and me." Grant pressed his lips together. That was the way it was going to stay. He couldn't hurt her. Not with that.

"I've got to go," he said.

Leaving the kitchen, he headed upstairs to his room. He opened the bedroom door and Aria was still fast asleep. Removing his pants, he slid between the sheets and pulled her against him. Aria didn't fight him. She curled up, snuggled in close, and went back to sleep.

****

"Did you know your dad beat him?" Maddie asked, stepping into the kitchen.

"No, I didn't." Bull should have known his woman wasn't too far. In the past few days, he'd struggled to sleep, and she always came to find him.

He opened his arms and she walked to him. The moment she was close, he wrapped his arms around her and drew her down onto his lap.

"You've got to stop sneaking around," he said.

She rolled her eyes. "Why would I stop doing what I love?"

Bull chuckled. "Because some of the guys might mistake you for a spy."

"No one will find me, and besides, it's only late at night that I sneak anywhere, when the bed gets cold. You're troubled."

"Grant's right. I've got four options in getting this guy to come to me."

"The one with Julio sounds dangerous," Maddie said.

"But it will be effective."

"I don't want you to use the dogs."

"Not going to happen." He remembered what happened the last time one of the rescue dogs died. Maddie had been inconsolable. It was what had alerted him to the dogfighting on his turf. Someone had made his woman cry, and he'd been determined to make that bastard pay, and he had.

"Which leaves Ranford and Grant," Maddie said.

"I can't use my brother."

"No, it wouldn't be good."

Bull sighed. "And Ranford won't play fair."

"Which brings you back to either Julio or Grant," Maddie said.

He had tried to keep the club business from her, but Maddie had been caught up in his world. There was no way he could keep her in the dark about all the shit that troubled the club. She was part of him, part of this world, and as much as he wanted to hide it from her, he couldn't. Just by being with him at this time, she risked her life.

"It's time for us to go to bed," he said.

"You know what you're going to have to do," Maddie said.

"I know."

"Bull, don't die."

He laughed. "Trust me. I plan to live a very long and healthy life."

Chapter Fourteen

Grant stood out in the cold, staring at the dogs as they sniffed around the backyard of the clubhouse. He had to head into town to Aria's house to grab her some clothes and personal items.

He loved seeing her in his clothes but knew there would come a point when she missed her own clothes. Shoving his hands into his pockets, he watched Wanda, Ernie, and Bruno. They were good dogs.

"Here you go," Maddie said.

He turned to see her holding a mug of hot coffee.

"Thanks," he said.

"Aria hasn't come down for breakfast yet."

"I told her to stay in my room," he said.

"You're going to keep her prisoner?"

Grant laughed. "No, but I don't need her talking to you."

Maddie snorted. "Please, I'm an adorable person."

"Exactly. I can't have you turning my woman against me."

"That's something I wouldn't dream of doing." She placed a hand on her heart. "I'm shocked you would even think that."

"I know you were there last night," Grant said.

"No, you don't."

Grant laughed. "And now you will never know if I did know you were there or not."

Maddie shook her head. "That is a cruel trick."

He winked at her.

"For what it's worth, I think you should tell her the truth about … you know."

Grant looked toward the clubhouse. "Maddie, Aria has a lot of … she has … body issues," he said.

"Don't we all?"

"Her mother has spent her whole life putting her on a diet, telling her she's fat. That she's ugly. When Aria looks in the mirror, all she sees is something ... that I don't."

Maddie sighed. "It's hard, Grant. I've been there, and even now, I still struggle. I gained quite a bit of weight with Lindsey, and I know I just want to lose it."

"I can't have her thinking I prefer her sister to her," he said. "I can't lose her."

"Then don't. Tell her the truth. Be honest with her. That's all you can do and hope she sees reason." Maddie put a hand on his arm. "And I hope your dad died a real horrible death for what he did to you. For what he did to us. We could have been great friends even before now. He cost us that."

Grant nodded. He felt the heat rising up the back of his neck. "You heard it all."

"I know this has been bothering Bull. I came to see how he was doing, but you arrived before I could take care of him."

"Take care of my brother, Maddie. He needs it." He finished off the hot coffee. It was freezing outside, so it didn't take long for the drink to get warm enough for him to down quickly.

Maddie had already gone into the clubhouse and Grant joined her, bringing in the dogs as he did so.

"Someone is going to need to hire someone to keep scooping dog shit," Rusty said, staring outside the kitchen window. "It's going to stink."

Grant ignored him and headed into the main clubhouse. The brothers were all there, enjoying their morning coffee. A couple of the women were hanging around, trying to garner the men's attention.

He left them to it, heading upstairs toward Aria.

She was sitting on the edge of his bed.

"You told me to stay here," Aria said. She got up and he wrapped his arms around her waist, pulling her close. "What is it?"

"I've got to head over to your place. You can't come with me, but I want you to stay here. Hang out with Maddie."

"Oh, okay. I could come with you, though."

"No, it's too dangerous."

"And you're going?" Aria asked.

"I know what I'm doing. I know what I'm up against."

"I don't like this." She ran her hands up his chest, wrapping them around his neck. "I don't want you to go."

"I'll be back before you know it." He gripped the back of her neck and kissed her hard. "I'll have my brothers at my back. They'll keep me safe. When I come back, we've got to talk."

"Okay." She nodded. "Wait, is this where you break up with me?"

"No. We just have to talk. I've got a few things I need to tell you."

"Sure. Yeah, okay."

He smiled. "Don't worry."

"It's kind of hard not to worry."

He kissed her again. "Don't worry."

Taking her hand, he led her out of the bedroom and walked her down toward the kitchen. Maddie was there with Lindsey.

"Take care of her."

Maddie winked at him and he didn't like that.

Leaving the kitchen, he made his way outside toward his bike. He'd not ridden it in a long time.

"Don't you think you should take your truck?"

Bull asked.

"If I do that, Wanda's coming with me, and she's got to stay here."

"I'll keep an eye on your dog."

"What about the shelters? Did the bastard go to them?"

"No, none."

Grant nodded, straddling his machine. "You've not tampered with it."

"Grant, I've told you once and I've told you a gazillion times, the only way you're going to die is by my hand."

He snorted, he couldn't help it. "Please, I'm living for eternity," Grant said.

"It's what scares me."

Grant blew his brother a kiss, reversed out of the parking space, and then revved his engine and took off, heading toward town. He was tempted to take the bike for a quick ride, but he was on a mission.

Arriving at Aria's place in town, he parked outside and made his way toward the front door. He pulled out the key and let himself inside.

He closed the door quietly, waiting, listening. The hairs on the back of his neck stood on end, and he just knew something wasn't right.

Grant made his way upstairs toward Aria's bedroom. Pulling out a bag, he began to fill it with her stuff. He picked the clothes he wanted to see her in. Jeans, dresses, skirts, he avoided the ugly-looking shirts that hid too much of her body. He didn't even bother with lingerie, but then he heard the sound of the fridge opening and closing.

Someone was inside the house.

Grant stopped.

Whoever was inside the house had heard him.

There was no doubt about it. He'd not heard the door, so they'd been there even before Grant had been. Hands clenched, his heart beat hard in his chest. Not fast. He wasn't scared, but ready, prepared.

With her clothes in the bag, Grant took the stairs. He didn't go to the front door, but straight to the kitchen where he saw him, the man who he witnessed kill that woman at the trailer park. Miguel Vito Carlos.

He was sitting at Aria's kitchen table. A bottle of water was open on the table.

"Hello, Grant," Miguel said.

His accent was thick but Grant understood him.

"Miguel."

By just saying his name, he saw the tic near the corner of one of his eyes. He had surprised him. "You know who I am."

He stayed silent. What the fuck was this bastard doing in Aria's house? It made no sense.

He'd seen the way Miguel looked at her, though. There was no doubt this man was interested in Aria, but why? Was it to get to the club? To get to Bull? To him? None of this made any sense.

"Ah, I see you're the quiet, silent type. Strange. I've heard so many things about you."

"What do you want?" Grant asked.

Miguel chuckled. "You're a guy who likes to get right down to business."

"I'm the guy that wants to know what the fuck you're doing in his woman's house."

"Ah, Aria Taylor. Sweet woman, am I correct? This was once her grandparents' house. I believe her receiving this in their will had caused quite the stir."

Grant smiled. "Nice."

Miguel bowed his head. "I like to be thorough when I do my research."

"Aria's not your concern."

"Oh, but you see, she is. She's part of Carnage and seeing as this town is very much my concern, I have every right to do my research."

"This town isn't yours," Grant said.

Miguel laughed. A full-throated, uncontrollable laugh, at least it sounded that way, but something in Grant's gut said this man was always in control. He'd never let his guard down.

Grant stayed perfectly still, watching him, waiting, trying to understand what was going to happen next. Was this the last day he got to see his woman, his brother, the club? Miguel was here for a reason and he'd already witnessed him kill before, so he knew Miguel didn't have any qualms about pulling the trigger.

Miguel sat back in his chair and as quickly as he burst out laughing, like a switch being flicked, he stopped.

"I have a business proposition for you."

"I'm not interested."

"Come on, Grant. I know that you and I are similar."

This made Grant laugh. "No, we're not."

"Fine. You kind of remind me of Julio."

"Do not mention that fucker's name to me," Grant said. He watched as Miguel's nostrils flared. "I'm nothing like him."

"No?"

"I don't kick a man while he's down, and I don't kidnap women, nor do I shoot them in the face," Grant said, staring right into Miguel's eyes as he made the last accusation.

A small twitch, ever so slight, and most people wouldn't have been able to catch it, but Grant did. He'd caught Miguel by surprise. How interesting.

"Aren't you tired of being under your brother's control?" Miguel asked. "He was given the Chaos and Carnage MC, but you were expected to wear the VP patch, with what? Pride? That doesn't seem like a fair deal to me."

Grant continued to stare at him. Yes, he and Bull had fought, and Grant, during one of his many pissed-off moments, had done the whole trying-to-stake-his-claim as Prez of the club, but it had been bullshit. Grant didn't want the role. He just wanted to piss off his brother.

Lame. But it was what it was. Brothers being exactly that—brothers. Grant didn't want anything else from Bull. In a way, he just wanted his brother back.

He smirked as he looked at Miguel. "And you think you can give that to me? Bull wasn't given the patch because of some older brother bullshit. He earned that patch."

"By killing your father."

"That must have been hard on you."

Grant didn't say a word. Was this man trying to reason with his sensitive side? Did he really think he missed his old man? Seeing that old man dead and gone was a huge fucking relief.

"What do you want?"

"I want to give you a chance to run the shop at Carnage. Bull is outdated and it's time for him to go. Hernandez was mistaken in thinking this town could be left alone. It's a wonderful bed for all kinds of business." Miguel got to his feet. "But I realize that you must need an incentive to see how important this is. Your woman, I promise you, no matter what, she will never see any harm come to her. For that, you have my word."

Grant snorted. "Your word. For that, you should stay out of town and approach me or my brother within the confines of the deal you made."

"That was not the deal I made. That was the deal Hernandez made and that's what got him killed." Miguel took a step forward. "I can offer you riches, Grant. I can offer you a future where you are king. Not your brother. You and I, we can build a fucking glorious empire. No more suspension. No more answering to your brother. No more seeing your patch on another member of the club. Someone who doesn't deserve it. You're a leader, Grant, and it's time for you to lead."

He stared at Miguel. There was nothing more to be said.

Miguel held his hands up. "There's nothing more for me to say. I only hope you consider what I have told you, and take it seriously. I mean it, Grant. I can offer you a kingdom, and security for your woman."

"And in return?" Grant asked.

"Well, all the details will be ironed out once we agree on our new relationship."

"And the club?" Grant asked.

Miguel smiled.

Grant didn't give a fuck why he was smiling, all he wanted to know was the details. "As you know, some men would not take too kindly to your takeover bid, but they can be easily dealt with. You'll have your own club, and we'll arrange to dispose of those that cause you trouble." Miguel pulled a card out of his pocket. "Here are my details. Contact me when you have the answer. I look forward to your call." He placed the card on the table, and then seconds later, Grant did nothing as he walked out the door.

****

Maddie was nice.

Aria smiled at the other woman as she flitted around the kitchen, trying to find her some breakfast. Men came and went as did a couple of women. None of them lingered the moment they caught sight of Maddie in the kitchen. She couldn't help but wonder what Maddie had done to make them so afraid.

"Ah, here we go. Grant would want you to eat something."

There were sausages, bacon, some tomatoes and lots of bread, also scrambled eggs. Aria smiled. This was not going to help with her weight. No, it was not.

"Thank you."

"I know there's a lot of food, but it's good."

Aria picked up her knife and fork and wondered what Jase would say about the breakfast she was eating. It didn't have a single piece of fruit or whole wheat bread. Cutting into a piece of sausage, she took a bite and smiled at Maddie.

"It's good, right?" Maddie asked.

"Yes, so good. I don't think Jase will be happy with me."

"Jase?" Maddie frowned and then her eyes went wide and she smiled. "Gym Jase?"

Aria stared at Maddie. "Gym Jase?"

"Yeah, the guy who owns the gym. Personal trainer type of guy?"

"Yeah, that's him."

Maddie chuckled. "Isn't he so sweet? When I went into the gym, determined to lose every single pound and inch, he was so nice about it. I always worried that I'd be laughed at and humiliated, but Jase is such a sweet guy."

"Do you still go to the gym?"

"Hell, no. Bull doesn't want me to go."

"How come?" Aria asked.

"A mixture of reasons. He loves my curves and I don't think he can stand the idea of me being alone with another guy."

"And you don't mind that?" Aria asked.

"No, I don't. I love Bull. It's strange, I know, but it is what it is."

She looked at the other woman and Aria saw the love shining in her eyes. She was happy. That was a good thing.

"I'm surprised Grant is happy with you going to the gym," Maddie said.

"He's not. In fact, he got himself hired at the gym, I think? I'm not exactly sure what Grant does or doesn't do." Aria shrugged.

"Yeah, when Bull and I were going through a rough patch, Grant was there for me. He even got hired at the diner." Maddie held her hands up and laughed. "I have no idea how he does it."

"You know Grant … well?" Aria didn't know why she hesitated with this woman.

"I, er, I don't know if you would say I know him well, but I do know him. We used to go to school together."

"Grant said you and he didn't always get along."

Maddie laughed. "You can certainly say that." She shrugged. "Did he tell you anything?"

Aria didn't know if there was something he shouldn't have told her. She didn't want to get Grant in trouble or cause problems between him and Maddie.

"Growing up, Grant was a … er … he was a bully. You know, that was just who he was. He has kind of outgrown it now. Sometimes I think he's a bit of a child and doesn't seem to take growing up seriously."

"I don't think he's that bad," Aria said. "Not that I can say much about him. You've known him longer than I have, but when it comes to the dogs, he's always there."

She thought back to him at the veterinary practice

239

with Andy and Phil. Yes, Grant flitted between jobs but he was always great at what he did. When he was around the dogs and at the shelter, he was in control. There was more to Grant than met the eye. Aria didn't know exactly what it was, but she saw it in his eyes.

"That's good," Maddie said. "I know Grant can be an ass and mean, and he can be cruel, but when he allows himself to open up, to be there, he's the best guy to have around."

"Do you and him have a past?" Aria asked.

"Me and him. Hell, no. Ugh, no. We've become friends, I think. It's hard to make sense of what we call ourselves."

Aria laughed. She just couldn't help it. The look of complete disgust on Maddie's face said it all.

"Grant was no saint. There were always a lot of women hanging around him, but you're different. He's different with you."

"He is?" Aria asked.

"Yeah, you're here because he cares about you. Grant doesn't care about women. They were…" She stopped and Aria chuckled at the cringing look on Maddie's face. "I should stop. He's your boyfriend?"

"We've not really said what we are," Aria said. "I guess we're dating, I think. I'm not sure."

They hadn't been on a date date. Not really. This was confusing.

"Look, Grant is different with you. He cares about you and I know for a fact no one has ever been able to hold onto him, not for longer than a couple of hours. That must mean something. You matter to him, Aria."

Nibbling her lip, she smiled at Maddie.

Bull came in with a young baby on his hip.

Aria cut up her breakfast, trying not to calorie

count in her head. She didn't want to be rude to Maddie or the club by not eating the food they'd provided.

She had to wonder if they had a gym, someplace for her to work out.

Finishing off the breakfast, there was no sign of Grant's return, so she made her way back to his bedroom.

She sat on the edge of the bed and then realized she hadn't called Lidia. Her best friend would want to know why she hadn't called or texted. Lidia was going to freak when Aria told her she was staying at the Chaos and Carnage MC clubhouse. Opening her cell phone, she saw that she had a video message waiting for her from an unknown number. Aria couldn't recall giving her number to anyone else recently.

When she saw the title of the message, "Who Grant really is," Aria hated the temptation. Before she could even question herself, she started to play the video. It wasn't longer than a minute and at first it wasn't even in focus.

"What are you doing?" She recognized Isabella's voice.

The camera suddenly stilled and then she saw them. Grant and Isabella.

"What happened nine months ago, you never speak a fucking word of it. As far as I'm concerned, I don't know you, you don't know me, got it?"

"I would never ... I promise. It was a moment of weakness."

"It wasn't weakness on my part. I was looking for a quick fuck, and you were there. You meant nothing to me. But Aria is the real deal. You say anything to hurt her, and I will end you, got it?"

"Michael, he can't know."

"Not a fucking word."

Then, as if the person who invaded the moment of privacy realized what they were doing, the video ended. It just came to a stop. Aria figured that was it, but then another video played.

"Who the fuck does she think she is?" That was definitely Grant's voice.

The video looked old, like it was taken with an old-fashioned camera rather than a cell phone. She spotted Grant, and then someone who looked like Maddie.

"Dude, come on, she's no good. She's way too innocent and sweet. Virginal."

"Nah, man, the only reason that fat ass is a virgin is because no one would want to see all the layers of fat to get to the pussy." Grant burst out laughing. *"Fuck, I hate fat people."*

The video ended.

Aria didn't know what to think. Grant had known her sister. He'd slept with her sister. All night long they acted like strangers. Aria didn't even realize that they could have known each other. She was so freaking stupid.

Tears filled her eyes. What had Grant been doing with her all this time? Was it a joke?

She hated that she allowed the tears to fall. This wasn't fair. None of this was fair.

What do you expect? Your mom is right. She is always right.

Aria got to her feet and made her way over to his closet. She found the clothes that she had been wearing and quickly changed out of Grant's into her own.

She was such an idiot. A fool. A foolish idiot. Ugh! She hated herself.

Once she was dressed, she made her way to the door and swung it open. There was no one outside waiting for her, which was a welcome relief. Taking the stairs down to the main room of the clubhouse, she stepped outside and then headed straight for the door that would take her outside. She was going home.

Aria stepped out into the freezing air. It was still quite early in the morning but she needed to get away.

Grant had pulled into the parking lot on his motorcycle. The machine sounded loud. He wasn't wearing a helmet.

"Babe, where are you going?" Grant asked.

All she kept hearing was the mantra of how much he hated fat people. She looked at him and had to wonder if it was all a lie. What was he getting out of it, lying to her? Not once had she thrown herself at him. He pursued her.

"Aria, babe, what's wrong?" he asked.

"Why did you do it?"

"Do what?"

She gritted her teeth. "Keep asking me out on a date when you hate fat people so much?"

"Hate fat people? Aria, I have no idea what's going on?"

"When were you going to tell me?" Aria asked.

Grant laughed. "I don't have a clue what you're talking about."

She shook her head. "Is that because it's convenient for you to forget?"

"For fuck's sake, Aria, tell me what's going on? I went and grabbed you some clothes. If the guys are talking shit, then you have to ignore them."

She pulled out her cell phone and then played the video. Once again, it took less than a minute but this time, rather than it break her heart, she watched Grant intently, hoping by some trickery of modern technology, it was all lies.

His face said it all. None of it was lies. It was all the truth. Grant had slept with her sister and he didn't like … fat people.

"Aria, I don't know how you got it—"

"Anonymous sender," she said. "Are you going to tell me none of this is true? That's you and Isabella, Thanksgiving night. Then I'm guessing that's you during high school? College?"

"Just after high school," Grant said.

"See, it's all real, and I have to wonder if you hate me so much, why did you insist on us dating? If we're so vile to you, why did you … why would you…"

"Aria, this was a long time ago. Trust me, I was a fucking asshole back then, and I didn't mean a single word I said."

"Trust you?"

"Yes."

"When were you going to tell me?" Aria asked.

Grant sighed. "I was going to tell you when it was the right time."

Aria reached for her bag. "Give me my stuff."

"You can't go out there," Grant said. "It's dangerous."

"No, it's dangerous if I'm still associated with you, right? Don't worry, Grant, I'll be fine because we're not together anymore."

"Aria, fuck, this is not … I'm not that person, at all. I don't hate you, I swear it. None of what I said was true. None of it. I … I fucking love you, Aria."

He wouldn't give her the bag and Aria stumbled back a little at his confession. She shook her head. How could she believe that? Turning on her heel, she headed for the gates.

Grant rushed toward her, wrapping his arms around her, and pulling her in close. Aria tried to fight him.

"I get that you hate me right now and you can do it, but please don't go. Do not walk through those gates. He will not care that you no longer want me, Aria. Fuck, do not fucking go."

Chapter Fifteen

Grant kept his distance for the next week. Aria didn't leave the clubhouse, but then, if it hadn't been for Maddie and Bull coming outside, he had a feeling she would have left.

Sitting at the bar, he kept his gaze on the main door leading up to the bedrooms. Aria was now staying in Pat's room. As for Pat, he was sleeping wherever he wanted to crash.

Fucking Pat. First his VP patch, now Aria.

Grant wanted a drink so badly, but he didn't want to mix his temper with alcohol. That wouldn't be the greatest way to deal with his problems.

"How are you doing?" Bull asked, coming to sit beside him at the bar.

"Fine."

"You've spent most of your time staring at a door the past couple of days," Bull said.

"Wouldn't you do it with Maddie?"

"I have done it." Bull sighed. "So she's the real deal then. Aria, she's the one you love."

"Yeah, she is," Grant said. "More than anything else in the world." He sipped at his coffee and even though it was scorching hot, it was not giving him the burn of alcohol he fucking wanted.

Everything had gone so fucking wrong in such a short space of time. He had every intention of telling Aria the truth, in time. Possibly when she was pregnant, post-orgasm, and kind of just sliding it in as a revelation that didn't mean anything. He didn't have a fucking clue how he was going to tell her.

"So, she found out the truth."

"Yes, in an anonymous fucking video," Grant said.

Grant thought back to that day—the meeting he had with Miguel. Aria couldn't leave, not until they sorted out the Miguel problem.

He tapped his fingers on the tabletop and then pulled Aria's cell phone out of his pocket. She had left it on the dining room table last night. She didn't have the thing locked and he was able to scroll through all the messages. Aria's main contact was Lidia, her best friend.

Grant clicked his tongue and then sent off a quick message to Lidia saying that he'd snuck out of the clubhouse and they were to meet around the back of the veterinary practice.

Maddie came out of the kitchen with Lindsey on her hip, giving the perfect distraction for Bull. Finishing off his coffee, he headed in the direction that Maddie had come from, and lo and behold, there was Pat.

"Hey, man," Pat said.

Grant ignored him.

Pat just laughed. "When are you going to grow up?"

He turned to glare at the other man. Pat had been sitting at the main table, but now he was on his feet and sending an almighty glare his way.

"Why don't you fuck off?" Grant said. "I've got nothing to say to you."

"This about the patch? Your woman?"

Grant's hands clenched into fists and he'd been near the door, but now he spun around to face Pat. "What the fuck did you say?"

"I want to know why you've got nothing to say to me. We've got no bad blood between us."

"No bad blood? You seem to want to take everything from me!" He slammed his palm flat against his chest. "You want to be Bull's brother, his VP. My woman's man, is that it?"

Pat smirked and shook his head. "You are way too emotional."

Grant swung, hitting his fist to Pat's face. The man barely moved.

He touched his face, next to his mouth, and came back with blood on a couple of fingers. "Now, I'm going to allow you to have that one, because clearly, you're going through some fucked-up shit. I've also heard that your body is covered in scars. I remember your old man. It doesn't take a genius to realize that he fucked your head up good."

Pat rarely spoke. He was known for being quiet. It would seem Grant had opened a dam.

"But you've got to learn to own up to your mistakes. You fucked up with Aria, not me. I'm not the one who pretended to not fuck her sister. You did. I'm not the one who's so fucking flighty he doesn't even stick to a steady job, for fuck's sake." Pat shook his head. "Bull loves you."

"Oh, fuck off." Grant had heard enough.

"What makes you think he doesn't?" Pat asked. "You're still around. You've challenged him enough times. Pissed him off. Come on, Grant, think. Time and time again, he lets you get away with shit. You're rarely at the shop. You're unreliable for anything but club stuff. Bull will always have your back here. You know that."

Grant had heard enough.

"And next time you throw a punch at me, make sure it knocks me clean out, because I won't be responsible for what happens next," Pat said.

The threat was real.

Heading out of the kitchen, he rounded the parking lot and went to his bike. Climbing onto the machine, he straddled the beast, and then headed his way into town.

It was nearing lunchtime, which meant Lidia was at the diner, so it wouldn't take her long to get to the veterinary practice.

Aria had once told him that Lidia was her closest friend. Since they were kids, they had shared a lot together. Not much had changed after they left high school, much to her mother's annoyance. Lidia was another person Joan Taylor couldn't stand. He figured it had to do with the fact that Lidia helped Aria escape the nastiness of her mother's words.

Heading through the main town, he went straight to the veterinary practice and saw Lidia's car already parked in the main spot. Andy and Phil's cars were there and he saw several customers inside.

Parking his bike, he climbed off, and then rounded the building to find Lidia waiting.

She turned to look at him and then he saw the instant change. Before he got a chance to say anything, she walked right up to him and slapped him across the face.

"You fucking asshole. I cannot believe you did that to Aria. Do you have any idea how she feels about you?" She went to slap him again but he caught her wrist, stopping her from connecting with his face.

"Enough," he said.

"Don't you tell me enough. I'll have enough when I'm damn well good and ready." She drew her hand back and was about to slap him again, but he captured her wrist before she made contact.

"I get it, you're pissed at me. I do. Trust me, you think I don't feel it."

"Do you even feel anything?" Lidia asked. "I should have known it. That you were playing some kind of game with my best friend. What was it, some kind of bet? Is that what you had planned?"

"It was no fucking game! I fucking love Aria. She is … everything." He'd never been good with words. Grant was used to hurting people and messing shit up, not talking about his feelings.

"Wait, what?"

He let her go and took a step back. "I love her, okay? I love her so fucking much it hurts to see her this way. I hate that she thinks I don't, that I … ugh. None of this was a game. Someone sent her a fucked-up video and yes, I was like that in the past, but not anymore. That was all lies. I lied a lot. I even hurt my brother's woman because of it. Trust me, I do not feel and I have never felt that way."

"Have you seen the video?" Lidia asked.

"Yes, have you?"

"No, Aria wouldn't send it to me. You really do love her?"

"Yes, I love her. I want to spend the rest of my life with her and I've been hoping to get her pregnant so she won't have a reason to fucking leave me."

Lidia winced. "You do realize that it makes you sound like a bigger asshole, saying stuff like that?"

"Do I look like I give a fuck?" Grant asked. "I mess everything up. Don't you see that? Bull's the one that keeps everything together, while I'm the screw-up."

"But you do love her?" Lidia asked.

"More than anything. Why do you keep asking the same fucking questions?" He was growing tired of this.

"Because it's nice to hear and I know you mean it when you say it. You're not lying. That's good."

He shook his head and pulled out Aria's cell phone. The video's on there as well as the number it was attached to. I don't recognize it and I've made a callback. The phone is dead."

"You expect me to know a number of someone who's trying to hurt my best friend?"

"It's a shot in the dark right now, but you're the only one who is closest to Aria, apart from me. Her sister isn't much good and after this, I'm not going to her."

"You do know this is a long shot," Lidia said.

Grant shrugged. "I've got other people I can use if you don't know it."

Lidia sighed and played the video. He heard his voice, once again.

Lidia winced. "Dude, you should have told her."

"Don't you think I know that?" He ran a hand down his face, finding himself getting more infuriated with every passing minute.

Lidia looked at the number and frowned. "Huh."

She pulled out her own cell phone. He saw her thumb flashing across the screen.

"That stupid prick," Lidia said.

"What?"

"It came from Sean's old number. I don't know why I didn't delete it before!" She pressed and then he heard the call doing the same. "He sent this and then he's gotten rid of his cell phone. Cowardly bastard. I should have known he was behind this. He tried to break up our friendship, saying all kinds of nasty stuff to Aria. When I see him, I'm going—"

"You're not," Grant said.

"Look here, Grant, you may wear that patch and think you're the boss of the town, but you are going to realize that you're not the boss of me."

"There's not going to be anything left for you to deal with. That piece of shit is mine," Grant said.

Lidia smiled. "Can I come for the ride?"

"No. Keep talking to Aria. I'll handle Sean."

"You're no fun."

Grant shook his head and then made his way back around the veterinary practice. He knew where Sean lived. Climbing onto his bike, he pulled out of the veterinary practice parking lot and headed out to the Wood Farm where he'd find Sean.

Grant had been struggling to figure out where someone could have gotten that video. It was taken close to thirteen years ago. When he'd been in high school.

Sean had a brother, Nicholas. He had left town several years ago. The last Grant had heard, he settled down with a woman he met in the city, or something like that. It had been a fairy tale story, and he'd never come back to Carnage. Sean, the younger brother, must have found the old video, going through the footage.

Wood Farm had once been a thriving ranch, but as the years went by, the Woods had invested their money into real estate as well as stock markets. They were a wealthy family, and kept the Wood Farm house, but most of the land had been sold off for potential redevelopment, which had never happened.

Arriving at Wood Farm, he parked his bike, climbed off, and headed up the steps that clearly looked like they had been recently painted. Grant pressed the doorbell and waited.

Sean opened the door and he watched as the man went visibly pale.

"Hello, Sean."

****

Aria wanted to go home. She had to leave. It had been a week. A very long week of trying to avoid Grant. She hated seeing him every single day, even when she tried to avoid it.

Tears filled her eyes as she held onto the pillow. She hated crying.

There was a knock at the door and she sniffled.

"Come in."

This wasn't her room, nor was it her house. She didn't feel comfortable taking someone else's room. Maddie stepped through the door.

"Hey," she said.

"Hey." Aria smiled at the other woman and then wiped at her eyes. "I don't suppose I can leave?"

"Not yet, I'm afraid." Maddie sighed and moved toward the bed.

"How do you stand this?"

"It's easier when you get to see the man you love every single day. I've been living in this clubhouse for a lot longer than a week." She sighed.

"Aren't you going crazy?"

"A little bit. I do get to go to the store, but I've got to have a couple of guys go with me. Bull's very protective."

Aria nodded. "I bet that's nice."

"Grant would do the same for you, you know," Maddie said.

"He lied to me. He had sex with my sister," Aria said. She sniffled. "It's fine. And I saw ... he was so mean. I know you said he was a bully to you, but I don't think I ... I didn't think—"

Maddie took hold of her hands. "Don't worry about it."

"How can you not be upset?" Aria asked.

"Grant is a strange kind of guy. Trust me, I had all these assumptions about who he was as a person, and I was so wrong on all counts. Yes, he was a bully. He bullied me about my weight for the longest time. Even when I dated Bull, in the beginning. He and Bull got into a little fight about it. Then it was like he changed." Maddie shrugged. "He went from being my worst enemy to one of my best friends."

"So which one is real?" Aria asked.

"I guess both are real to a point," Maddie said. "Does it really matter that he slept with your sister?"

The tears filled her eyes. "Isabella's the pretty one. Everyone wants her."

"That's not true."

"Isn't it?" Aria asked. "Grant already had my sister. What if he's comparing us?"

"Stop it," Maddie said.

"My mom always said that I was never going to match up to my sister. That men would never want me, not after they had seen Isabella. I figured Grant was different."

Maddie grabbed both of her hands. "I don't like your mother. She sounds almost as bad as mine."

"I'm so sorry for your loss," Aria said. She had heard that Maddie had lost her parents.

The other woman chuckled. "She wasn't my real mother," Maddie said, surprising Aria.

"What?"

"They adopted me from Beatrice and Carl."

"The owners of the diner?"

Maddie nodded. "It's not common enough knowledge but they're my real parents. Times were tight and they didn't want to give me up, but they couldn't run a crumbling business and raise a baby. They didn't want to leave town, and so they gave me to my mother. She was a horrible woman. She told me all the time how fat and ugly I was. She really messed with my head and I'm guessing your mom has messed with yours." Maddie sighed. "Bull helped me to see reason. He got me to think about my own daughter. This was before Lindsey, and if I would say those horrible things to my daughter. If you looked at yourself and saw your daughter in the mirror, would you tell her the same things your mother told you?"

The tears fell down Arai's cheeks. "No, hell, no."

"Then you've got to stop believing them. You're a beautiful woman, Aria, you're sweet and kind, and I know for a fact that Grant loves you, so very much. He messed up. Guys are going to mess up. Bull did and still does, but I love him. I love him enough to stay at his clubhouse until he thinks it's safe for me. I'd do anything for him."

She loved Grant, so much. But it was hard. He had lied to her.

"He should have told me the truth," Aria said.

"Yeah, he should have and he's a dick because he didn't. Believe me, Grant knows what he did wrong and I bet he even regrets it."

Aria sighed.

"You're telling me I need to forgive Grant?"

"No, I'm not telling you that. Yes, I'd like you to forgive him, but only when you're ready to." Maddie smiled. "I better head downstairs. I'm pretty sure Lindsey is already driving everyone crazy."

Maddie got to her feet and left.

Aria sighed.

Lidia had asked if she would ever forgive Grant. She wanted to.

Reaching for her cell phone, it wasn't there. She frowned and got to her feet. She checked her pockets and then quickly left the bedroom, going to the bathroom. Knocking on the door, no one called out that they were in there, so checking through the laundry basket, she tried to find her cell phone. It wasn't there either. Where did she have it last? She made her way downstairs and went to the kitchen. There was no sign of her cell phone.

"You okay, Aria?" Pat asked.

"Yeah, I was looking for my cell phone."

"I haven't seen it. I think Grant might have taken it."

"Grant?"

"Yeah, and look, he just pulled up."

Aria looked toward the window and saw Grant turning off his bike. She stepped out of the kitchen door and headed in his direction. Grant turned toward her and he stopped. Aria stopped. They hadn't spoken in over a week.

"Aria," Grant said.

"Grant."

"What's up?"

"Pat said that you, er, that you have my phone."

He chuckled. "Leave it to Pat to tattle."

"Do you have my phone?" Aria asked.

He reached into his pocket and she saw his knuckles were bleeding. "Are you okay?" Aria asked. Deep down, she knew she shouldn't care. Grant had lied to her. He had put her in this position. And yet, she couldn't help but be concerned seeing the state of his hands.

"It's nothing."

"Grant, that's not nothing. You're hurt."

"Sean sent you those videos." He held out the cell phone for her to take. "The guy's a piece of shit. I used to go to school with his brother. Sean likes control, and he wanted to remove all of Lidia's friends and family, but you wouldn't leave, so you ruined his plans."

"Seriously?" Aria asked.

"He won't be bothering you anymore."

"You beat him up?"

"I taught him a lesson in respect. Also, I called his brother," Grant said. "They're coming to deal with him. It would seem he's been causing the family a lot of worries."

Aria nodded. She should have known it came from Sean.

"Aria, I know I messed up."

She shook her head. "I don't want to do this now."

Grant nodded. "Fine. I can wait."

"All my life, I've been told I was never good enough, that my sister was the one who—"

"Stop it," Grant said.

"You had sex with her."

"And I don't remember it. Aria, I never claimed to be a saint before I met you. I was a piece of shit and I still am a piece of shit. I messed up but that night with your sister didn't mean anything. It was before I met you, before I felt this way. She was easy."

Aria shook her head. "You still don't get it, do you?"

"Get what? Tell me what I can do to make this right. I'll do anything."

She stared at him and the tears filled her eyes once again. "You didn't trust me."

"What?"

"You didn't believe that I could handle it."

"Can you?" Grant asked. "You found out and look what's happened to us? You can't even look me in the eye!"

"Because I was hurt!" She screamed at him. "How would you feel if it turned out that I had sex with Bull, but then I hid it from you?"

"I know that's not possible," Grant said.

"Ugh! Why are you being a giant pain in the ass? Of course I've never had sex with Bull. I'm asking you to take a chance at feeling what I'm feeling." She shook her head.

Ernie and Bruno came out of the kitchen. Pat had

opened the door. Wanda also. Her dogs had been staying with her, but she knew they missed Wanda, who went to stay with her best friend, Grant.

"I know what you're saying," Grant said. "I just don't like it."

"And you expect me to?" Aria asked. "You didn't have enough faith in me or in us, where does that leave us?"

"I made a mistake."

She shook her head. "We have moved way too fast, Grant. We need to stop."

"No," Grant said.

"Yeah, I think we do."

Grant closed the distance between them, cupping her face, tilting her head back, and then he slammed his lips down on hers. "No, we don't need to slow down. We don't need to stop. I fucked up, Aria. I know that. I will never do anything like that again. You want to know every single woman I've fucked? I'll point them out. I'll tell you."

"I don't want to know every single woman," Aria said.

"I love you," Grant said. "I love you more than anything else in the world. I don't need you to change. I don't need you to be different. I love you for who you are." He pressed a kiss to each of her cheeks. "And I'm not going to stop. This isn't over."

He took possession of her lips and Aria couldn't fight him. She didn't want to fight him.

****

"Another dead body was found last night," Bull said. "Dylan called me." He looked around the church table, seeing the grim look on his men's faces.

Lockdown right now was not working. They were not drawing out the enemy. He couldn't allow Maddie to go out there, knowing Miguel waited for them.

"Three spots around town, all on the outskirts. First, we have the trailer park, then the old barn, and another outside of the woods, where Ernie and Bruno were found," Bull said.

"Is he trying to tell us that we're surrounded?" Sweets asked.

"That's what I believe." Bull turned toward his brother. "Miguel went to Aria's house a week ago. Grant had gone to pick up some clothes for her. He wanted to make a deal."

Grant had come to him immediately. Bull threw the calling card onto the main table.

"You're only bringing this up now?" Rusty asked.

"Grant came to me. I wanted to know what to do with this information before I acted on it." Bull looked toward his brother. "I want Grant to respond to this call."

Grant looked up. His brother didn't look good. He hadn't shaved in several days, nor did it look like he had slept. This shit with Aria was affecting him.

"What?" Grant asked.

"It's well known you and I don't have the best relationship. I want you to call this in."

"You're crazy," Grant said. "He'll see right through it."

"Will he?" Bull asked. "He reached out to you. We need to get rid of this fucker, Grant. You're the only one who can do it."

No matter what he thought about this outcome, none of them were as good as Grant. Not even one of the other guys could pull this off, but Grant could.

"You're to make the call, follow his instructions, learn everything, and then we're going to take them out. I need to know how many there are in town. I need to know where they're staying, and then we're taking this fight to them. I'm not going to be at their mercy anymore. I'm done making deals like our old man."

Bull slammed his hand down on the table.

"And I'm done keeping us all locked up. The clubhouse, you brothers, you mean everything to me, but I need my wife, alone, without hearing one of you fucking farting outside my bedroom."

Rusty held his hand up, and Rip was the one to high-five him.

"Rip bet me fifty bucks to do that. We wanted to see if you'd still be able to get your nut off with a bunch of dudes farting."

Bull shook his head. Even when they were in danger and the threat was very fucking real, the guys still found the time to make jokes. Assholes.

"This is dangerous," Pat said.

"I'm not going to put Aria at risk."

"That's the thing," Bull said. "To help, I've already gotten Jase to spread the rumor."

"What?"

Bull wasn't proud of this. He'd called Jase, asked for a favor, told him what had happened between Grant and Aria, and her sister. Aria and Grant had been the talk of the town. He'd heard the people gossiping about his brother, and it was the perfect fuel to help word get back to Miguel. It would protect Aria, and Grant would be able to do this.

"You had no fucking right," Grant said.

"It's done. Aria is already on her way home," Bull said. "I let her go. I told her that with you and her no longer together, the threat is not real to her."

Bull tensed up as Grant threw himself across the table, charging at him.

"You son of a bitch. You had no fucking right."

Grant threw back his arm. This time, Bull allowed him to have the first punch, then the second, but then, with Pat, Rusty, and even Stacks's help, they had to pull Grant off him. "Do you know what you've done?"

"I've saved your woman and I'm saving this club."

"No one else knew!" Grant yelled. "No one knew that I had fucked her sister and now they're all going to know. You've humiliated her. Now she's never going to fucking forgive me."

He tried to pull out of the confines of the brothers' arms.

"This way, my way, you'll get chance to make it right with her. You can't make it right while she's avoiding you in the clubhouse."

Grant gritted his teeth. "I hate you."

"Good. You can channel that hate into doing your job."

Bull knew he'd done the right thing, but it had come at a cost to his brother and Aria. He only hoped that Aria was so in love with Grant that she'd be able to forgive him.

Chapter Sixteen

"Aria, what are you doing here?" Jase asked.

Aria looked up at her personal trainer and the truth was, she didn't have a clue. Bull had sent her home only yesterday.

Nothing was disturbed. Her house was fine. The food in the fridge had to be thrown out, which she had done when she got home. Her life had gone on as usual.

Eating was not high on her list of things to do. The thought of food made her feel sick. She'd been able to eat a slice of whole wheat toast for breakfast, half of a sandwich for lunch, nothing, so far, for dinner. Nothing appealed to her.

"Er, isn't it our scheduled appointment?" Aria asked, glancing down at her wrist, but her watch wasn't there.

Jase frowned and then nodded. "Yes, it is. I ... I didn't put two and two together. Yes, it is time." He paused and looked down at his desk.

"I'll go and get changed." Aria disappeared into the changing room. There were several women chatting amongst themselves. When Aria stepped through, they looked in her direction. She gave them a polite smile and made her way into one of the private rooms. She couldn't stand to get changed with someone close or watching.

"Was that Aria Taylor?"

She froze. Did they realize that their whispering was loud?

"Yeah, I think it was."

There was a giggle.

"Do you know what I heard?"

"What?"

"That Grant Reynolds, the super hot bike guy, wanted to see what it was like to take on the two sisters.

He screwed Isabella and then he did Aria."

"I heard he ended up vomiting afterward."

They knew. How did they know?

Aria stood in the changing room wishing the world would open up and swallow her whole. She had no idea how they knew, but Aria didn't know how she'd be able to step out of that room. Would they just leave?

The sound of their voices started to fade and Aria was thankful for that. Sitting down on the floor, Aria felt the tears fall down her cheeks. If those women knew, then others did. Probably the whole town. Which explained the pitying looks she was getting by several of the customers.

"Aria, are you okay?"

"This is the ladies' changing room," she said.

"I know, I got one of my female employees to see if it's all clear for me to enter." Jase's feet appeared near the door.

Aria stared at them.

"Are you okay?"

"Yeah, I'm fine."

"Do you want to come out?" Jase asked.

"I'm not changed."

"That's okay, we can talk through the door."

"Do you know?" Aria asked with a sigh.

"Do I know what?" There was hesitation in his response and this only made her laugh.

"Of course you know."

Jase sighed. "Yes, I know."

"Great," Aria said. "So everyone knows that Grant had sex with my sister before me." She pressed her hands to her face. All she wanted to do was scream. Could this get any worse?

"Are you going to hide in that stall forever?" Jase asked.

"I can't go out there."

"Why not?"

"Because they all know."

"So they know that shit happened," Jase said. "It's not the end of the world. Trust me, it's not. You can hold your head high, and you can ignore the shit they're saying. You're in control of your own life, Aria. Not anyone else."

Aria got to her feet and she quickly changed out of her clothes into her gym suit. Opening the door, she came face to face with Jase. "Fine."

"You might want to splash some water on your face."

Aria nodded. "You're right."

Walking around Jase, she went to the sink and splashed water on her face. Afterward, she stood up and stared at her reflection. Why should she run and hide?

****

Aria's body hurt by the time she finished at the gym. All she wanted to do was go home, have a nice, long shower, forget what her body felt like, and then eat a ton of ice cream. Vanilla or chocolate, whichever was available in her freezer.

Lidia had been calling her, asking if she wanted her to come over. No. All she wanted was to be left alone.

Arriving home after the gym, she pulled into the driveway and then groaned. Her mother was standing on her doorstep. She hadn't spoken to her since Thanksgiving. This couldn't be good. At least she had taken the time to change into clothes rather than leave the gym in her workout ones. She didn't want her mother to know she was actually putting her thoughtless gift to use.

"Where have you been?" Joan asked, her hand on her hip. "What time do you call this?"

"I don't live in your house, Mom. I can come and go as I please."

Joan tsked. "I don't know what's gotten into you, Aria Taylor. Where has my respectful daughter gone?"

Aria couldn't help but laugh. "You mean the doormat? The one that puts up with all your insults? The disappointment? The waste of space. Shouldn't you be at Isabella's right now, telling her what she should or shouldn't be eating?"

She had no idea where this was coming from. Aria had never, ever spoken to her mother like this. Never.

"How dare you?" Joan folded her arms across her chest.

Aria didn't care to continue talking to her mother outside for whichever nosy neighbor was close by. Too much of her dirty laundry had already been shared with the town of Carnage. She wasn't ready for more.

Opening her front door, Ernie and Bruno were there to greet her.

"Disgusting. I cannot believe you adopted those filthy animals."

"They're not filthy animals. You're good boys, aren't you?" Aria kissed their heads and then made her way into the kitchen.

She heard her mother close the door.

Opening one of the cupboards, Aria grabbed some dog food and their two bowls. Her mother's annoying little tsk followed her.

She spun around to her mother and held her hands out. "What do you want? What have I done wrong now?"

"Do you have any idea what that vicious rumor has done to Isabella?" Joan asked.

"What rumor?" Aria asked, but she had a rough idea which one.

Joan growled. "You know which one, Missy, and don't you dare take that tone with me."

"You're in my house, asking me about a rumor that I'm part of, but instead of coming to ask me how I'm holding up, you only care what's going on with Isabella."

"She is married. Pregnant, Aria, I'm not sure you understand the severity of the situation."

"Oh, I understand it. So long as Isabella is fine, you don't give a crap about me. I'm not perfect, I'm not beautiful."

"How could you do this to her?" Joan asked. "Is it because she has a lovely husband? Is it out of jealousy? Spite?"

"I wasn't the one that made her screw Grant!" Aria yelled. "I wasn't the one to tell that rumor to anyone. But thanks, Mom, thanks for showing me once again that I'm not a good enough daughter for you. That I will never be good enough. That I don't measure up to Isabella's standards. You know what, get the fuck out of my house." Aria had never cursed. She had never yelled at her mother. This was a first.

Joan's mouth opened and closed. "You have no idea who you're talking to!"

"Funny you should say that. I never thought a mother should treat her daughter the way you do me. I guess you don't know who you're talking to either. Get out of my house. You're not welcome here. I don't want to ever see you again."

Her head lifted.

"I cannot believe he went from Isabella to you."

"Get out," Aria said.

Joan turned on her heel and Aria followed her, slamming the door closed as she did so. Her hands shook, her heart raced. Pressing her back against the door, she tried to take a deep breath, but it was impossible. She felt sick to her stomach.

Her mother had come to accuse her. Not to console her, but to point the finger. She just couldn't take it anymore. Years of being ignored, of being told how she didn't measure up, and she finally had enough.

Joan Taylor had said her last words to her. Aria was never going to forgive her.

Ernie and Bruno came toward her and snuggled up against her. Aria laughed. "I still have you two boys, don't I?" Aria asked.

They each put their head on her knees and she couldn't help but laugh. "I love you guys too. So much." She pressed kisses to their heads.

****

Grant didn't like this. Going to an abandoned farm was not fun. Nothing good ever came from a building that looked like it had been haunted for generations. He didn't scare easily but he didn't like Bull's plan. It was thoughtless.

Running a hand down his face, he turned as he heard a car approaching. He could die today. Miguel could have been lying about his offer and all of this could be just to lure him out here to die.

He couldn't help but think about Aria.

He'd called Jase and the personal trainer had confirmed the rumors were spread around town. Aria would be alone when all of this happened. He had no choice but to call Lidia and ask her to keep an eye on his woman for him. Lidia had promised him a quick swift kick in the balls was heading his way. He didn't care, so long as Aria was protected. He'd take any punishment she was willing to dish out.

"Grant, we meet again," Miguel said.

"And as you can see, I came alone, but you decided to bring a party."

Miguel chuckled. "You're young and still foolish. You remind me of Julio. Search him."

Grant glared at Miguel, but lifted his hands, locking them together and placing them behind his head. Next, he spread his legs wide.

"Go ahead. Be a little paranoid. It's textbook, right?"

"Betrayal happens in all forms."

"Trust me, I get it," Grant said, thinking of Bull spreading the rumors about him and Isabella.

He'd wanted to break his brother's face. Using his woman's pain like that.

"Your brother has betrayed you?"

"Took my woman from me," Grant said. Might as well stick to truth. He and Bull had been through a lot together, and something told Grant that Miguel wouldn't believe that he'd suddenly turned from the club. If Grant hadn't left the MC before now, he wouldn't just magically do it, not even for control of the club.

One of the large guys came forward and Grant glared at him. "Don't touch my dick."

Miguel laughed.

The man patted him down, roughly as he did so. Grant was going to take great pleasure in killing him, as he was the other guy.

Seconds passed and they turned to Miguel. "He's clear."

"So, no wire."

"Why the fuck would I be wearing a wire?" Grant asked.

"You expect me to believe that out of the blue you're going to turn against your brother, your club?" Miguel asked. "I gave you that card over a week ago and now, after you have time to plan, you expect me to believe you."

Grant shrugged. "A lot can happen in over a week. Your brother can cost you a great deal."

Miguel's brows went up. "True. Julio cost me time."

"Time? You went to prison?"

Miguel laughed. "No, he cost me time in taking what was mine. His petty dogfighting ring brought too much heat. I wasn't ready to take on Hernandez. It's cost me a lot of good men."

"Brothers." Grant put his hands on his hips. "Bull has cost me for the last time."

"Your woman?" Miguel asked.

"Yeah. Aria's gone," Grant said. "She's not coming back to me. Bull has seen to that."

"I can help you," Miguel said. "I can give you everything your heart desires. The club, your town, riches, and your woman."

The only thing he wanted was Aria.

"How?"

Miguel smiled. "That will come in time, but first, I need you to take care of two little problems."

"What?" Grant asked.

Miguel clicked his fingers and the bodyguards placed something in his hands. Grant watched and it looked like a little box, but there was nothing distinctive about it.

"Bull killed my brother and he cost me dearly. Before he dies, I want to see him suffer." Miguel stepped toward him. "I want you to give this to Maddie and Lindsey."

"What is it?" Grant asked.

"Poison. Not the kind that will make them go to sleep. The kind that will make them suffer right in front of his eyes. You give this to them, and then we'll talk."

"A test?" Grant asked.

"Of course."

"Seriously, why bother reaching out to me? You want Bull dead, say the word."

"All in good time. I don't believe in being rushed. This will go my way."

Grant squeezed the vial in his hand.

"Kill Maddie and my niece," he said.

"Yes. To be the leader of Carnage, Grant, you need to learn to strip away everything that matters to you. No one can be a weakness." Miguel smiled. "I expect them dead by nightfall."

Grant nodded. "Consider it done."

Miguel got into his car and drove off. As for Grant, he stood there waiting.

Pat was the first one to make it to him.

"Did you hear?" Grant asked.

"Yeah, I heard."

"Bull better have a fucking plan, because right now I don't know what the fuck to do." He would never harm Maddie or Lindsey. Never.

He held the vial out to Pat. "Well? What the fuck is he thinking?"

"We should go," Pat said.

Grant shook his head. This was some messed-up shit. Killing dogs, now women and kids. Grant wanted to kill this son of a bitch, and soon. First, though, he and Bull had to find a way of faking Maddie's and Lindsey's deaths.

Great, fucking great.

Chapter Seventeen

Aria walked with Ernie and Bruno through the woods. She had already passed the park and stopped to see a couple of the kids playing. She loved to watch them and couldn't help but admit that she'd love to have children of her own.

This made her think about Grant and what he'd been doing since she left. Aria tried to think of how long it had been since she last saw him—it had been easily a couple of weeks. She hadn't even seen him around town. He'd not been the one from the animal shelter to bring the dogs in for a checkup either. The person who assisted the dogs had changed every time. She recognized Rusty and Sweet, as well as Bud and Rip, but other than that, they were different people.

Gripping her shoulders, she stretched out her neck while the dogs kept sniffing the ground on their way home.

Jase wasn't happy with how fast she was losing weight. He wanted her to keep a food diary of everything she consumed, which, in fact, wasn't a lot. She just wasn't hungry. Her diet the past few weeks had consisted of toast, sandwiches, and probably some crackers if she felt like it.

Ernie came toward her and Aria suddenly realized she'd come to a stop. She had just stopped walking. Crouching down, she gave him a stroke behind the ears. "You're a good boy, aren't you?"

Bruno came toward her and wanted his turn as well. "I love you both so damn much." She felt the tears start to well in her eyes.

Everyone in town knew about her sister and Grant. The rumor had spread faster than any gossip she could recall. She didn't have a clue who had said anything. Was it Grant? Was it the club?

Someone must have heard them arguing, or Grant told them. Either way, it was so humiliating to have the town know her business. The pitying looks, the giggles, and of course the snide comments were all a little too much. She had stopped going to the diner. Beatrice had threatened to expel anyone who made her feel uncomfortable but Aria refused to allow that to happen.

So, she stayed at the veterinary practice. She either ate her lunch inside at her reception desk if there were no customers, or she made her way out to the car if there were some.

Lidia also tried to have lunch with her at every available moment. She had wanted to go and kick Grant's ass, but she wouldn't let her friend do that. What was the point? Nothing would change. The whole town knew her business.

Getting to her feet, she breathed out a sigh, and then wrapped her jacket around herself even tighter. Snow was set to fall any day now. Christmas was around the corner. Aria hadn't even bothered with lights or a tree this year.

She wouldn't be going home. For the first time ever, she planned to spend Christmas on her own.

Arriving back home, Aria paused when she caught sight of her sister standing on her doorstep. She'd not seen or heard from Isabella at all.

"Isabella," Aria said.

"Aria, thank God, I was starting to worry when you didn't answer your door. I didn't know if I should call the sheriff or an ambulance." Isabella rushed over to her and hugged her. "I'm so pleased you're all right."

"I don't know why I wouldn't be."

"Mom told me what she did. Ugh, I can't believe she did that."

Aria pulled away. It was way too cold to be having this conversation outside on her doorstep, and way too many nosy locals lived nearby who pretty much fed themselves on local gossip. She wouldn't give them any more ammunition.

She invited Isabella into the house. She had already switched the heat on before she went for a walk so it would be nice and warm by the time she and the dogs got home.

The dogs went to their water bowls, took a nice big drink of water, and then like all the other times before, took themselves over to the sofa in the living room and snuggled in. They wouldn't leave their cushions until food was served up. They were so predictable and cute.

Hanging up her jacket, she took Isabella's and then headed toward the kitchen to make them both a hot drink.

"Tea? Hot chocolate?"

"Do you have whipped cream?" Isabella asked.

"No, I have tea and hot chocolate."

Isabella pouted. "I'll have the hot chocolate."

Aria chuckled.

She would have the fruit tea that Jase had insisted tasted nice. She'd been drinking it for over a week and so far, the taste was still nasty, but Jase had told her it takes some time to get used to.

"Mom has been to see you?"

"Yeah, she told us what happened and, well, I've come to invite you for Christmas," Isabella said.

This made her pause and quickly spin around to face her sister. "What? Won't you be going to Mom's?"

"Hell, no, and I mean that. This year, Michael and I will be cooking Christmas dinner and we're doing the works. A huge turkey, stuffing, mashed potatoes, maple roast parsnips, pigs-in-blankets, and I won't have anything green on my plate. Oh, roast potatoes as well, and I'll be making the gravy." Isabella looked so excited and happy.

"Sounds amazing."

"It will be."

"You're not here to berate me over what happened?" Aria asked.

"The gossip? No. Why would I? It's not like you spread the rumor yourself, did you?"

"No, I didn't."

Isabella sighed. "How did you find out?"

"Someone saw you two. They must have been filming you without you guys realizing it. I got the video sent to me."

"Wow," Isabella said. "That must have hurt?"

Aria turned back to the kettle. "It did."

"Is it true? You and Grant are no longer together?"

"We're not."

"It's not because of me, is it?" Isabella said. "Because I swear to you, Aria, nothing happened, not since I got married. This was before I did. Michael and I, we went through a rough spell, and no one else knows but we did separate. It was hard and I went out drinking because I didn't know how I was going to tell Mom, and then I saw Grant. It was a one-time, and I mean, one-time thing. He didn't even know my name. It was a giant mistake. One I do regret."

Aria finished making the tea and hot chocolate. She turned toward her sister and slid the hot chocolate across the counter for her.

"Does Michael know?" Aria asked.

"Yes, of course he does. We've talked and he admitted that there was someone else during that time.

We both made mistakes and it was when he realized he didn't want to be without me."

"I can't imagine the two of you arguing. That picture doesn't seem right inside my head."

Isabella laughed. "It was about you."

"Me?"

"Yeah. It was after several Sundays of him sitting opposite you, watching what Mom did to you. The way she talked to you. He hated it. He hated her being so obsessed with weight. We argued. I said she didn't mean anything by it and that you didn't mind and Michael, he went … he was so angry. He made me see you and made me realize that everything she did affected you. I watched you and I saw he was right. He said he couldn't marry into a family so cruel. That if I thought for a second he was going to allow her to give us a diet sheet for our children, I was very much mistaken."

"How did he take the pregnancy diet?" Aria asked, a little warmed by the fact Michael had seen her.

"He burned it. When she came to us the other day and started to yell about you, calling you horrible names, I realized she had been doing that all our lives. I never really got to know who you were because she always kept us apart."

Aria forced a smile to her lips. "That was her way. I wasn't allowed to hang out with you, because I didn't measure up to her standards."

"She's so awful and I am so sorry I didn't see it before. I know this makes me a horrible person."

"No, it doesn't."

"But, it should. I never got the chance to be a big sister. We didn't hang out in each other's bedroom, talking about boys or our favorite movie star crush. Neither of us got to really know each other, and I hate that."

"I don't have one," Aria said.

"What?"

"A movie star crush. I don't watch a lot of movies. I like reading, romances mainly. I've got two dogs, Ernie and Bruno, who take up a lot of my time and I just love them. I work at the veterinary practice which is a job I love and hate, and right now I'm so damn miserable because I broke up with my boyfriend because he slept with my beautiful sister."

Isabella's eyes filled with tears. "No, we didn't sleep together. It was a few minutes, that was all. It wasn't great, I swear."

Her sister got to her feet and started walking toward her. Aria was tempted to refuse the hug that was coming her way, but what was the point? Their mother had stopped them being close. She would no longer be the cause for them not being close. Wrapping her arms around her sister, she held on tight, not wanting to let go.

"I love you," Isabella said.

"I love you too."

"And don't let what happened between Grant and I spoil you two. I saw you together on Thanksgiving. You both have a special bond. There is love there, and that kind of feeling shouldn't be squashed. That should be embraced and cherished." Isabella stepped back and stroked her cheek.

"I don't know how the rumor spread."

"I don't care," Isabella said. "It has done me more good than not. The truth is out to Michael and we're working through everything. I've finally gotten rid of Mom's toxicity, I'm going to get to know my sister, and we're going to get to eat together. Good food. Not damn vegetables!"

Aria burst out laughing.

There was a sudden honking of a horn.

"That's Michael. Our food is ready. We ordered takeout." Isabella hugged her tightly. "You're coming for Christmas dinner and I'm not taking no for an answer."

Aria laughed. "Okay, fine. Christmas dinner."

Isabella pulled away and Aria went to the door with her, watching as she rushed down the garden path. Michael was there and Aria raised her hand to give her a wave. Just before she got into the car, she turned. "Next time, don't forget the whipped cream."

She couldn't help but laugh at her request. Whipped cream.

Closing her door, she flicked the lock into place and stepped toward her sitting room, seeing the dogs looking all snug and cozy. Aria clicked her fingers.

Feeding. That's what she had to do. She made her way into the kitchen, grabbed a couple of cans of dog food, opened them up, and mixed in a few dry biscuits for them as well. With their bowls ready, she put them on the feeding mat as someone knocked on her door.

Aria frowned. Who could it be?

She walked to the door and this time checked through the peephole to see who it was. Opening the door, she was still a little taken aback. "Grant?"

He stepped inside and she was so shocked that she didn't even try to stop him. He closed and flicked the lock on the door. She didn't argue with him. Didn't stop him.

He cupped her face and then slammed his lips on hers.

****

Bull didn't have a good enough plan as far as Grant was concerned. Finding two bodies and dressing them up in Maddie's and Lindsey's clothes wasn't going to work. Miguel wanted more than dead bodies. He wanted actual proof, footage of him poisoning the two loves of Bull's life.

Grant couldn't do it. There was no way he was going to kill his best friend or his niece. Not going to happen.

His plan might not work, or it might, but it could also cause a lot of casualties. It was the only way, though. To strike fast and at Miguel. To bring him to them. It wouldn't take out all of Miguel's men, but it would be a start. Either way, his plan would involve a lot of time. The only problem he had initiating his plan was this woman, with perfectly plump lips—the woman who haunted his dreams.

She had every right to fight him and push him away, but she didn't. At first, he had taken her by surprise. She could pummel at his chest, scream at him, tell him to fuck off and get out of her life, but Aria didn't do that. She also didn't pull him in closer.

She did kiss him back and he considered that a bonus. Aria's kisses were addictive.

Sinking his fingers into her hair, he tilted her head to the side and pressed her up against the door at the same time. Thrusting his pelvis against her stomach, he heard her slight intake of breath.

That's right, baby, I'm here for you.

Aria might not want him, but her body did. There was no taking that away from him.

"Grant?" she said once they had broken the kiss.

"I know right now you hate me, and I get that. I hate myself. I should have told you but I didn't want you to get hurt." He pressed his head against hers. "I've missed you, Aria, and right now, shit is about to go down at the club, and I don't know … it's bad, and I just had to come and see you."

"What do you mean?" Aria asked.

Grant pulled away and smiled at her. "It's

nothing."

"No, you can't say stuff like that and then … where's Wanda?" Aria asked.

"In the car."

Bruno and Ernie had come to sit near them, clearly waiting for their other family member.

"Damn it, it's cold outside. You can't leave her out there. She'll freeze." Aria opened the door and Grant went to his truck.

Wanda was underneath a thick blanket but when she realized she could come inside, she didn't have to be instructed to move. She darted into the house and he quickly got inside the door before Aria could close it. He closed it, locked it, and then stepped toward Aria. He cupped her face, tilting her head back, and looking into her eyes.

"You're so beautiful, you know that, right?" he asked.

She licked her lips. Taking possession of those luscious lips, he kissed her hard and another moan escaped her, which he swallowed down.

His cock hardened. Thick. Solid. Wanting inside her.

"Tell me to stop," he said.

Aria wrapped her arms around his neck, and slid her tongue into his mouth.

That was all the permission he needed. He broke the kiss, taking her hand, and then, leading her upstairs toward her bedroom.

"I know this doesn't mean that you forgive me," Grant said once they were inside.

"Shut up."

"Do you want me to fuck you?" he asked.

"Yes."

He pushed her hair out of her face. "Then we

keep the lights on. You don't get to hide from me. I want to see every single part of you."

She didn't argue.

There were times when they had been together when she tried to insist on turning them off. Not happening. He'd waited patiently for this woman and he wasn't going to waste a moment making love without the light on.

Moving his hands to her shoulders, he went to the buttons of her shirt. He tried to be patient in opening them, but there were too many and they were getting in his way. He grabbed the shirt and tore it from her body. The buttons sprayed all over the floor and she gasped.

"I'll buy you a new one."

She rolled her eyes and that soon turned into a moan as he cupped her tits over her sports bra. It had to be the least sexy thing he'd seen her wear.

He grabbed the bra and eased it off over the top of her head and threw it to the floor, where it deserved to be.

"Oh, fuck me, I've missed you." He cupped her tits, lifting them up in his palm and running his fingers across the tight buds.

Each time he did this, she let out a little noise of complete pleasure.

He needed those nipples in his mouth. Holding one up to his lips, he sucked hard and deep. Aria hissed and he used his teeth to create just enough bite of pain, but then soothed it out as he sucked on her tit.

"Grant?"

Oh, he knew what he was doing, so he moved to the other nipple and did exactly the same. He loved her tits. Loved how responsive she was to his touch. He couldn't get enough of her.

Sliding his thumb back and forth across the

mound, he wasn't sucking. He needed to feel her sweet cunt so he stroked his hand down, going toward her pussy. He fingered the edge of her jeans. He found the latch of her button and flicked it open. Next, he tugged her zipper before he crouched down and slid the jeans over her thighs.

Aria stepped out of them. The panties were a problem. He grabbed them and tightened his grip, tearing them off her body. Aria let out a gasp and he smiled.

This was how he wanted his woman. Naked. He stayed on the floor, but instead of crouching in front of her, he knelt. Gripping her hips, he moved her back until she had no choice but to sit on the bed. Once she did, he spread her thighs wide, and stared at her pretty pussy. So soft. So wet. All his.

There was no way he was going to let another man have her. No way at all. Aria was all his. His woman. His everything.

He couldn't give her up. Refused to. When all this shit was over with the club and he'd made it out alive—if he made it out alive—he was going to fight for her.

Running his fingers up the inside of her thighs, he touched the lips of her pussy and spread her open. Staring at her cunt, he groaned. Perfect.

The scent of her was intoxicating and he couldn't wait another minute. Sliding his tongue between her soaking wet slit, he touched her, then went straight down toward her entrance. He tongued her hole, stroking around it before plundering her cunt. In and out, he worked his tongue, hearing her slight intake of breath as he did so. She was a fucking dream.

Drawing his tongue back up to her clit, he worked around, across, back and forth, heightening her arousal, her need. Using his fingers, he plunged two deep inside her, feeling how tight she was. His woman was always so tight.

Twisting his fingers, he stroked across that precious spot that had her gasping his name. He didn't stop teasing her clit and he felt the change within her in just a few seconds. Her orgasm started to build and he drew it out as long as possible, but when she came, he felt his own desperate need.

Grabbing his dick even before she had finished her release, he lifted up, and then, in one smooth stroke, thrust to the hilt within her pussy. They both moaned.

She felt so good. Better than good. Perfect. So fucking perfect.

Pulling out to just the tip of him inside her, he waited and then thrust hard and deep. He did this for several thrusts, taking her harder than before.

Grant was so close, but he didn't want to come so fucking fast and ruin the moment. This could potentially be their last time.

In and out, he thrust inside her, going harder, and this time as his orgasm started to build, he didn't try to stop it. When it came to Aria, there was no stopping this need. It consumed him. He thrust into her one final time and filled her, wave upon wave of his cum. Grant prayed this one took. He wanted to knock her up and make her his, for them to have something that bound them together.

Grant stayed inside her, but he moved them both up the bed, until they were lying against the pillows. He didn't want to leave her pussy. He wanted to keep his dick like a plug inside her pussy, so she couldn't go shower, giving time for his seed to do its job.

Aria stared up at him and he saw the tears in her eyes. "Why didn't you tell me?"

"Because I'm a big fuck-up, Aria. That's what I

do. I mess shit up."

Her lip quivered.

"Don't, baby. Don't cry. I can't stand it when you cry. I don't want to ever see you cry."

She sniffled and he groaned. "I'm not crying."

"It looks like you are to me."

"I'm fine."

He pressed his lips to her head. "I love you, Aria," he said. "So fucking much."

"I love you too."

Grant closed his eyes. They loved each other, but it didn't mean they were fixed, not yet.

Now he had to do something he didn't want to do. He pulled out of her pussy and leaned over her. "I've got to go now."

"Grant?"

"I've got some shit that I need to do, but I will come back. You and I, we will have this time together."

She took hold of his hand and he pressed kisses to her knuckles. Fucking her and leaving wasn't what he wanted to do. It was the last thing he wanted to do, but he had no choice.

Running a hand down his face, he grabbed his clothes and stepped out of the bedroom. He changed and quickly made his way into the sitting room. Wanda was there, snuggled with Bruno and Ernie.

What he was about to do was dangerous.

He stepped over to her and ran his hands across Wanda's head. "I love you, girl, but I need you to stay here for me. I need you to take care of my woman for me. To protect her while I'm not here."

Wanda gave a little whimper. He smiled. This was dangerous. He got to his feet and looked at all three dogs. They'd protect Aria.

He stepped out of Aria's house, headed toward

his truck, pulled out his cell phone, and dialed Bull.

"I'm ready."

Chapter Eighteen

"This plan is not going to work," William said.

Grant didn't know why his brother had contacted William fucking Ranford, but either way, he'd arrived at Bull's house, along with the crap he was spewing.

"Why are you here?" Grant asked.

"I think we should listen to him," Maddie said. "He's faced this person before. We haven't."

"Are you all seriously doubting my ability to keep you alive?" Grant asked.

"We're not doubting it," Pat said. "But it would be good to get another's input on who we're dealing with. Miguel is a new enemy."

Grant ran fingers through his hair. "Do you guys not get the fucking timeline right now? I had twenty-four hours to kill Maddie and Lindsey. We're now down to like seven and I'm not going to have fucking corpses and shit. It was a horrible idea. You have to admit that was a bad idea," Grant said, looking from Bull, to Maddie, to Pat, then to William.

Rusty and Rip agreed with him. "Sorry, Prez, but Grant's right. That was bad."

"And you think bringing Miguel and his men here is going to work? My daughter is right fucking there!" He pointed toward the crib that was currently protected with some pink cushions.

"I told you. That's why Rusty and Rip are here. They're going to create enough of a distraction for Pat to swoop in and take Lindsey before all the guns start going off. It's going to be touch and go, but it requires you to be tied up and perhaps take a few punches," Grant said.

"Your whole plan revolves around you going off the rails, right?" Pat asked.

"Pretty much." He looked toward Pat and waited.

"You got a problem with that?"

"With your reputation, I'd say this is a dangerous one, but in all honesty, I think it's the only one that will work."

Bull rolled his eyes. "You cannot seriously think this is going to work?"

"Why not? Your plan was going to get us all killed. No doubt about it. Using corpses is like the oldest trick in the book. Even in movies, that no longer works. With Grant's record of being flighty and then the loss of Aria, this is probably the best solution."

Bull threw his hands in the air and Grant couldn't help but feel that sinking sensation in the pit of his stomach. His brother wasn't going to let him do this. He didn't trust him enough to do it. He stood and waited.

"This is dangerous, Grant."

"I know."

"You, me, we could all be killed." Bull's hands were clenched into fists.

"I know, but I'm not going to let that happen."

Bull shook his head and then moved to Maddie. He cupped her face and kissed her.

"I trust him," Maddie said.

"So do I," Bull said. "But I'm sure he understands my nervousness. If this was Aria, he'd be questioning me."

"Without a doubt," Grant said. He missed Aria. Could still smell her on his skin. He wanted her again.

This had to work. Once they took out Miguel, the plan was to go straight on the attack. They already had the boys on call, not just at Carnage, but all Chaos and Carnage charters. They were ready for the call.

Grant wanted this done. He was tired of Miguel and the Cartel hanging over their heads. It was time that the last area of control from their father was gone. Chaos and Carnage MC belonged to Bull. He needed to run it without that threat.

"Okay, let's do this."

"It's going to need to look authentic," Grant said.

"How?"

Grant slammed his fist against his brother's face as hard as he could. Bull hadn't been expecting it and so he fell to the floor. "Kind of like that."

"You fucking … I mean it, Grant, this better fucking work."

Grant put his boot on Bull's back and he cringed as he did so. "Don't get up quite yet. I've got to make it look like you've been dragged."

"Is this really necessary, Grant?" Maddie asked.

"I've not started on you."

"If you punch my woman or hurt her in any way—"

"Shut up, Bull. I won't hurt her." With his boot print on Bull's back, he then turned his brother over and hauled him up. "Have you put on weight?"

"Fuck off, Grant."

He chuckled. He couldn't help it. After some serious tugging, he got Bull into the chair and then tied him up with the rope, being sure to knot it as he did so. "There."

Blood dripped from Bull's mouth.

"You've got to spit at me," Grant said.

"Seriously?"

"I wouldn't tell you to spit on me for shits and giggles," Grant said.

Bull rolled his eyes but did as he asked. The spittle landed near his face and hit his neck. Grant swiped it off and then rubbed it on Maddie's shirt.

"Hey!"

"Sorry, Pumpkin, you're next."

Grant shoved his shoulder into her stomach and then lifted her up.

"You can fight and wriggle a bit."

"You're going to drop me," Maddie said.

"No, I'm not."

After she began to growl at him, Grant chuckled and then placed her in the chair opposite Bull.

"Now I need you to look like your hair has been pulled," Grant said.

Maddie sighed but then ran fingers through her hair and tugged it in all directions.

"Great, slap your face."

"You do realize there's going to be payback for this," Maddie said.

"Yeah, I know, but if it means you can get out of the clubhouse and not be locked up again, don't you think that's a bonus?"

"This is all fucking crazy," William said. "There's no way any of this is going to work. You're acting foolish."

"You think my brother and Maddie are the only targets?" Grant asked. "Trust me, Ranford, you're next."

He slid a fist into the man's guts. He recoiled.

"You're also part of the plan."

Rusty whistled. "I do not want to be you right now."

"Yeah, well, I'm fucking bored with this shit." He pulled out his cell phone, complete with Miguel's card. "It's showtime."

He found the number and clicked the green button to put the call through. Grant waited. By the fifth ring, Miguel answered.

"Grant, so good to hear from you."

"Change of fucking plans," Grant said. "If you want to see this fucker die, then you better get to Bull's house. I've got a couple of prizes for you." He hung up the call.

Pulling his gun out, he attached the silencer and did a few shots at certain points. Two around Bull, another around Maddie. He didn't point the gun at his niece.

Pat, Rusty, and Rip left as well. They were all in their positions.

"Did you go and scc Aria?" Maddie asked.

"Yeah, I did."

"And?"

"And ... I don't know. I told her I'm going to try and make it back to her, but I don't know how tonight is going to play out. I could die tonight."

"Don't say shit like that," Bull said. "You don't get to tie me and my wife up and say that shit. You're going to make it out alive. We're all going to make it out alive."

"I love your optimism." Grant removed the silencer after a few minutes.

"You got this, Grant."

He wanted to burst out laughing.

"You're a waste of space. They'll kill you at the club. You're a good-for-nothing waste of fucking space. You piece of shit."

His father's words came back to haunt him, but he shook them off. They didn't have the time and this certainly wasn't the place to be thinking about his old man. He was still trying to deal with the shit their old man did.

"Could you imagine what Pop would say right now if he saw us?" Grant asked.

"No, because he wouldn't have said shit."

Grant laughed. "He would have."

"No, you don't understand, everything that

bastard said was shit, Grant. Everything. You need to forget the shit he said. He was a fucking monster, an asshole."

Grant smiled.

"Incoming!" Pat said.

The time for smiling was over. With the gun held steady, he went to the front door. It had started to snow and it sent in a gust of cold air. This was another reason he'd put cushions around Lindsey's crib. He didn't want to hurt his niece, but at the right moment, Pat was going to get her out of harm's way.

This had to work.

Grant turned away from the door and headed back to where Bull and Maddie were waiting.

"Nice of you to stop by," Grant said.

"What is going on?" Miguel asked, holding his hand up, stopping his men from moving.

Grant saw that they had guns. "Oh, I know you wanted me to poison them, but that isn't happening. No, I've got other plans."

"This is the prize?" Miguel asked. "You didn't follow my instructions."

"Instructions are overrated. He never trusted me. He'd never have allowed me to take the club. I'm going to shoot him in the fucking face and then I'm going to take Carnage. It's mine. My town."

Grant had no idea what he was saying. He was just throwing words. The last thing he wanted was the town.

What he needed was for Miguel and his men to step inside the house. Once they had them surrounded, it would be easy pickings. Rusty and Rip were ready for the distractions. Bull wasn't happy that this had to take place at his home, though.

William was on the floor, also hiding a gun.

Grant had also given Bull a knife to slice through the rope. So long as he didn't make any sudden movements, this was going to work.

"What's the matter?" Grant asked. "Are you afraid of a tied man?" He threw back his head and laughed. "I always told you I was going to take the club."

"You're an asshole, Grant. He's not going to let you have the club. You think you're going to be in charge, but you're not. You're going to die, just like me."

"No, I'm not." He gritted his teeth.

Miguel stepped inside the house, as did his men. Grant counted six. Six men to come to one house. Why? Grant tried not to overthink that kind of shit. Miguel was known for being paranoid.

"Kill them," Miguel said. "I have grown bored with this. I want you to shoot his wife, then his child."

"First, before I do that, I wanted to give you another little present. Over there," Grant said.

He wanted Miguel on his own, but the guards seemed to move as one. This was not part of the plan. The guards were supposed to cover the door, Miguel moving on his own, checking William, which would allow William to grab Miguel, and for him, Rusty, and Rip, to get the guards. *Shit. Fuck.*

Grant kept his gun trained on Bull.

"Ah, I see you have finally located Mr. Ranford." Miguel clicked his fingers and Grant watched as one of the guards was about to hand over the gun to Miguel. He had seen this happen at the trailer park.

"Now!" Grant yelled the word at the same time he fired his weapon, taking out the hands of the guard who was about to give up the gun.

William spun away, drawing his weapon. They were outnumbered, currently. Pat had already swooped in and taken Lindsey.

Miguel tutted. "Grant, you disappoint me."

"You knew," Grant said, staring at Miguel, who looked bored.

"Of course I knew." Miguel smoothed out his suit jacket. "I was hopeful that you would see sense, but all the evidence pointed to you taking your brother's side." He tutted.

Grant didn't like how happy Miguel looked. Something was going on right now, something else was in play.

Rusty and Rip were ready, guns pointed. Bull stood up and stepped in front of Maddie. He reached into Grant's jeans and pulled out another gun.

"Do you really think my brother would turn on me?" Bull asked.

"I have to admit, I doubted it, but what are you going to do, shoot me?" Miguel asked. "Will that help you get Aria back?"

Grant tensed up.

"Ah," Miguel said. "You really think a little rumor around town would stop me from taking her, from using her?" Miguel chuckled. "It was all so easy. You kill me, you lose her."

"But we don't need your men," Grant said.

He fired his gun and hit the guards. With him, Bull, Rusty, Rip, Pat, and William, the guards went down fast. There was nowhere for Miguel to run.

Grant threw his gun aside and charged at Miguel who was trying to head for the front door. He grabbed him, spun him around, and landed a blow to his face. He couldn't stop hitting him.

"Grant, Grant, stop!" Bull grabbed his arm, stopping him.

"He's got Aria."

"First, we need to make sure he has Aria. Then

we deal with him."

"Your woman is going to die," Miguel said. "Carnage will burn to the ground."

****

Aria's head hurt. Everything hurt. She was also cold, so freaking cold.

Rolling onto her back, she frowned as she stared up at a ... holey ceiling. What? It took her a few moments to remember what had happened. Grant had paid her a visit, they had sex, then he'd left. She had cried. He had sex with her and left, just like he did with those other women.

She had gone to the kitchen to make herself a drink when the door had been kicked open. Her dogs had growled. There were men all dressed in black, and she had fought them. She had grabbed a knife, hurt one of them in the process, but it hadn't been enough. One of them must have hit her, and they had done so real fucking hard. The back of her head hurt so damn badly. She reached out, touching her head, wincing.

"Aria?"

At the sound of her name, she tensed. "Hello."

"Aria, it's me."

She turned to see Lidia. She sat up and then realized the reason her body felt heavy. Chains were wrapped around her feet and her wrists. They were both chained to the beds.

"What is going on?" Aria asked.

"I don't know. I was taken during my lunch break," Lidia said. "A weird guy, wearing a suit and an accent. He stopped by when you arrived. He said it would be rather touching for two best friends to die together."

"Die?" Aria shook her head but even that hurt.

Lidia sat up in bed.

"We're in the old abandoned hotel, Aria," she said.

She couldn't recall a time she had seen her friend look so afraid. "Lidia, what's going on?"

"The man that came. He didn't tell me his name but he said if Grant didn't do as he asked, if he tried to act foolishly, then you and I were going to pay the price. This building is set to burn."

"What?"

Aria tried to get off the bed to walk, to move, to do anything, but the cuffs kept her on the bed. There was not enough give in them. She let out a scream. The scent of mold and decay hung heavy in the air.

"This can't be happening." She sat on the bed and tried to take deep breaths.

"What does Grant have to do?"

"I don't know," Aria said. "I know the club was in trouble and that was why I had to stay at the clubhouse but … I don't know. He came to see me tonight. He said something was going down." She rubbed at her temples trying to think of what it could be, but nothing was there. Not a damn thing.

Lidia sniffled.

"I don't understand," Aria said. "Grant and I are not together."

"Come on, Aria, you and I both know the rumor about Isabella and Grant had to have been spread on purpose," Lidia said. "He must have been trying to protect you."

"Why?" Aria asked.

"Look around you. This is clearly club business. He was trying to save you from it."

Aria felt tears fill her eyes. "My dogs."

"What?"

"Before I was knocked out, I heard a gunshot. My

dogs." She knew it probably wasn't the right time to be thinking about her dogs, but she didn't want anything to happen to them.

"Aria, we need to get out of here."

Staring down at the cuffs on her hands, she tried to pull her wrists through, letting out a yelp as the metal cut into her wrists. She whimpered.

"I've tried that." Lidia held up her wrists. "I ended up cutting myself. Ankles too. Also, the chains have been cemented to the beds."

"What?"

"Yeah, tried to lift the beds. It's not working."

"So we're trapped here."

"Yeah, we're trapped."

Aria sat on the bed and took several deep breaths. "Grant will come," she said.

"Does he even know you've been taken?"

"He will."

"Aria, you know that Grant is not … he's…"

"You don't know him like I do. He will come for us. He'll save us." Aria knew he would.

"How can he come when he doesn't know we're here?"

"I know him. He'll come. He will." Aria kept nodding her head at the same time trying to pull the cuffs from her wrist.

Tears filled her eyes. This was a nightmare. She loved Grant so damn much. Her heart raced.

"Aria, do you smell that?" Lidia asked.

Yes, she did, but she wasn't going to let her friend worry. "Smell what?"

"Aria, don't lie to me."

"I don't smell anything."

She did. The scent of smoke. The fire had already started. What did that mean? Did they have minutes?

This hotel was falling down. She couldn't remember if it had been condemned or not. It wouldn't take long for fire to travel, so they didn't have long.

Aria felt the tears falling down her face. "Isabella invited me for Christmas."

"That's good. What about your mom?"

"She's not invited but Isabella looked really excited about making dinner. Everything, the works."

"Sounds great."

"I lied," Aria said.

"I know."

"I smell the smoke."

"I know." Lidia let out a whimper.

"It's fine. We're going to be fine."

Aria sat on the mattress but she couldn't allow herself to just wait. Spinning on the bed, she saw there were metal bars. There was enough give for her to be able to reach up with both hands. She grabbed onto the bars and pulled.

The beds were quite flimsy from years of rusting, not being used, exposed to different weather. She held on tightly. Her arms ached but she couldn't give up. The smoke had started to push through the bottom of the door. They had to get out.

Prying the bar off the bed, it bent forward just a little. Aria laughed. This didn't bode well. If she could pull it off the bed, all she needed was to be able to slide between the cuffs and create enough give for her to wriggle out of them. The metal pole was too big.

"No. No. No. No!" She screamed.

"Aria?"

"It's fine. It's totally fine."

It wasn't.

Grant would come for them but it would be too late.

With the smoke filling the room, Aria tried tugging at her wrists and ankles, hoping to find some weakness within the cuffs, some design fault. Anything that would allow her to get out and get free. Lidia did the same. Why did they have to take her best friend as well?

"Aria, it's not working," Lidia said, sobbing. "There's no use."

"We're going to get out of here, Lidia. We are."

"Stop saying that. You and I both know it's not true. This is what happens. We die."

Aria couldn't stop the tears.

"Do you remember when we were kids?" Aria said. "Your dad had just built you that tree house."

"We spent a lot of time in that tree house."

"We did. Well, imagine we're back there right now. This is part of our game."

"Aria, we always got out alive," Lidia said.

"I know. We will."

Aria stared at the smoke. She breathed in and tried to control the cough, but it wouldn't stay inside. She let out a cough. As she did, so did Lidia.

"Cover your face."

The coughing got uncontrollable and Aria was certain she heard the fire crackling. Was the room getting warmer? She was going to die tonight. Die without seeing Grant again. Without telling him that she loved him and forgave him.

Do you forgive him?

What was there to forgive?

Yes, he had sex with her sister. Yes, he lied about it. Well, did he lie? He just didn't tell her the truth. Why did he do that? He didn't want to hurt her.

The smoke was coming thick and fast.

She felt the room getting warm.

Collapsing to the bed, she tried to preserve her

strength. Curling up in a ball, she felt like she was choking.

This was how her story would end.

Chapter Nineteen

Grant looked through the hospital room window at Aria. She was hooked up to several machines. He'd gotten to her before the fire had been able to touch her, but he'd not been able to control the smoke.

She had smoke inhalation and was currently in a coma. Lidia was also the same. Both friends were in the hospital, in the same room. He'd insisted. Lidia's parents had hugged him tightly, thanking him and the club for saving them.

He'd nearly failed. Dylan had gotten the call from a couple of drunken kids about a fire at one of the old abandoned hotels.

"You made it," Bull said, slapping him on the back. Miguel was currently at the Chaos and Carnage MC clubhouse chained in the basement with the men taking turns to watch him. The club was on guard. They knew his men would come for him.

"He was going to kill her. Burn her," Grant said.

By the time he got to Aria, she had already been passed out on that filthy-looking bed. Pat had been the one to suggest taking the metal clippers. It had been a hunch of his to take them and it was a good thing he had. Chained to a cemented bed. Miguel had planned it. The chains had been cemented on and given time to set. All he'd needed was the bodies of Aria and Lidia.

He put Aria's life at risk. Him, no one else. He should have kept her at the clubhouse, protected her.

"You had no way of knowing."

"I should have known. My plan was fucked up from the start."

"No, it wasn't."

"I nearly got us all killed."

"Grant, your plan didn't get us killed. Did it have

a few hiccups, yes, but what plan doesn't? Nothing always goes the way we hope it will. We got Miguel. Six of his guards are now gone. We're bringing an end to his control on the club. This is a win. Your plan worked."

"And what if she doesn't wake up?" Grant asked. "What if I failed her?"

"You didn't."

"It's my job to protect her. She's my woman."

Bull put his hand on his shoulder. "We can't be everywhere all the time. I know this. If that was Maddie, I know I'd be feeling exactly the same way right now, but you cannot allow this to swallow you up. You won today. This is a win."

He shook his head. It didn't feel like a win.

A win was when nothing went wrong.

"I bet our old man is laughing at me right now."

"No, I bet our old man, the one before he got hooked on the dope, would be fucking proud of you. Dad wasn't always an asshole, Grant. Money, drugs, power, it got to him, turned him into the monster that he is."

Grant could rarely remember the man he was before those vices gripped him. The bad in his world far outweighed any of the good in the early years.

"She's gotta live," he said.

"She will, but you know our job isn't finished, don't you?" Bull asked.

"I know."

"Are you coming?"

Grant was tempted to say no, that he'd stay here with his woman.

"We're here. How is she?"

Isabella and her husband Michael rushed toward them.

He glanced at them both then turned back to look through to his woman. "She's in a coma." Staring at

Aria, she looked so lifeless and he hated how thin she looked. It had only been a couple of weeks, but already her extreme dieting had taken a toll.

When Miguel and his Cartel bastards were gone, he was going to fix this.

"Your mom's not allowed here," Grant said. "I've got to go and take care of something. I need you both to watch her."

"Of course," Isabella said, reaching out to touch Michael's chest.

Grant watched him take a deep breath, his nostrils flaring. "Are we going to have a problem? I don't care about her. The only woman I care about, the only woman I want, is laying in that hospital bed. There's no competition here. There never was."

"Michael, babe, please, we talked."

He nodded. "We'll take care of her."

Grant turned to look at Aria. He was going to be back before she woke up. That was his fucking determination. Bull waited for him, but Grant couldn't just leave. He stepped into the hospital room, walked up to her bed, and placed his hands beside her head.

"I've got to go and take care of something and while I'm gone, you're going to rest. You're going to sleep, and whatever you need, you got me. You're going to take all the time you need and when I get back, you can wake up. You can come back to me and then we'll sort this out. You and me." He pressed a kiss to her forehead. "Fuck, Aria, please come back to me."

He had no choice but to pull himself away from his woman and leave the room, giving Isabella and Michael a chance to enter.

Leaving her was torture. It was the last thing he wanted to do, but he had business to attend to.

****

"Cut his dick off!" William yelled from the corner.

Grant watched as his brother looked at Miguel. The man would be dead soon. He'd already taken so much, and he was still keeping his secrets.

Bull was growing impatient. Grant was as well. He didn't have time for this. He wanted to be in the hospital, taking care of Aria, not listening to this piece of shit screaming. Running a hand down his face, he listened as there was another grunt as Bull started in on the teeth. Miguel still believed he had all the power.

Grant cleared his throat and moved over to the tools that were displayed on the table. He picked up five knives. That was it, five.

"Can I have a go?" Grant asked.

"You're asking for permission to torture the man that nearly killed your woman?"

"Yes."

Bull looked at Miguel and then him. Grant was bored. He waited.

"Fine, but you can't kill him."

Grant walked over to the far corner and grabbed one of the large wooden chairs stacked up there. Lifting it off the pile, he carried it across the room in front of Miguel. His movements were very relaxed. He sat down and stared at Miguel.

"Do you think you scare me? The younger brother. The mistake."

Grant stared at Miguel.

Miguel laughed. "Are you trying to bore me to death?"

"I'm watching you because I enjoy seeing in person how the mighty fall." Grant smiled. "It's a good look on you."

"Fuck you."

Grant shrugged. "You see, the difference between my brother and me is he's getting impatient because he thinks you're going to get to a point where you'll tell us everything. What good are you then, we can just kill you. It still sounds like a lot of fun, but after all the shit you've put us through and this town, that doesn't sound like a nice idea." Grant held one of the blades up toward the dim light. It was sharp. Pat would make sure every single item was. There was no room for sloppiness in their line of work.

In one swift move, Grant imbedded the knife all the way to the hilt within Miguel's thigh.

"But you see, I don't give a fuck about the rest of your Cartel. It'll take them a while to get their shit together, needing a brand-new leader, and then they'll come back. We took out Julio and now you, so I don't see you guys being much of a problem anymore. Someone will realize taking on the club means death, and everything will go back to normal. We'll have our lives back, and maybe the next guy that takes over will keep his position long enough to get his dick sucked. As for me, you took Aria, you kidnapped her and her friend, and chained her to a cemented bed, and then got your men to set fire to the abandoned hotel. That for me means you're not leaving this basement. She's in the hospital, in a coma. I don't know if she's going to wake up, and while I don't know what will happen to her, I've got to get my entertainment somehow, and the only way to do that is to deal with you." Grant held another knife and did the same thing to the other leg, slamming the blade in to the hilt and watching Miguel as he tried not to scream.

"Do you think this scares me?"

"I hope not," Grant said. "I've got three other knives and a whole lot of other tools, as you can see. I won't get to cutting until I'm really bored. For now, I'm happy to just sit back and watch."

"Grant, we don't have time for this," Bull said.

"Why not? They're not going anywhere and he wanted me to poison Maddie and my little niece. We've got all the time in the world."

Grant whistled and held the other knife. Where should he put the next blade?

Miguel's hands got the next two blades and as for the final blade, he decided to slam that through the man's cock.

Pinned to a chair, screaming, writhing in agony, and faced with a man who showed nothing but boredom, after an hour of Grant not changing, other than to pull the knives out and place them somewhere else, throwing alcohol onto his wounds, for him to feel every single burn, Miguel cracked.

He told them everything. Every single detail of the Cartel.

Grant stared at Miguel. He wanted to end him, but that wasn't for him to do. Getting to his feet, he put his hand on his brother's shoulder, and then left the basement.

"Are you okay?" Pat asked.

"Fine."

"Are you sure? I don't think I've ever seen you do something like that."

"There's a lot you don't know about me, Pat," Grant said. "That didn't bother me. My woman, alone in a hospital bed, that's what bothers me."

Bull came up from the basement. "It's been taken care of."

"What's the plan?" Grant asked.

William appeared as well, face set in stone. "It's time for us to go to war."

"You don't have an army," Grant said.

"But I do."

****

"Come back to me."

"Come back to me."

Aria moved her head from side to side, confusion clogging her thoughts. She was so tired.

Grant … he was speaking. She wanted to follow the sound. To hear him talk, listen to his voice, but the sleepiness was too much. She had no choice but to close her eyes and go to sleep. Sleep was a good place to be.

"Do you think she's going to be okay?"

Was that her sister? What was her sister doing in the burning hotel?

"I think she will be. The doctors are hopeful. We've just got to think positive."

Was that Michael? What was he doing in the burning hotel as well?

"Is he good enough for her?"

"That's not your place to say. If Grant makes her happy, then you can't come between the two of them."

"I know that, but she's my sister and I want her to be happy. She deserves to be happy."

"And she will be."

Grant, she missed Grant. Where was he?

"Aria, I know you're sleeping and this will be helping you to mend, and to be … right, but I need you to come back to me. Please, baby, I need you to come back to me right now."

Grant. She wanted him. She wanted to hold him. To tell him that she didn't care, it was all in the past, and that she didn't want to waste a moment. But she was so tired. She'd tell him as soon as she woke up.

"Hey, bestie, I'm awake but it would seem that you are not."

Lidia? Why was Lidia talking to her? They were

trapped together in a burning building.

"Come on, Aria, you've got to wake up. You've got to come back to us. Grant wants to ask you something and you need to come back because he is ... the smell is really bad. I'm hoping Maddie can convince him to leave, and you know, shower, to do something."

Did Lidia touch her hand?

Aria flexed her hand, opening and closing it, but nothing was there.

So tired.

"Hey, Aria, I know you and I haven't been friends long, but I'd like to rectify that. You've missed Christmas and New Years. There are a ton of presents waiting for you. The doctors have asked for the flowers to stop, but I think once you get out, you'll be able to plant them in your garden."

Presents. Flowers. She never got flowers.

"Hey, babe, so I did it, I'm working at the club's garage, permanently. I go there after I take care of you, and then I come back here. I have washed, so you can tell Lidia to fuck off with that shit. I'm clean. Bull and Maddie convinced me that stinking up the place wouldn't help you wake up."

Grant. He was here.

She wanted to hold him and tell him she loved him and didn't want him to leave her side, not now, not ever.

Grant.

So tired. Always so tired.

"Will she ever wake up?"

Aria frowned.

That was so clear. Not far away. Not distant, but it felt like he was right in the room with her. Aria no longer felt numb or alone. Taking a chance, she opened her eyes and looked around. She wasn't in the burning hotel room. There was no smoke. The room was white and there was light coming in through the window. It was bright. Machines beeped all around her.

"Right now," someone said.

Aria turned toward the voice.

"Miss. Taylor, good morning…" His words filled the air but Aria turned toward Grant, who moved to her side. He took one of her hands within his and kissed her knuckles.

"Aria, baby, you're awake."

"Mr. Reynolds, I'm trying to—"

"Grant," she said.

"You know who I am?" he asked.

She smiled and nodded.

"That's good." He looked toward the doctor. "That's good, right?"

"Yes, it is good news."

"What date is it?" Grant asked.

Aria smiled and tears filled her eyes. "I don't know." Her throat felt scratchy. "Do you have any water?"

"Yes, of course."

"Mr. Reynolds, she wouldn't know what day it is as she's been asleep." The doctor looked at her. "I want to run a few tests, Aria. I'll be back with a couple of nurses in a few moments, is that okay?"

She nodded.

The doctor nodded at her and then left the room.

"Asshole. I thought he'd never leave." Grant reached past her and then brought back a glass with a straw. "Here you go."

She took the straw between her lips and sucked at the liquid. She felt instant relief.

"For a moment there, I didn't think you were going to wake up." He reached out, tucking some hair behind her ear. "I've got to text Lidia, Maddie, and your sister. They wanted to know when you woke up as soon as you did."

Aria took his hand.

Grant looked up and stared into her eyes. She wanted to look at him.

"Nothing is going on between me and your sister, or Maddie, or Lidia."

"I nearly died," Aria said.

"I know, I'm so sorry I wasn't there to stop it. I would do anything for you. Oh, Andy and Phil as well. They've been so worried about you."

"Grant, shut up," Aria said.

He frowned.

She chuckled. It tickled her throat a little and she asked for some more water. Grant wouldn't allow her to lift the cup, so she had no choice but to drink as he took care of her.

"Can I speak?" Grant asked.

She shook her head. "No, I want to speak."

"Okay." Grant put the cup back down and then he took hold of her hands again.

"I nearly died and as I was in that hotel room, seeing the smoke fill the room, all I could think about was you." She stared into Grant's eyes. "I wanted to see you, talk to you, tell you that I forgive you. I have no idea who let out that rumor—"

"My brother."

"What?"

"Bull, he called Jase, who then did as my brother asked and spread the rumor. He didn't want to. I don't know if that makes you feel any better. Also, he's the one that left the roses." Grant pointed toward a bouquet of flowers in the corner of the room. "He did also send some healthy kind of chocolate but I ate that, then the trash bin ate the rest."

Aria laughed. "Your brother?"

Grant sat on the bed. "It was club business. The guy that took you was an enemy of the club."

"We can talk about that some other time, outside of the hospital, where other people can't hear." She smiled at Grant. "I love you."

"I love you too. I'm so sorry."

"I forgive you."

"You forgive me?" he asked.

"Being in that bed, chained up, unable to escape, all I could think about was seeing you. Loving you. Being with you. That was all I wanted. Just you."

"And now?"

"Now, I just want to be with you, Grant. All of you."

"Then marry me," he said.

"What?"

"Marry me. That's all *I* want. You and me, both of us. I want you to be my wife."

"You're serious?"

Grant reached into his leather cut and pulled out a ring. "Deadly serious." He held up a diamond ring.

"You just carry around engagement rings in your pocket?" she asked.

"Ever since I saw it at the jewelry store, I have. I got it just before Christmas and I've been wanting to give it to you for some time. Will you marry me?"

"Oh, my God, we're here for the proposal."

Aria turned to see her best friend rush through the door. Isabella and Michael were not far behind. Then she saw Maddie, Bull, and Lindsey enter the room. They were not the only ones. Aria looked out the door to see several of the Chaos and Carnage MC. They had all come to visit her.

Lidia kissed her head and then smiled. "You're awake, finally."

"We've all been taking turns visiting you," Maddie said.

"We're your family," Bull said.

Tears filled Aria's eyes. "Thank you."

"No need to thank us," Pat said.

"We always take care of one of ours."

She didn't quite know who said that last part but then she turned to Grant, who still held the ring in his grip.

"Aria Taylor, will you marry me?" he asked.

"Yes."

"What did she say?" someone else asked.

"I said yes," Aria said, laughing.

Grant took her finger and slid the ring on it. It was a perfect fit.

"Okay, so who's going to tell her about the baby?" Lidia asked.

Chapter Twenty

Three Months Later

Aria stepped out into the warm summer air. It was going to be a good day. A warm one, according to the forecasters.

"Come on, Bruno, Ernie, Wanda." She gave a whistle and all the dogs followed her outside.

It had been three months since she had gotten out of the hospital. During that time, Grant had moved in with her. That had been a whole new experience for her, moving in with her fiancé. The Chaos and Carnage MC had helped. With Grant and Maddie's help, they had been able to keep everyone fed and happy, which was a good thing.

That hadn't been the most exciting part of the last three months. Nope, the most exciting part had been the wedding that took place on Valentine's Day. Yes, Grant had been insistent on it being that day. February 14th. Aria had figured it was to make it more romantic for the two of them.

Nope. Not for Grant. No, he wanted that date because he'd remember it, and even if he didn't remember, which was unlikely, he'd at least get her a box of chocolates and flowers. Aria had found it so adorable. Grant had seen it as practical. He already knew he was going to be in trouble for a great deal of their marriage, but he wanted to get some things perfect.

The other interesting news she had gotten was that she was five months pregnant. She rested her hand on her swollen stomach. Grant had wanted to throttle Lidia for letting that little detail out of the bag, but Aria was grateful.

Her pregnancy was going well. The doctors had been checking her throughout her stay in the coma, and they believe her body had been repairing itself, healing. Either way, Aria was so freaking happy.

She was pregnant with Grant's baby. The club had teased him, telling him the baby would be doomed, which wasn't very nice of them. He had admitted he was terrified of being a crap dad. His words, not hers. He was worried he'd turn out like his father.

"My dad wasn't a good man, Aria. I don't ... what if I turn out like him?"

"Are you going to tell our child that he can't be friends with people?" she asked.

"No."

"Are you going to beat him? Punish him? Lock him in a dark room until he forgets about him?"

"Fuck, no."

"Are you going to love him or her?"

"Yes."

"Then I'd say that's a good start."

She didn't know if she was having a boy or girl. On the last scan, the doctor had said it was possible for them to know, but she wanted to wait and for it to be a lovely surprise. That was what she looked forward to.

Heading across the path, she took the dogs out toward the park for a long walk. Grant hated it when she went for walks, but their dogs needed the exercise. As she made her way across town, she saw Jase with one of his clients, and she gave him a wave. She no longer visited his gym. The one time she tried to, Grant had left his job at the garage, picked her up while he'd been covered in grease and oil, and then carried her out of the gym. From that day forward, Aria had only ever waved at Jase.

With her hand on her stomach, she thought about her sister who was only a few weeks from giving birth. Isabella spent a lot of time with her. Their mother had cut them both out of her life. Aria didn't care. She didn't miss her mother and from what her sister said, neither did she. There was no more toxicity in her life. No one constantly telling her she was ugly and wouldn't measure up.

She was free.

They both were.

Finally.

Aria saw the garage up ahead and like all other times, Wanda went first, rushing to see Grant. She rounded the garage and stepped inside. Grant was on his knees. The cloth he used to wipe his hands was on the floor.

"There's my big girl."

Not only did Grant work at the garage full time, he also still took his role at the animal shelter seriously. Aria continued to work at the veterinary practice. Phil and Andy had proven to be popular and the town had started to trust them. They had become the stop for all animal care.

"What have I told you, Mrs. Reynolds?" Grant asked. He got to his feet but made sure to pet both Ernie and Bruno.

"You tell me a lot of things," she said.

He chuckled. "How are my woman and my child?" He put his hand on her stomach.

Grant had changed so much. She knew several people around town were shocked by his transformation. Even Maddie had noticed how different he was. Responsible. Grown up. Reliable.

"We're doing fine. We needed a walk and so did the dogs."

"I don't want you doing too much," he said.

"I'm not." She rolled her eyes. "I was thinking about heading to the shelter."

Grant groaned. "Don't do it."

Aria frowned. "Why?"

"There was a litter of puppies found abandoned by the side of the road. Maddie has already sent me pictures. I'm staying well clear of them. Honestly."

"A litter of puppies?"

"Yes."

"Are they okay?"

"I think so."

Aria cupped his face. "Are you sure you don't want to go and check if they're okay?"

Grant rolled his eyes. He'd told her how much he loved all the dogs at the shelter and wanted to take care of them, to make sure they got their forever homes.

"You don't help me," Grant said.

Aria laughed. "It'll be good."

Grant kissed her. "I've got a couple more hours here."

"That's okay. I'm going to meet Lidia for lunch, then I'll take Wanda, Ernie, and Bruno over to the shelter and check them out. You can pick me up there."

"Hey, Aria," Bull said.

"Hi, Bull." She couldn't believe Bull, the Prez of the Chaos and Carnage MC, was her brother-in-law. She also couldn't believe she wasn't afraid of him.

"Grant, I need an update," Bull said.

Her husband rolled his eyes. "Duty calls, babe. You're deadly. We can't have any more dogs."

Aria agreed with him, but that didn't mean she couldn't go and shower lots of love onto the new dogs.

By the end of the day, Wanda, Ernie, and Bruno had two new sisters, Izzi and Lizzi. Grant chose the names, not her.

****

Four Months Later

Grant had been beaten by his dad. He'd been kidnapped and beaten. He'd gone toe to toe with his brother. He had faced scary, vicious dogs, gone against the Cartel, risked certain death.

None of that was as terrifying as watching his wife scream in agony. Getting her pregnant had been the fun part. He enjoyed that part. This was not fun at all.

"I've got you, baby, I've got you."

"Ouch, this hurts so much…"

"You're doing good, Aria, just a few more pushes and everything will be fine," the midwife said.

Aria whimpered and Grant kissed her head. He wanted to take the pain away from her, to tell her it was going to be okay, but there was nothing he could do. Nothing. This was all up to her. All he could do was sit back and watch and hold onto her hands, praying it was over soon.

"I've got you, baby. You're doing so well."

She turned her teary eyes to him. "I'm so bad at this."

"No, you're not. You're doing great. So freaking great. I love you, baby. I love you." After this, he was cutting his balls off. They were not having another child. Not now. Not ever.

Aria grabbed his hands, lifted up, and then pushed. Her face went red and he saw the pain in her eyes, and he hated himself. So fucking much.

"I've got you, baby. I've got you. That's it, push. Come on, baby, push." He had no idea what he was saying, but the midwife and doctors had encouraged him to be supportive, to try and help her through the process. He did that. But he didn't know if he was helping or just annoying her.

Then, Aria collapsed against him and he heard the sound of a baby's scream. The midwife lifted the baby from between Aria's thighs, cut the cord, and then handed the baby to the nurse.

Grant watched the nurse.

"That's a good thing, right?" he asked. "Our baby has a good set of lungs?"

Aria squeezed his hand. "Is everything okay?"

"Yes, I think it is."

The midwife stepped away from the table and moved toward the baby. Grant watched, hating the time it was taking them to show him his baby. Then, as if by magic, the midwife walked toward them, and the baby was swaddled in the yellow blanket Aria had insisted on.

"Congratulations, Mr. and Mrs. Reynolds. You have a beautiful baby boy."

The midwife put the baby into Aria's hands, and Grant stared down at his son. A boy. He'd been so freaking afraid of this moment. A boy or a girl.

Was he going to be like his dad? A fucking monster?

Staring down at his son's head, his little boy opened his eyes, and Grant knew he wouldn't be. He didn't know how he knew it, but it was deep in his gut. He was going to protect this boy's life with his own.

"Grant, we have a son," Aria said.

Gant kissed her head. "Thank you so much."

"What are we going to call him?"

This was up to him and as he looked at his son, he smiled. "Alex," Grant said. "Alex Reynolds."

Epilogue

Five Years Later

"Alex, Lindsey, stop fighting, I mean it," Grant said, stepping to the clubhouse kitchen door and calling out to his son and niece.

"They're fine," Maddie said.

"They're not fucking fine," Grant said. "Lindsey's about to kick his ass."

"He's five," Aria said. "I'm sure he'll recover."

Aria moved up toward him and wrapped her arms around his waist. He felt her swollen stomach pressing against his back.

He had tried to be strong, to not have another baby, but this would be their third. Their second baby, a girl, was in Lidia's arms, around the back with Isabella and Michael's kids.

Aria had never reconciled with her mother, neither had Isabella. The club more than made up for that, though. They had accepted Aria as well as Isabella and Michael, and even Lidia was one of their own.

Bull stood by the grill. He looked toward his brother who held his hand up in a wave. The past five years had been tough. The Cartel was not as big a problem. With William Ranford's help, they were able to keep the threat at bay, but there was always someone vying for turf.

With his head out of his ass and focused on his family, Grant saw the bigger picture. He and Bull still argued, that was what brothers did. But it no longer interfered with the running of the club. Grant had then made it his mission to earn the VP patch on his chest. He didn't want Bull looking at him as if he shouldn't have the patch. He wanted to earn it, and so he had. Whenever Bull needed his VP, he was there.

He saved his disagreements for when they were alone. Bull respected him.

Wanda, Bruno, and Ernie were much older, and he knew their time was going to come to an end soon. He would cherish every moment with them.

Reese giggled as Wanda wiggled down to his level and started to lick his face. Bruno and Ernie were trying to get Lindsey's affection. As for Izzi and Lizzi, like always, they were near the food.

Like he could only settle for five dogs.

They had three others who were near him and Aria. He had brought them from the shelter as like Wanda, they had withdrawn into themselves. Trixie, Marsha, and Bowen. They had eight dogs, three kids, and a whole lot of happiness.

Pulling Aria into his arms, he stared into her beautiful blue eyes. This woman had been the love of his life. He should have known the moment he walked into that veterinary practice all those years ago, he was doomed.

She had changed his life. For the better.

"I love you," he said.

She smiled up at him. "And I love you."

"Daddy, Daddy!"

And that was a name he fucking loved as well.

The End

BESTSELLING BBW ROMANCE
SPICY ROMANCE FOR REAL WOMEN

DAMAGED SOULS

EVERNIGHT PUBLISHING ®

www.evernightpublishing.com